Consequences and Repercussions

E. MARIE SANDERS

Printed by CreateSpace for E. Marie Sanders Ink. Publishing

Cover photo: Phaylene McKinnon
Cover Model: Norman Anderson
Author photo: Tasha Prescott-Wilson
Lexile Level: 1050L

Sanders, E. Marie. 1974—
Consequences and Repercussions/E. Marie Sanders.-1st ed.

ISBN-13: 9781492113515
ISBN-10: 1492113514
Library of Congress Control Number: 2013915135
CreateSpace Independent Publishing Platform
North Charleston, South Carolina

Acknowledgments and "Shout Outs"

God, again I say thank you. It's an awesome thing to walk in Your will, and I find great pleasure in it. Thank You for the ideas, the motivation, and the support. I know I could not do this writing thing without You.

Eric, who would've thought that we would do this again for a third time? In case you didn't know, you are a phenomenal husband, and when it comes to that little game we play, I have to admit that I'm the one who got the better deal. I love you!

Tara, Kenyon, and Tasha, my book confidants, you are so special to me. I love you and thank you from my whole heart!

Charles BKA (Chuckie to me), thanks for putting up with all that annoying contact from me years ago on Facebook and those text messages. Your openness within that last message really blessed me. I needed your help and you came through for me. Beyond that, thank you for just being real. It takes a genuine person to be real with me, and I appreciate it. I love ya', fam!

Mar, you are invaluably special to me. Thank you for sharing your promoting gifts and talents with me.

Phay, my manager who has bigger dreams for me than I have for myself, I am so thankful our paths crossed some sixteen years ago. You are so much more than a friend, and the sister I never had. Thank you for encouraging the gifts God placed in me. Now, it's my turn to do the same for you!

To my entire family, thank you for being who you are! I love you.

To my editor, who made this book so much tighter than it was when you received it, Janet A., Project Team Three at CreateSpace, Sara Zola, and John Rieck, thank you for making me feel like my project is as important to you as it is to me.

Again, I must give a shout-out my church home, Faith Tabernacle Christian Center in St. Pauls, North Carolina (www.ftccenter.org), where Earl and Denise Goings serve as our founders and pastors. I'm still thrilled to be joined to you and to witness all that God is extending from this local body of believers.

To my former coworkers at the Public Schools of Robeson County (who I miss dearly), my present coworkers at Robeson Community College, and all the students I have had over the years, thank you. You will never know how much of a blessing you have been to me.

To my Lesley University doctorate classmates and my professors, this book was supposed to be done before I met any of you. When did I find time to finish this novel while posting comments to discussion boards, delving into scholarly journals, decoding Brookfield, and creating annotated bibliographies? Regardless of the time it takes for us to complete assignments and take steps closer to this terminal degree, I must say that I'm glad that I'm walking this journey with you—the Twelves forever!

To Spellman College and Emory University, I appreciate what you did for me. Without you, I would not be me.

Accolades for *Blindsided*, a best-selling novel by
E. Marie Sanders

"In my opinion, *Blindsided* is one of the best Young Adult novels that I have ever read. As a literacy specialist in the public school system, I'm always looking for engaging material to peak my students' interest in reading. In addition to the ease in readability, I found the book to be a timeless piece of literature that uniquely delves into many of the modern-day situations that plague our youth. The language is rich and the characters are highly believable. I recommend using this book as a class read for struggling readers and for those students who can never seem to find anything of interest to read. This book is sure to captivate their interests."

-Moneike, a Barnes & Noble Reader

"E. Marie Sanders did it again! She left me sitting on the edge of my seat with the end! If you have a teenager, this is a DEFINITE read as well! The things I love about E. Marie Sanders' books are the Love of God, and also not forgetting the temptations that people have even when they have a relationship with Him."

-Latasha Prescott Wilson, Amazon Reader

"I was left on edge throughout the entire read. The chapters flowed together so smoothly that I did not notice the transition. I was able to visualize everything that you exposed to your reader. Thank you for sharing your amazing gift with us. I'm excitedly trying to secure funding to order this text for my students during the summer as well as during the school year. Keep up the great writing and inspiration. You are jewel in the midst of awesome authors."

-Vanessa Robinson, Amazon Reader

"I have been a follower of E. Marie Sanders and her work since *To K(no)w Avail,* and just like her first book this one did not disappoint. I was extremely impressed by the ease of the characters and how the storyline flowed. It wasn't rushed or pressed; it was as if I was following Marlena and her family through this time in their lives. I especially appreciate how the subject matter was handled while still contained within the boundaries of a Christian fiction heading. That in itself is a true rarity."

-Yolanda Gaston, Poet

For more information about Blindsided and other projects by E. Marie Sanders, visit www.emariesanders.com

Consequences and Repercussions

BOOK TWO IN THE K(NO)W SERIES

If you have yet to read *To K(no)w Avail,* Book One in The K(no)w Series, you may want to read it before you read this book, *Consequences and Repercussions,* which is Book Two in the series. That way you will begin the series by getting to know Kyle Thompson, the charismatic football jock who fell for Avail Andrews, the slightly naïve and intelligent coed who struggled between keeping her vow to God and giving in to her desires. Her friends, Raine and Shea, provided the sisterly advice she never got growing up with two older brothers, and Frick, Grey, and Reese, the ultimate upperclassmen, showed a level of attractive sophistication unmatched by anyone younger than them. Camden and her crew delivered just enough interference to cause problems in a budding relationship while Celeste, Kyle's ex-girlfriend, made a powerful, threatening promise to Avail.

Part One

One

Her Way

"Avail, if you need anything, let me know," Mom called through the door.

I had to do my best to assure her that I was okay, so I replied, "Thanks, Mom. I'm just going to take a nap." Sitting on the edge of my bed, I took my hands out of my lap and smoothed the comforter directly next to my legs. I tried to settle myself, but that proved to be a difficult task with everything that had transpired over the past twenty-four hours. Last night, I was in a beautiful hotel room with Kyle after what turned out to be a minor car accident. I thought that we could have lost each other, thus throwing me into a romantic ambiance between our college campus and home with my incredibly sexy boyfriend who sent me into a lustful whirlwind just by getting out of the shower. Our undressed bodies' desires rode the wave of emotion we both felt. All scruples, morals, and vows flew out the window for the sake of us experiencing each other for the first time, even though we had agreed not to go there. I couldn't believe that we lost control so easily.

An intense kiss turned into gentle pecks as Kyle loosened my ponytail; he preferred my hair down so that he could play in it. As the directions of his kisses aimed for my neck, I briefly opened my eyes to take in the atmosphere of the moment. Shadows danced on the walls from the candles placed around the Jacuzzi tub in the bathroom. White and cream linens surrounded my body, and Kyle's glowing skin cross-sectioned mine in ways that made it feel as if an electric current was passing between us. I couldn't articulate how Kyle was feeling, but I felt like I was on the brink of explosion. I wanted more, but I didn't know how much more I could take.

"Do you want me to stop?" Kyle asked as he caressed my hips and kissed my neck in synchronization, both hot spots for me. Almost desperately, he asked again, "Do you?"

My mouth admitted, "No, don't stop," despite the warnings in my heart.

So we continued with full consent for one another. He started kissing areas that he'd never kissed before, and I felt like a virgin, embarrassed but totally engulfed in the enjoyment of this new feeling. Minutes before, I felt him stiffen against my leg, and I knew what came next. I just had to invite him in by spreading my legs just enough....

And then it happened. Kyle's cell phone sang the ring tone that he'd programmed for both Raine and

Shea. Before Kyle and I left, I told them that if they needed me, they could hit me up on his cell until I got home. I directed them not to call the house because it was supposed to be a surprise that I was coming home a day earlier than expected. Kyle, recognizing the ring tone, stopped his pursuit and asked, "Do you think we should answer that? It may be an emergency." He lingered around my belly button, but then he looked up questioningly as I reached for the phone. Kyle eventually pulled his bathrobe to cover me before getting up to get the other one in the bathroom. After confirming that Raine's number was on the screen, I hit the button and said," Hey girl, what's up?"

At first, all I heard through the line was sniffling and light crying. Before I could inquire what was wrong, Maurice's voice chimed in and said, "Hey Avail, it's Reese. Raine wanted to call you, but she can't stop crying right now."

I knew enough to understand that Maurice didn't do anything to hurt her, but I still didn't understand why she was so upset. "What's wrong with Raine? Why is she crying?"

I heard Maurice console Raine, and she managed to quiet her small whimpers. "She wanted you to know that we just found out that we're pregnant."

"Pregnant?" I repeated. I felt like I shouted my surprise.

It was a sign from God for Kyle and me at that critical moment, freezing us from continuing in the act we'd so hungrily pursued. It gave us such a harsh, tangible jolt of reality that everything came to an immediate stop, and suddenly, Kyle and I had what we'd always lacked: self-control.

Eventually, Raine talked to me on the phone, letting me know that she was okay but very shocked. I managed to make her laugh a few times, and I offered to come back to campus, though really, we had no way to get back since the mechanic had agreed to work on the car overnight. Kyle spoke with Maurice and Raine, and then he settled next to me after disconnecting the phone call.

The news itself was sobering, but the timing of it could not have been a coincidence at all. It was divine and planned. Now, the question was what to say to Kyle.

As it turned out, I didn't have to say anything to him, because once I returned from dressing myself in the bathroom, he had made himself comfortable on the pullout sofa bed. I didn't want to disturb him, so I crawled into the bed where we had almost consummated our relationship, and fell into a nervous, uneasy sleep.

When I woke up the next morning, Kyle had already been to the mechanic to pick up the car. I found a note on the nightstand instructing me to meet him in the lobby when I was packed and ready. I understood his need to take precautions because of everything that almost went down the night before, but it seemed that he was being a little too cautious. Nonetheless, he was my ride home. If I got down there, we could talk about it and get all the awkwardness out in the open.

Kyle was still as courteous and loving as he usually was, but I knew something had changed when quiet consumed the first ten minutes of the ride. I couldn't take it anymore, so I asked, "Are you thinking about last night?"

A good portion of the man I knew before this incident returned to reality by glancing over at me and replying, "Honestly, Avail, I can't believe that I tempted you to break the promise we both made." He shifted his vision back to the road and said, "I'm so disappointed in myself."

I really could not believe that Kyle blamed himself for everything that had happened. He didn't plan for us to have a car accident or to get tremendously romantic in a hotel room. He didn't choreograph anything that went down between us. It did—and then didn't—happen, but now he saw the fault in what had almost happened. I did too, and I wanted him to know it.

"Kyle," I began carefully, "you were not the only one involved with everything that almost went down last night. My urges are just a strong as yours are, and I totally threw aside everything that mattered to me for the sake of one night with you. You can't possibly take this totally as your fault. I'm at fault too."

It was as if what I had said brought him no comfort whatsoever. "I should have stopped us. Thank God, really, that Raine called when she did, but her news didn't make our situation any better."

Kyle is being really hard on this. I have a feeling that some changes are coming to our relationship...strict changes that I might not like.

7

"The important thing is that we stopped, and just like you, I am thankful that we did," I offered. "If we hadn't, we could be in the same predicament as Reese and Raine."

Now, why did I say that? That flipped Kyle out just a little. "I know, and if that had happened to us, I would man up. I wouldn't ask you to do anything like terminate the pregnancy. I'd have to man up, for real." I didn't mean for my last statement to send him into a hypothetical scenario that had him rising to an imaginary challenge, but it was reassuring to know that he would handle his responsibility of our fictitious child.

"But Kyle, we don't have to worry about being pregnant because we're not."

Kyle didn't hear a word I said. "There's no way I would ask you to abort my child; no way under any circumstances. You wouldn't be able to go through with it anyway. You couldn't handle it. You're way too loving and caring, and there's no way you could do it." And suddenly it hit me why Kyle babbled on and on the way he did: It was because of Celeste and the child she aborted that they had conceived together. I reached over to stroke the back of his neck to show him that I understood, but my touch only made him flinch and continue his stream of imaginary consciousness. I returned my hand to my lap and sat silently.

When we pulled in front of my house, my parents ran out to greet us. Kyle felt obligated to explain the car accident as the reason we had stayed the night in a hotel room together, and he reassured them that nothing had happened between us. As frantic as he spoke, I was almost sure that he would give them blow-by-blow details of everything that went down, but he restrained himself, looking painful as he did it.

"And what exactly gave the two of you the bright idea of leaving campus that late?" my father demanded of me once Kyle left.

I had spent all my nerves on the situation with Kyle, but it wasn't like I could just go off on my father. Calmly, I said, "We wanted to surprise you and mom and his parents by coming in a day early." Adding a little embellishment, I said with puppy-dog-daughter eyes, "We learned about our grades and wanted to come home to share them with you. It seemed like a good idea at the time." Maybe that would soften up my father a bit.

It didn't work, but my mother chimed in. "Well, I'm thankful that the accident was no worse than it was and that you two only came out with minor injuries. How long will it take Kyle's gash to heal?"

"I think the paramedics said only a week. It's amazing how those liquid stitches work," I commented.

I don't think my father was falling for any of this part of the conversation purposed to divert him from the whole I-spent-the-night-with-my-boyfriend thing. "Did anything else happen?" I knew exactly what my father was asking, but I'd best be careful of what I said.

"Daddy, Kyle was a perfect gentleman, and we slept in separate beds." I didn't lie, but the details of what led up to sleeping separately would kill my father.

My answer seemed to satisfy both my parents, and I headed for my room where I sat for the moment, reviewing everything that happened, especially how close I came to getting a piece of Kyle.

I want to call him, but there's no telling where his head is. I'll just give him some space for now.

$\mathcal{O}ne$

His Way

$\mathcal{M}$om and Dad were not home when I arrived after dropping off Avail, and that was a relief. If there is one thing that annoys me about my parents, it's the fact that they can see straight through me when I'm troubled.

I can't deny that right now; troubled seems to be a light word for the way I'm feeling.

Instantly, I flashed back to my explanation to Avail's parents; I had attempted to be open with them while not saying too much. "When I lost control of the car," I shared nervously with Mr. Andrews, "we slid off the road and hit a tree head on. Since the car was damaged badly and the mechanic who came with the tow truck said that he could fix it overnight, Avail and I shared a hotel room for the evening instead of bothering you or my parents."

Even as the last bit came out of my mouth, I knew that Avail's father wasn't going to like it. I didn't mean it the way it sounded. Before I could clarify what I really meant, I heard Mrs. Andrews say, "Well, I'm just glad the two of you are okay. What you did was dangerous; just know that next time, maybe you should wait until the roads are officially cleared."

"Yes, ma'am," I replied thankfully, mainly because when she interjected, I managed to escape the wrath of Mr. Andrews.

Avail and I said our goodbyes as her parents went into the house. As much as I don't want to admit it to myself, this whole incident has changed our relationship, and I'm not convinced that it's for the best right now. Just last night, I exposed myself to her, and I enjoyed parts of her that I knew would drive me crazy. Even as I contemplate the state of uncertainty of our relationship, I remember how her back arched to make her slightly sculpted abs meet southern-bound kisses from my lips. The drive home gave me time to remember Avail's body and the ways it projected its excitement to me, and I couldn't deny that I had taken pleasure in every moan and sigh that escaped her mouth.

If she had said no when I asked her if she wanted to stop, it would have been hard—and it was hard—for me to stop, but when we were totally in the moment, she didn't turn away from me.

How aroused I was appeared to be no secret, especially when her legs relaxed and opened just for me to enter—to the sound of a ring tone I set for both Raine and Shea on my cell phone. I felt like having an adult temper tantrum, because after withholding myself from this woman for almost four whole months, I finally was going to get some from her. I was going to connect with her in a way that only I would be able to—even though I knew that we had agreed not to go there.

When she reached for the phone, I was pretty sure that our action had come to a complete stop, especially because I know how her long her conversations with Raine and Shea tend to be. I pulled the robe I had on over her and walked swiftly into the bathroom to retrieve the other.

From the bathroom, I heard Avail say, "Pregnant?" *Oh no, who is pregnant?* I wasn't sure whether Avail was talking to Raine or Shea.

Upon my return to the main room, completely robed, Avail continued her conversation with the party on the other line, and my head began to spin. Just a few minutes ago, I was in the process of making love to my girlfriend for the first time, and now, as if by some act from God, one of our friends has told us that she's pregnant. I didn't think that Frick and Shea got down like that just yet, but I was pretty sure that Reese and Raine had taken the plunge. They were on an entirely different level from every couple I knew. Reese had the reputation for being deep, and Raine adapted his persona to a certain extent. Nonetheless, no level of deepness could prepare anyone for an unexpected, first-year-in-college pregnancy. I didn't have the skills to handle it when I got Celeste pregnant, and we were just in high school.

"Kyle, it's Raine. She has some news she wants to share with you too," Avail said quietly as she handed me the phone. *So, it's Reese and Raine.*

I sat next to Avail and began, "Hey, sis," because, really, I didn't know what I was going to say to her. How could I comfort a friend who had just found out some life-changing information, since only minutes ago, I was attempting to perform the act that got them in their situation? "What's going on?" seemed appropriate.

"Hey, Kyle." Raine sounded a little more chipper than I thought she would be. I guess she was laughing on the other end when Avail laughed on this end. "I didn't mean to interrupt your time with Avail—especially after your accident. Are both of you ok?" Avail must have shared a brief portion of what happened with us tonight. Judging from Raine's general concern about our car wreck, it was obvious that Avail hadn't let it slip that we were going at it hot and heavy when she called.

"Are we ok?" I asked rhetorically. "I should be asking you that question. I heard Avail mention something about someone being pregnant."

"Yeah, I just took a home pregnancy test and found out that I'm pregnant," Raine said, as if she was trying to maintain her composure with me. "Of course, I took it here in Reese's room, and once we found out, I really fell to pieces. I don't know why, but I wanted to tell Avail and you immediately."

You may not know why, but I'm sure that God wanted to use your phone call to stop Avail and me in our pursuit of having sex for the first time.

14

I thought this, but all I said was, "I'm glad that you did," and truly I was, even though my body still ached for Avail. I knew stopping was for the best. "You know that if there's anything we can do for you, just let us know." I meant that sincerely. Raine is more than a friend. She's like that annoying sister who tells you the truth when you don't want to hear it, but it's exactly what you need at the time.

"Just do me a favor; say something to Reese. He's okay, but Avail's support made me feel better. I'm sure you'll do the same for him."

Reese and I were on speaking terms, but we never engaged in extensive conversation. Since she's my sister, I obliged by saying, "Okay, put him on the phone."

As Raine passed the phone to Reese, Avail gathered the robe around her, picked her clothing up from various places in the room, and headed to the bathroom to get dressed, I assumed. Just as she entered the bathroom, I heard Reese say, "Hey, Kyle, thanks for talking with Raine. The news hit us both pretty hard, but I know we'll be okay."

I shared with Reese the same thing I had told Raine. "Well, man, if there's anything we can do to help just let us know. Raine's like my sister, so that automatically makes you fam. For real though, just let us know what we can do."

I think I threw Reese off with my remarks, and I didn't know anyone could do that. He simply thanked me for my offer and said that he had to get back to Raine, and then he ended the conversation abruptly.

I was still a little miffed about what had happened between Avail and me, so I decided that it would be in our best interest to sleep in separate beds. As I made up the sofa bed, I rationalized in my mind about not sleeping on it. I wanted to be in the same bed with Avail so much it hurt, but then I kept thinking that all it would take was for one of us to accidentally roll over and initiate physical contact to find ourselves in the same position we were in before the phone call.

But the phone call settled everything in my mind. I jumped into the sofa bed and pulled the covers up to my shoulders in an instant flashback of the time Celeste was pregnant. She had thrown the test at me from the doorway of the bathroom and screamed, "See, I told you I was pregnant!" I had forced her to take the test because of all the fake pregnancies she'd had in an attempt to hold on to me. I remember staring at the plus sign on the test stick verifying the pregnancy hormone in her system and secretly beginning to panic. Not only had I created life with this woman I loved—though I hated the things she did in the name of love—but now I was tied to her for life through our child. We hadn't graduated from high school yet, which meant college would be out the question, and I would have to take any job I could find to raise a child with Celeste.

We argued about it that very night. She claimed that I would leave her for one of the other girls I dated on the side, and I did my best to convince her that I would step up to my responsibilities. Days later, she accused me of the very act, argued with me again, slammed the phone in my ear, and from what I understood, she made the call to set up the appointment for an abortion immediately after she hung up on me. When she told me what she had done, my first instinct was to choke her. I wanted to choke the life out of her, just as she allowed my baby's life to be sucked out of her, and without my consent! She didn't lie down by herself! That was my son or daughter too.

Yet now I lay here perplexed in my feelings, because the act that Avail and I almost ventured into had the potential for her to get pregnant. I had no condom. I know that she's not on any form of birth control—and even so, bigger than all of this, we almost reneged on our vow to God. What does that say about my lack of self-control—my lack of self-discipline?

I know one thing that it does say: I have to make some pretty serious changes in this relationship, if we can still have one at all.

$$\sim$$

$\mathcal{S}$leep did not lift a single thing off my mind. I felt heavy, as if the weight of the world slept on my chest and didn't move when I got up to take a shower. Even though Avail was in a deep sleep, I closed and locked the bathroom door, wore a robe to and from the shower, and dressed in the bathroom. When I saw and heard the message on my cell phone from the mechanic stating that the car was ready and I could pick it up anytime, I wrote Avail a quick note to let her know that I had gone to pick up the car and that she could meet me downstairs.

When I returned to pick up Avail, she wasn't in the lobby yet, which gave me time to reflect on the good that came out of this whole situation. Raine called at the right time. Avail and I didn't break our vow. I can't think about what I'm "missing" since I didn't experience Avail last night, and now I'm thinking about the limitations we'll have to place on our relationship. Knowing Avail the way that I do, I will have to be the enforcer of these new restrictions. When I remember the night I asked her to be my girlfriend, I know for a fact that if I hadn't stopped our physical pursuits then, Avail and I would have made love. I don't know where I got the strength the stop us then, but I know I'll have to pull from that source until we both can maintain a level of self-control.

When Avail exited the elevator, I rushed to grab her bags. I would do my best not to let the evening's events bother me. I had to take responsibility for dealing with how I felt, including the flashbacks of my unborn child. I also had to face the fact that I still wanted Avail even though I knew I couldn't have her. I opened her door to seat her, loaded her luggage in the car, and began the drive home.

Planning as I drove, I figured that Avail and I could handle being around each other, but I knew that we would have to cut out our all-night study sessions. Sleeping over was definitely out of the question. I didn't think we would have to put an end to being alone completely, but we couldn't tease our desires by being alone at night. This all seemed very reasonable to me, but I hoped that Avail would see the reasoning behind it.

I don't want to be the one that she'll regret sleeping with. I want what we have to last.

I guess my internal planning created too much silence in the car because out of nowhere, Avail said, "Are you thinking about last night?"

I wasn't trying to avoid the subject. I knew we'd talk about it eventually, but I was still trying to develop a plan so that we wouldn't find ourselves in that situation again. Putting on my best front, I glanced over at her and said, "Honestly, Avail, I can't believe that I tempted you to break the promise we made." I returned my attention to the road and added, "I'm so disappointed in myself." More truth than she probably realized came out in that statement, but at this point, she should know what I mean.

"Kyle, you were not the only one involved with everything that almost went down last night. My urges are just a strong as yours, and I totally threw everything that mattered to me to the side for the sake of one night with you. You can't possibly take this totally as your fault. I'm at fault too."

I did my best not to look at this as whose fault last night was, but everything in me said that the responsibility lay with me. I was the one who insisted on getting on the road early. I was the one who initiated that tender moment in the bathroom. I was the one who took sensual liberties that I knew she didn't want to experience before marriage. I was the man in this relationship. I offered, "I should have stopped us. Thank God, really, that Raine and Maurice called when they did, but her news didn't make our situation any better."

In an attempt, I think, to make me feel better, Avail said, "The important thing is that we stopped, and just like you, I am thankful that we did. If we hadn't, we could be in the same predicament as Reese and Raine."

For no reason whatsoever, her statement sent me into a state of panic, and I brainstormed aloud. "I know, and if that had happened to us, I would man up. I wouldn't ask you to do anything like terminate the pregnancy. I'd have to man up, for real." I heard Avail chime in, but I have no idea what she said. I continued to ramble, "There's no way I would ask you to abort my child; no way under any circumstances. You wouldn't be able to go through with it anyway. You couldn't handle it. You're way too loving and caring, and there's no way you could do it. I want you to be the mother of my children, just not now. I know that you would be great. I would be a great father. You couldn't…you wouldn't kill my baby. I'm not saying it would be easy, but there's no way we would take the easy way out by having an abortion. You would need me to be there with you, and plus, you wouldn't be able to do it anyway." When I realized that Avail had retreated from the conversation and I was babbling, I just stopped without another word until we reached the front of Avail's home.

I flopped onto my waterbed, returning to the present, knowing that, after our close call last night, and my issues concerning my experience with Celeste, things would never be the same with Avail no matter how much I wanted them to be.

Two

HER WAY

The nap that turned into full sleep managed to refresh me and help me pop out of bed early the next day. Before reaching the kitchen, I smelled evidence of scrambled eggs, sausage, and hash browns—my mom's perfect breakfast food that was sure to extinguish my morning hunger. Mom stood there, dressed for work and pouring herself a cup of coffee. Since I'm on vacation, she asked me, "What do you have planned for the day?"

Having noticed that my parents had not set up the Christmas decorations yet, I suggested, "I'll probably do some general cleaning and pull the Christmas lights out to make sure they work."

Mom looked a little shocked when she said, "You didn't get my message before you left campus, did you?" I simply shook my head no. "One of my cousins who I haven't seen in years called us to see if we wanted to spend the holidays with them. Your dad liked the idea, and we made plans to spend the Christmas holiday with them."

I had so many questions. "Who is this cousin I've never heard about before? Will there be anyone my age there? And where are we going?" Mom chuckled at my rapid-fire questioning skills.

"To answer all of your questions, it's my first cousin on your grandfather's side, Bryan, and yes, he does have kids close to your age, a set of twins. He lost his wife a few years ago and moved from one part of Maryland to another. In fact, he doesn't live that far from his old home in Baltimore…Hagerstown, I believe it is."

The possibility of a road trip for the holiday never crossed my mind, but I was sure it wouldn't be that bad. At least I would get to see another part of the county and meet some new family members. The only drawback was that I wouldn't see Kyle while we were gone.

I couldn't really guarantee that Kyle wanted to be bothered with me now anyway. It seemed my existence served as a reminder that he had almost coerced me to break my celibacy vow to God, but I really didn't want him to beat himself up about it too much. I was in that bed with him. I undressed him. I invited him to experience more of me. The worst he did was to accept my invitation.

Then my thoughts turned to Raine and Reese. To find out that they're pregnant the night before leaving campus for the holidays must've been devastating.

I had no idea what they were going to do, but Reese gave me the impression that he did not condone abortion. He valued life, and now that they had created one, I was sure he would handle his responsibility with keen attentiveness.

Breaking into my thoughts, my mother confirmed as she walked out the door that my father had pulled an early shift and that they both would return home close to 6:00 p.m. Since it was my first day back, I thought I would use the day to prepare for this unexpected trip. First things first, I needed to see where this town was. The name itself made it sound tiny and insignificant, but what did I know? Meeting new family in a new-to-me city might prove to be a great thing for this much-needed break from school. I started a general search on the computer, checking out maps that gave me some interesting information. Hagerstown is not that far from Baltimore, and in Baltimore are my boys, Frick and Grey.

Before all the snowball fight events went down, Grey and I exchanged home numbers and private email addresses so that we could stay in touch over the break. Flashing back to a key moment in the snowball fight, Grey confessed that he had feelings for me, but he hadn't moved forward on them since Kyle and I had become an official couple. I could almost admit to myself that, in that moment, something sparked within me in terms of my feelings for Grey. He was honorable and upstanding. It didn't hurt that his athletic six-foot-four basketball frame, chocolate brown skin, dark brown eyes, high cheekbones, pretty lips, and dazzling smile made him easy to look at. And it only helped that he was smart and a great friend.

Since I was on the computer, I thought it would be a good idea to send Grey an email. An email was all well and good, but I had to have a reason for sending it without it looking staged. I didn't want to just blurt out that I would be in Hagerstown for Christmas. Understanding that he would know that it's not that far from Baltimore combined with the fact that I was just thinking about his inner and outer appeal, I just felt like getting in contact with him—no biggie! After signing in to my account, I composed the following note: "Hey Grey. I just thought that I would drop you a line to thank you again for helping me with my prob and stats class." That seemed like a good way to start. "I don't think I would have passed without your help."

Okay, we're easing into the friend zone now.

"I was just wondering what your plans are for the holiday since we didn't talk about it. My mom just told me that the family will be traveling to Hagerstown, Maryland, to spend Christmas with one of my mother's cousins." I paused here because I really wasn't sure if I should mention the fact that I knew it wasn't that far from Baltimore. Then, as the thought developed in my mind, I typed, "I know that it's not that far from Baltimore."

I hope that statement isn't inferring that I would like to see him if he's close by. Pausing again, I laughed at myself because I was analyzing this email way too much.

Let me wrap this up in a quick closing paragraph.

"Well, regardless of your plans, I hope you will enjoy yourself and your family. If you have any basketball tournaments during the break and you're playing near Pittsburgh, let me know. I'll be home before the New Year. Tell Frick I said what's up, and you take care. Avail."

I reread the email and concluded that it carried an innocent and friendly tone, and clicked send with a smile on my face.

⌒

*I*n the late afternoon, I was immersed in my regular chores of laundry and cleaning the bathrooms when the phone rang. I scrambled to the closest cordless set and checked the caller ID before I picked it up. It was a 937 number, which meant it was either Raine or Shea calling. I hit the flash button to connect the call and almost desperately greeted, "Hello!"

"Hey girl," Shea greeted. "What are you up to?" I gave Shea just a quick review of the day's events, nothing major, when she interjected and said, "I guess Raine has called you since you left campus."

A quiver dropped in my stomach. "Yeah, she told me about the pregnancy. How is she? I mean, how is she really? I know you saw her before you left campus."

"I sure did," Shea confirmed. "Frick and I went over to Reese's room after she called me. On the outside, she looked okay, as much can be expected when someone receives news like that. But I have to admit that I'm a little concerned about her."

I didn't like how this was sounding. "What aren't you telling me, Shea?"

Shea hesitated, but continued. "I can't put my finger on it. Before we left, she grabbed my arm and asked if I would be there for her regardless of what happens or what goes down. She seemed desperate, and I think she's going to do something desperate."

I didn't want to jump to conclusions, so I offered, "Maybe she just wants to be sure that we have her back; you know, that regardless of the pregnancy, we'll all still be tight."

"That's not the impression I got." Shea paused. "I think she's thinking about terminating the pregnancy."

"An abortion?" I questioned. "No way! There is no way that Reese would consent to that. The act itself is contrary to everything he believes."

"If she does it before we come back to Whitaker, he'll have no say in the matter. He lives in Georgia. She's up here in Ohio with...."

I cut Shea off and asked, "Did she give you any indication that she would abort the baby?"

"Directly, no, but I can tell that it's a thought in her mind. It's just something that I picked up in the few times we talked before our parents came to get us."

Of the three of us, Shea is the most intuitive, so I take what she senses seriously. "Have you talked to her since you got home? I mean, I know it's only been a day, but still."

"That's the thing. Raine always answers her phone, even when she's sleeping and my call wakes her up. Either she's not taking my calls or she's not thinking about anything other than the baby."

Panicking a little, I insisted, "We've got to make sure she knows that we'll be there to help with the pregnancy and the baby as much as we can."

We continued talking until we resolved that during fall semester, if necessary, we'd take classes around the needs of the baby, eliminating the need for day care, and the three of us would get an apartment off campus. I was sure that Reese would jump into the mix somehow, but there was no way we were going to leave our girl hangin' in her time of need. We weren't going to abandon Raine just because she was pregnant. If anything, we were going to do everything to hold her up. Now we just had to make sure she knew that, but with Raine not answering her phone, letting her know would be a challenge.

Two

His Way

Being in the house was driving me crazy, but a large portion of me didn't want to get out of the bed simply because I thought that would mean having to deal with some fierce realities in my life. Whether I want to admit it or not, there's a huge part of me still grieving the abortion of my child, and that happened years ago. I don't care how things were at that time between Celeste and me. I still can't understand how any situation on this earth could make anyone want to destroy a defenseless child. Even if we couldn't have taken care of the baby, we could have placed the child up for adoption. Sometimes I wonder if Celeste did it for purely selfish reasons. After all, she would be the one showing physical evidence of what we did and what we created. I would not have had to live with the same level of shame that she would have faced. Or, like she enjoys saying, maybe she did it to get back at me.

Either way, my child is dead, and I never really dealt with it. Around the holidays, it's even worse because I'm surrounded by family and friends…and their children. What tops it all is that our child was due right around Christmas.

There was also the whole idea that I could have impregnated my current girlfriend, Avail, who I'm sure is wondering if I'm okay. We haven't said a decent word to one another since I dropped her off, and even then, our conversation was so tense. I should call her, but I'm ashamed of how I pushed her into dropping her vow to God like it's nothing. I placed her in that situation, but we did stop thanks to a phone call from Raine. Her situation just makes me think of my unborn child again and sink a little lower into a quiet, dim depression.

I was never one to wallow in my own pity for too long; plus, whether I did it enough or not, I knew that prayer could fix a lot of this. So, I slid my limp body out of bed, and knelt on the floor as I leaned against the edge of the bed. The side of my face made contact with the warm, water-filled mattress, and I began my chitchat with Jesus: "I need your help, Lord. I'm in this depressed mood, and I know you didn't put me in it, but I know that if I repent, You'll help me out of it." I then lifted my head, propped my elbows on the bed, clasped my hands in a traditional prayer stance, and leaned my forehead against my hands. "I know You have forgiven me for my ways with Celeste, for the creation of the baby, and even for the abortion of the baby. I got that—I just have issues with it, issues that

I don't quite know how to handle. I mourn the loss of my baby every year around this time; I feel like I can't control my sexual desires; and on top of it all, I almost asked Avail to break her vow to You by having sex with me. Please forgive me for that. You gave me these desires; You designed me this way, so I know that with Your help, I can control my urges. Look out for me in this area, please. Until I can fight it off, keep me from temptation. One more thing: please continue the process of healing me of the hurt of losing my child to abortion." I sighed heavily and wished I could hear God say something, anything to me. Refocusing on the underlying issue that bothered me the most, I wrapped up the prayer with, "Thank You for Your warning that kept Avail and me from sleeping together, but I do want to lift up Raine and Reese for the situation they are now facing. Help them and show them exactly what they need to do. Thanks for listening. Amen."

As I knew it would, the prayer helped, but I still felt the need to share these issues with someone, so I got dressed and headed straight for The House of Refuge, my church home. At this time in the afternoon, my pastor should just be finishing his lunch.

⌒

"Hey Kyle, it's good to see you. You must have just got home," my pastor, Rev. Johnson, greeted through his traditional man grip and hug. "How did you finish up your semester?"

I laughed and replied, "No sir, I've been home for a day, and I finished up with a high B average. Not too bad for a first semester in college." I took in his approving smile and nods, and then I said, "I've had some things on my mind, and that's why I came to see you."

The joyful look on his face turned into slight concern as Rev. Johnson offered me a seat across from his desk. As he sat down, he asked, "What can I help you with, Kyle?"

"Well, there are a few things on my mind...." I drifted for a moment and eventually said, "I really don't know where to start."

"I do remember that around this time of the year, you tend to reflect on the child you and Celeste conceived that resulted in an abortion."

I really appreciate the fact that my pastor not only listens to me, but he remembers issues that I have. He's a great confidant.

"I can understand why you're still dealing with it."

"Well, Pastor, it has hit me in a harder way this year. It just surfaced more strongly because of something that almost happened," I admitted.

"What was that?"

I swallowed hard and slowly began explaining to him about the vow that Avail and I had made to remain abstinent, and then I told him about the car accident and the events in the hotel room, ending with the phone call from Raine and the news she shared with us. Rev. Johnson concentrated on every detail that I shared with him, knowing that I was being totally transparent with him. When I ended, he leaned back in his chair and said, "Knowing you the way I know you, you've already reflected on every part of this issue and have probably come up with some strategies as to what you need to do in the future to avoid these situations."

"Yes, sir, I have."

After clearing his throat, Rev. Johnson began. "Let's take this issue by issue. If you have really repented about the abortion of your child, then you shouldn't be walking around in condemnation. The Bible says there is no condemnation for those who are in Christ Jesus. That means you should not dwell on the past when God has forgiven you." I choked back a tear, and he continued. "That's the thing about sin. Even though we walk in God's forgiveness, the enemy uses the past to make us feel less than a child of God. It's one of the many consequences and repercussions of sin."

Rev. Johnson continued, and I heard every word he said, but the phrase "consequences and repercussions" kept echoing through my mind.

Three

Her Way

After winding down my cleaning, I thought I would give Kyle a call. It had been almost a whole day since I spoke with him, and I couldn't recall us ever going that long without speaking. Surely, we weren't mad or upset with each other, but I wanted to respect the space he was in. Lots of conflicting feelings were running through him now, including the fact that he and Celeste once were in the predicament that Reese and Raine were in. I picked up the phone and decided to let him know that he could count on me for support while he dealt with his issues.

While attempting to dial his home number, I accidentally hit a key on the keyboard that made my screen saver disappear, revealing a message in the lower right-hand section of my computer monitor notifying me that I had some unopened emails. I put the phone receiver on its base and reviewed my emails.

Of the twenty or so unopened correspondences, the one with Raine's name on it caught my attention first. I immediately opened it. "Shea and Avail," it began, "I know you well enough to know that you have been trying to call me. I just wanted to let you know that I'm okay. I just need a few days to process everything that has happened and figure out how to tell my family. I'm not casting you to the side—you mean too much to me to do that. I just need this space. I'll be in touch before we return to Whitaker. Have a great holiday with your family. Love ya. Raine."

I know she said she needed the space, but I felt compelled to email her. After all, she didn't have to open it until she was ready to read it. "Hey Raine, I know you got a lot on your mind, but I want you to know that Shea and I are your girls. We're prepared to do whatever we got to do to help. We can talk details later. Enjoy your time off, and I'll see you in January. Love ya. Avail." I wanted to say enough but not too much. There was no need to alert her of our suspicions in her fragile state.

I reviewed the inbox list one more time before I clicked Delete All, and I was glad that I did because an email from Grey caught my eye. A motivated grin came across my face, and I know I lit up. I inhaled through my nose like I do when I'm in a yoga session, and I clicked on his reply. "Hey Avail, it's good to hear from you, and I'm glad that you made it home safely. I heard about the accident Kyle and you were in, but I'm glad you didn't sustain any bad injuries."

Okay, I know Whitaker is small, but I didn't know that our accident was public knowledge. No biggie, but Grey's concern for my safety was a biggie for me. How sweet of him.

His next paragraph read, "As for Christmas, my family will gather at my grandfather and grandmother's home and hang out just about all day. It's nothing terribly special, but there's enough for us to enjoy each other during the season. Frick and I have plans to hook up that evening, but again, nothing terribly special." Next paragraph: "So, you'll be in Hagerstown? Yeah, you're right. It's not that far away from B'more, but there's not too much to do there being that you're used to Pittsburgh. I'm sure you'll find the normal stuff to get into."

Wow, that really doesn't make me look forward to the trip, but there's nothing I can do about it.

Grey closed his email by writing, "I hope you enjoy your time off. You deserve it since you worked so hard this semester. We don't have any basketball tournaments during the break, but the first Wednesday we're back, we play at Waynesburg. I hope you'll come to the game to cheer us on. If I don't talk to you before the end of break, I'll see you back at Whitaker. Y'boy, Grey."

My cheeks grew warm as I reread the email twice. I was glad that Grey had emailed me, but it was also clear that I was trippin' over him. I needed to calm down. He was my friend, and that was all.

Kyle is my boyfriend—who I was going to call before I opened up these emails. I better give him a call now.

Three

His Way

Rev. Johnson and I examined every issue we discussed and I left feeling as if a major burden had been lifted. I saw hope again, even within the parameters of our relationship that Avail and I would have to honor, but it would become a habit worth establishing. Speaking of Avail, I need to give her a call. This must be the first time since we've known each other that we've gone more than twenty-four hours without speaking.

Standing on the steps of the church, I pulled out my cell phone and dialed Avail's home number. Just before I hit the Send button, Celeste walked around the corner and trekked up the stairs. I made eye contact with her without making a connection with her. It was as if she was a shell of her former self, and I knew why. She was probably experiencing the same mood swings that I'd just gotten over. "Hi," I managed to whisper.

When she lifted her head fully, I could tell that there was something else wrong. This had to be beyond the mourning of our child. She looked sickly, as if she had lost weight. Her eyes bulged slightly and looked to have released fresh tears. It's nothing to see her in a sweat suit, but usually she takes too much pride in her appearance to dress like that when she comes to church, even on an off day. In an instant, she attempted to snap out of it, and she mumbled, "Hey, um, Kyle. How are you?" Almost in an attempt to prove nothing was wrong with her, she didn't wait for me to respond. "I haven't seen you since homecoming. I imagine you and that Avail chick go together by now…." Her voice trailed off.

I never enjoyed this part of breaking up with anyone, but I admitted, "Yes, we're together now." The words seemed to have no effect on her, and that's when I knew something huge was wrong with her. Typical Celeste wouldn't let a comment like that slide by without throwing a miniature fit, even with us standing on the church steps. I had to ask, "Celeste, what's wrong?"

Snapping a little, she answered, "What gives you the right to ask me what's wrong? I'm not your girlfriend anymore, so you don't need to be concerned about me." I didn't like the reply, but she did sound like her normal self.

"We may not date anymore, but because of our history, I figured…."

She cut me off. "You figured what?" Again, not waiting for a reply, she demanded, "No, really, what did you figure, Kyle? You can't have it both ways where you have the girl you claim to want and have me standing on the sidelines. I'm beyond tired of that mess, and trust me—you won't have to worry about me lurking in the shadows, waiting for you to come to your senses. I have bigger things to worry about now."

Attempting to rebound after that verbal slap in the face, I came back with the stupidest, most typical, post-breakup line. "I was sorta hoping that we could be friends."

If showing concern for her well-being made her flip, the friends comment made her go off. "See? You're doing it, and you don't even know it! You want me to say something like, 'Sure, we can be friends,' but in the past eight years, whatever friendship we developed always ended in us getting back together. I'm not going to be fooled by that again." Celeste stared into my eyes and pierced me by saying, "We're not going to be friends. You and I can't and won't work on that level. And like I said before, I have bigger things on my mind." With that, she walked up the steps and headed into the church.

If I had not talked with Rev. Johnson before running into Celeste, I think I would have felt even worse. I knew I couldn't make things better for her; I got it. I'd been a source of pain for her recently and through the years. But still, I was sincerely hoping that we could still be friends because, unlike Avail, she knows the agony I feel around this time of year. Flashing back, I can remember two New Year's Eves ago when no one could find me. My parents hadn't purchased a cell phone for me yet, and no one could contact me. Of course, one of their concerned calls went to Celeste, and when she heard that I was missing, she knew exactly where to go.

She found me under the same tree I sat under in Point State Park when I found out about the abortion. When she arrived, I was shuddering with cold, even in my down coat. My tear-stained face looked up at Celeste, and all I could do was shed more tears. I blamed her, but at the same time, I blamed myself too. The nature of our relationship made her feel as if the only answer to our mess was to get the abortion. She took a tissue out, wiped my face, and encouraged me to come with her. Celeste and I went back to her house where she soothed my pain in ways that only she could do, and I snapped out of it. That was the first year I felt her sorrow, too, and I felt compelled to comfort her in ways she knew so well.

It's amazing the bond people have when they share a tragedy, and the things they do because of it. After her comments today, I have a feeling that our bond is now broken. It's not a bad thing, but for some reason, I don't feel completely healed from it.

"And how is my girlfriend today," I practically sang into the phone after answering Avail's call.

"Much better now that I'm hearing from you. I was worried about you. Honestly, I was worried about us, Kyle," Avail admitted immediately. It was so good to hear from her; just the sound of her voice helped release some of the tension that had built in my shoulders after my brief encounter with Celeste. She sounded like her cool, calm, collected self, and I was thankful to have her in my life.

Attempting to play with her, I asked, "Well, why didn't you call me sooner?" We both laughed, and then I shared, "My head wasn't in a good place, Avail. I wish I had hit my head harder in the accident. Maybe then I would have had the sense to prevent what almost happened between us." I didn't mean to jump right into this topic, but I haven't hidden a thing from Avail the whole time we've known each other. I told her about my meeting with Rev. Johnson and everything we talked about. I thought it was important to share with her my vision of our relationship in the days ahead.

I heard a tiny, audible sigh before Avail spoke. "I understand and agree with all our restrictions. If we want this to work, this is what we have to do." I could feel the sincerity in her voice, and I knew she'd have no problem joining me on this venture, which she had first presented to me. I became excited about what we could have together if we managed to honor God this way.

Catching myself before I got emotional, I cleared my throat and announced, "Well, now that we have that established, let's figure out what we're going to do this Christmas holiday. Traditionally, I spend it with my family, just like we did for Thanksgiving, but for Christmas, we always go over to another relative's house. Then after everyone is full and is tired of the

Dallas Cowboys football game, the teens in the family go to the Riverfront movie theater and pick a flick to watch. I know you'll have your time with your family, but I'd love it if you came with my cousins and me to the movies. We can exchange gifts then, too!" I paused for a moment when I realized I was running off at the mouth, and then I posed, "How does that sound to you, love?"

This time, Avail's sigh was much heavier, and she sounded as if she had just rejoined the conversation after drifting away. "Kyle, my goodness, I should have called you…." Her voice trailed off, and it concerned me a little.

"Avail, what's wrong? Will family obligations keep us from seeing each other on Christmas? If that's the case, don't worry about it; we can get together Christmas Eve or the day after. It'll still be our special time together."

I could sense her lowered mood before she responded. "In a way, yes, but not like you think. Very rarely do we go out of town for Christmas, because we usually have my extended family here at our house on Christmas Eve and Christmas Day, but…." She paused. "But this year, my mother's cousin in Maryland called and invited us to spend the holiday with them."

She was silent then, waiting for me to respond, and all I could think was *Wow—it's our first Christmas as a couple, and we'll be spending it separately.* There wasn't too much I could do about it, so I offered, "Well, Rie, that leaves Christmas Eve. What day is your family leaving?"

I didn't know if I really wanted to hear the answer, because most families travel on Christmas Eve.

"Well, Al, that's the thing. We're leaving on the twenty-third, Sunday after church."

"That's only a day and a half away!" I tried not to sound too pouty, but just came out that way, especially because she'd called me Al, her pet nickname for me.

"I know, baby, but what can I do? I haven't even gone shopping for you yet!"

I almost blurted out that I hadn't picked up her gift yet either, but instead I said, "Okay, okay...that gives us tomorrow night. Make no other plans; tomorrow will be our holiday."

"Okay, then. That sounds great. Do you want me to find a place for us to go or anything like that?"

She must have forgotten how much I enjoy planning things like the private homecoming we shared earlier in the semester. "No, Avail, I got this. I'll let you plan our next celebration, but I'll handle the arrangements for this one." My excitement got my blood pumping full of possibilities, and I told her, "I better get started on these plans. If I don't talk to you tonight, I'll definitely give you a call tomorrow to let you know what's going on. I love you, Avail," I said again, almost singing the phrase.

She sang right back to me, "I love you too, Kyle. Bye!" We both disconnected the call, and I could see Avail panicking a little in my mind's eye.

Since she hasn't shopped for a gift for me before, I'm sure she'll put a large amount of thought into this one. Unlike my

45

girl, I know what I'm getting her; I'm sticking with the idea of getting her a cell phone.

Now that I had my own phone account that I paid for and not my parents, it was just a matter of adding another line and picking out the right phone. In order to have enough time to do this, I made her gift the first thing I needed to do on my list for the remainder of the day.

Four

Her Way

Before making the call, I grabbed one of my favorite Pittsburgh Steelers blankets and sat in a comfortable chair that my mother normally sits in when she is home. With a slight bit of anxiousness, I tried Kyle's house number first just to see if he was home. Knowing him, he was probably running here or there making preparations for the holiday.

Once the familiar voice greeted me with the traditional hello, I responded with, "It seems like it has been forever since I spoke with you! Hey love!" I couldn't hide my excitement.

"And how is my girlfriend today?" There was something about him calling me his girlfriend that made me feel all bubbly inside. I smiled as if he was looking at me right now.

"Much better now that I'm hearing from you," I jumped right to it. "I was worried about you. Honestly,

I was worried about us, Kyle." I knew that he needed some time to deal with his personal issues about the accident and, perhaps, the abortion of his child a few years ago. I wanted to respect that space, but at the same time, I had to wonder if he had second thoughts about us being together.

"This morning when I woke up, I wasn't feeling all that hot. I felt like I was slightly depressed and that I had to get that mood off of me. I prayed, and I knew that it worked, but I still wanted to talk to someone about it."

Well, he knows I'm here for him, so why didn't he call me?

I tried not to be moved by that when he offered, "I just came back from a meeting with my pastor."

Oh, okay. I understand.

"I told him how I was still feeling about the abortion of my child, and then I told him what happened to us—what we almost did—and how this whole unexpected pregnancy with Reese and Raine got me thinking about all that. All of it is connected in my mind, and I needed some wise counsel on it."

After hearing all of that, I realized it was silly of me to wonder why Kyle hadn't called me. He needed some serious direction in his life right now, and I'm too close to the situation.

Without saying a word, he continued. "When it comes to us, Rie, there must be some changes." It was good to hear him call me by his nickname for me.

I didn't know where he was going with this, but I knew that we had talked before about knowing our limits. It looked as if we now had to define them. With everything swimming through his mind, I could understand why we had to make these limitations tangible. "What changes do we need to make, Al?"

With a little more hope in his voice, he proclaimed, "Only three simple things. First, we can't be in each other's rooms alone. Second, we can't be out at night together by ourselves." He stopped and took a deep breath before saying, "And third, we can't do anything in private that if our parents were watching, we'd be ashamed of doing." We both talked about how these three rules should strengthen our relationship and our desire to please God. If we were in either of our dorm rooms alone, that created a level of intimacy that we didn't want to provoke this early in our relationship. The alone time at night would have the same effect. The rule about the things we would and wouldn't do in front of parents—I understood that one very well. A long time ago in youth church, I learned that parents are what my youth pastor called God's watchmen. God gives them insight into many of the things their children do without them really knowing. They're a form of spiritual authority, and if we don't want to let God down, then we shouldn't let our parents down either by doing things we know they would disapprove of. We should be willing to keep our relationship motives pure in front of our parents and behind their backs as well.

I'd been holding my breath bracing myself for limitations that I thought I couldn't handle, but all of these were reasonable. We could do this. I exhaled lightly and said, "I understand and agree with all of these restrictions. If we want this to work, this is what we have to do." I knew we wanted this to work, and it would!

Kyle discussed plans we could have for the Christmas holiday when it hit me; since we hadn't spoken in a day, he had no idea that I wouldn't be in town at all. My parents told me to prepare to leave for Hagerstown in less than two days. I broke into his explanations and share with him my family's plans.

When I told him we were leaving on the twenty-third, he almost yelled in to the phone, "That's only a day and a half away!"

"I know, baby, but what can I do?" I said, seeking to comfort him a little. "I haven't even gone shopping for you yet!"

I could almost see the gears turning in Kyle's head. "Okay, okay…that gives us tomorrow night. Make no plans; tomorrow will be our holiday."

Didn't he just say something about us not being alone at night? I'm not going to bring it up now. I'm sure he has a plan.

"Okay, then. That sounds great. Do you want me to find a place for us to go or anything like that?"

"No, Avail, I got this. I'll let you plan our next celebration, but I'll handle the arrangements for this one!" It's weird, but I could see him rubbing his hands together as if he was thinking of a master plan. "I better get started on these plans. If I don't talk to you tonight, I'll definitely give you a call tomorrow to let you know what's going on. I love you, Avail."

"I love you too, Kyle. Bye!" This was a lot to process in a little bit of time. We'd spend our Christmas celebration together tomorrow night, but our new rule was that we were not allowing ourselves to be alone together at night. I couldn't wait to see how this worked out, but I didn't have time to daydream about it. I had to figure out what to get him for Christmas. This was the all-important first Christmas gift in our relationship. If I got myself together now, I might just be able to miss the rush-hour traffic around the mall.

Four

HIS WAY

On the way to the phone store, I had plenty of time to think carefully about what type of phone I wanted Avail to have. I wanted to make sure hers had the same capabilities as my phone so we'd be able to communicate easier. Unlimited texting and access to the Internet were a must. If I got her the same plan as mine, she should be in good shape.

When I walked in, the salesman, Tim, a friend of mine from Perry High, greeted me and asked what I needed. "I want a smart phone for my girlfriend; it's her Christmas gift from me," I explained.

"Okay, then; I can help you with that," Tim said, full of enthusiasm. "I thought Celeste already had a phone. She came in the other day to pay her bill, but I didn't help her." Just when I was going to correct him, he said, "And I guess congratulations are in order."

"Nah, man, Celeste and I don't go together anymore, so there's no need to congratulate me on that…." For some reason, the last part of his statement hit me late. He didn't know that Celeste and I didn't go together anymore, so why was he congratulating me?

I started to ask him, but he immediately introduced me to the model of the phone he recommended for Avail. It was basically the same phone I had but a prettier, slender, more feminine version. Once I approved it, he went to the back to get it set up for use. Just to occupy my time, I looked at the other phones on display, but my mind kept floating back to what he said about congratulating me. What was that all about? I would call Celeste myself, but she probably wouldn't take my call. She made it crystal-clear that she didn't want to be bothered with me. I decided I'd just ask the dude when he returned with the phone.

A few moments later, a young woman in her midtwenties tapped me on the shoulder and asked, "Are you Kyle Thompson?" Once I indicated that I was, she held out a bag with the phone and accessories in it. "Tim, the guy that helped you earlier, had an emergency, and I finished up your order. The phone number is on the box of the phone. Now, you just wanted to add this line to your account, right?" I robotically went through the motions of paying for the phone and making sure I had everything I needed, but my mind was distracted by what the guy meant when he congratulated me. The cold air hitting my face as I walked out the store brought me back to my focus, which was designing an evening for Avail and me. Now, being that the event would take place at night, we would need someone with us, and I knew the perfect couple who would enjoy an evening out as well.

"Why do you want us to come along with you and Avail? I'm sure you guys would rather spend this time with each other without us tagging along."

"I'm curious too. What's the deal, Kyle?"

I took a deep breath and stated, "Mom, Dad, because Avail and I don't want to overstep any boundaries we shouldn't, we agreed on three things we would do to make sure we wouldn't go too far in our relationship." I paused just to behold the countenances of my parents, who looked shockingly thrilled. "We agreed not to be alone at night, not to spend time in each other's rooms by ourselves on campus, and not to do anything we wouldn't do in front of our parents." I paused again, and if I recall correctly, I can't remember seeing either of them blink! "So, what do you say? Will you guys go out on a double date with Avail and me to see *The Nutcracker* tomorrow night?"

I began to translate the expressions on their faces as pleasantly pleased. I'm sure that various thoughts ran through their minds from times past of ways I'd snuck out to be with Celeste or another girl, and they were definitely aware that I'd been sexually active, especially when Mom found a condom wrapper in the trash. I think a piece of them was just waiting for me to come home and announce that through one secretive act or another, I had made them early grandparents. Now, here I stand, asking them to chaperone Avail and me in order to prevent any such act from happening. The pride beaming from their faces provoked both of them to speak, though ironically enough, Mom claimed, "I'm speechless."

"If that's the case, then, man, we'd be more than glad to go out with you and Avail." My father propelled his hand toward me and shook my hand like a real man would. "If you don't mind me asking, what brought this on? I'm just curious."

They might as well know everything—well, just about everything. "Back when Avail and I were just talking about dating, she let me know that because of some past experiences in her life, she didn't want to get involved in pre-marital sex if that's what it would take for us to have a relationship. I understood where she was coming from, so I agreed. Recently, I took it a step further by saying that we didn't need to put ourselves in situations that would make us want to have sex. One of those stipulations is that we wouldn't go out alone at night, so I need someone to go with us."

My mother burst out with, "I knew I liked her for a reason!" All three of us shared a comfortable laugh as she continued, "We would be foolish not to support you in this, so of course we'll go out with you guys tomorrow." She paused and looked toward my father. "My God, it's been years since we've been on a date." Almost in a panic, she ran up the stairs saying, "I've got to find something to wear!" leaving my father and me downstairs shaking our heads and grinning.

I finally made eye contact with my dad, and I sensed a "I'm proud of you, son" comment coming any moment. Instead, his eyes held back tears of pride that spoke volumes, whispering in the air that he had just witnessed a "from boy to man" moment. I was rooted in place because I couldn't recall ever seeing a reaction from my father like this, even when I graduated from high school in the top ten percent of my class. This was a type of pride that evoked an emotion that my father obviously hadn't had a lot of experience with. I almost got caught up in the moment too, and then he cleared his throat, wiped a tear while looking away, and said firmly, "Do you need any money for the tickets?" We had returned to manliness.

I told him, "If you cover your tickets, I'll take care of mine and Avail's."

"Well, we've got to get ready for this date!" he responded. "I think I'll take this opportunity to show you how an old player does it," he added, punctuating the statement with a smug grin.

I laughed. "Oh, so you think you got game?" Playing with my father, I said, "You're game's rather dusty! There's some new things out here you don't know about!"

Chuckling, my dad said, "Man, the game ain't changed—just the players! We'll see who can romance his girl the best tomorrow night." With that, my father cool-walked away like we'd made a silent bet or something.

Tomorrow, both he and Avail will find out how it's done!

Five

HER WAY

I sat on the side of my bed playing with the delicate treasure that would soon become Kyle's first Christmas gift from me, a gold cross charm hanging from a corresponding gold rope necklace. My only concern was whether Kyle's football neck would allow the cross to dangle. If not, I'd have to get a longer chain.

I placed it in a velvet jewelry pouch and then I put it into the box the jewelry store gave me. Being that Kyle was a big kid at heart, I knew that I had to wrap it so that he could enjoy opening his gift. I carefully picked up the package and headed for the dining room table to wrap it.

As soon as I started cutting the paper, my father came into the room and asked, "Are you ready for the trip to Maryland? You know how slow you can be when it comes to packing, and you know that I'll be ready to

get on the road as soon as you get back from church."
Daddy had a point. Whenever we went on a road trip,
he did two things: he slept at least eight hours the
night before, and he always wanted to leave at the time
we said we'd leave.

I smiled and answered, "I have all of my stuff packed
already. When I get back from church, I'll throw my
toiletries into the bag and I'll be good to go!"

Dad took a seat across from me, and referring to
the gift, playfully asked, "Is that for me?"

"No," I dragged out. "This is my first Christmas
gift to Kyle. I got him a necklace with a cross charm."

"How thoughtful of you," my dad commented. "Just
out of curiosity, what prompted you to get that particular gift?"

I quickly debated how far into the real story I should
go, knowing that my father couldn't handle everything that I normally told my mother. Since my father
was pretty much a straight-to-the-point kind of guy, I
summarized the story in very general terms. "Kyle and
I have been working hard to keep God in the midst
of our relationship. I told him some things that I expect us to refrain from doing, and he shared with me
some things that we won't do in order to make sure we
don't tempt one another." I broke my eye contact with
my father and went back to wrapping the gift because
without saying it, I knew my father understood what I
was talking about.

After a long pause, my father remarked, "Hmmm…
okay. That's good to hear. In that case, I think it's the
perfect gift." It was weird. Whenever my father felt a

mixture of pride and being uncomfortable with sensitive subjects, he found a way to leave the scene, and this conversation was no exception. He escaped to the kitchen claiming he was looking for something to eat, though I knew he couldn't possibly be hungry since he'd had a snack an hour before.

When I returned to my room with the neatly wrapped package, I noticed that the hour was getting late and Kyle had not called me with details about tomorrow evening. I had to give it to him: he knew how to put together a special occasion. The private homecoming dinner he hosted in his room last semester overwhelmed me. I couldn't believe that he went through all that trouble just for me. Reminiscing about the dancing, foot massage, and cuddling afterward, I also knew that nothing like that would take place tomorrow night since we now have these three stipulations on our relationship. There's no doubt that we can still enjoy each other's company while maintaining our standards, but I have to admit: it will be different.

⌒

The repeated ringing of the house phone made me pop out of bed wondering why no one had answered it. Mom and Dad must have left the house early to get some shopping out of the way, but I was in a deeper sleep than usual. Immediately, I ripped the comforter and sheets off my body and searched for one of our cordless phones. Usually, we return each one to its base, but sometimes we leave them in the kitchen, living room, or in our separate bedrooms. Thankfully, I found it resting on its charger.

Being that I hadn't uttered a word yet, my broken voice greeted, "Hello."

"Good morning! We're you sleep?"

"Umm, yeah," I replied a little sarcastically, after I caught Kyle's voice. Waking up a little, I added, "I'm in vacation mode, so I'm sleeping much later than I do at school. What's so important that you had to call me this early?"

"Early?" Kyle questioned. "It's seven thirty. The sun's been up for hours!" He laughed, but I just smiled since I was working my way into consciousness. "Besides, I can't believe you slept so soundly without knowing what we're doing tonight." He sounded so excited, so I knew it had to be good.

I also understood that he was trying to get me to ask a million questions about our celebration because he loved being able to hold a surprise from me. *Let's see if I can turn the tables on him a little.* "Yeah, you're right, but I'm more excited about seeing you open your gift that I wrapped last night."

"What did you get me?" he asked with enthusiasm.

I laughed to myself because I had no idea it would be that easy to bait him.

"You will see tonight when we meet. Speaking of which, I want to be dressed appropriately, so can you tell me what we're doing or at least give me an idea of what to wear?"

I heard Kyle lightly chuckle before he said, "I won't tell you what we're doing, but you should dress up. I plan to wear a shirt, tie, and some dress pants."

Oh wow, I need clarity. "You don't necessarily mean like prom dress up, right?"

"No, not that formal!" We both laughed.

"Okay," I said, "but I need to know what time I need to be ready."

"I'll be at your front door around a quarter after seven tonight. We'll have to leave immediately because we need to be in our seats…I mean we need to be in place by eight." *Did Kyle just give me a clue? Hmmm…he let the word* seats *slip out.*

"Sounds good, but I have one more question."

"What do you want to know now, Avail?" Kyle asked playfully.

I didn't want to seem as if I'd forgotten about the three standards that we'd agreed on, and since he instituted them, I doubt he did either, but I had to inquire. "Well, one of our new rules for our relationship said that we wouldn't be alone at night. We're already breaking that rule if we go out alone tonight. I know it's a special occasion, but that should be no exception." I was serious. If we were going to do this, we might as well do it right.

"Avail, there's no need to worry. We're double-dating with another couple, and I explained to them our situation. It's okay; I have it covered."

That was a relief, but I had to wonder who this other couple was. I hadn't met many of Kyle's friends, and I could imagine that a few of them might size me up and compare me to Celeste—not that I was intimidated or anything, because I could obviously hold my own. This whole double-dating thing would have its positives and negatives anyway, and I honestly believed that the sacrifice was worth it in the long run.

We chatted for a few more minutes before we both concluded that we needed to get ready for tonight. As soon as I disconnected the call, I noticed that my neglect of my hair since I'd been home was evident in how it looked now. Surely, a deep conditioning and hot oil treatment should do the trick.

And it did when coupled with my hair pulled back into a ballet bun toward the back of my head. A few long strands twisted their way to my shoulders while a part on the left side of my head helped offset a swoop into the bun. When I checked myself in the full-length mirror, I was pleased with the effect: my red, long-sleeved, sparkling, wrap-style top coupled with my black, velvet, mid-calf pencil skirt and black silk hose accentuated my figure perfectly. I was grateful that it hadn't snowed to the point where I couldn't wear my black patent leather four-inch heels. I hadn't worked out since leaving Whitaker for the holidays, but my silhouette had not suffered from it.

I grabbed my long, black wool coat, matching scarf and gloves, and my purse, and set them near the door so that I could expedite our departure. I returned to my room to pick up Kyle's gift just as the doorbell rang. I grabbed the small treasure and walked quickly down the hallway since I was the only one home. My parents had headed over to an aunt's house hours ago.

I opened the door after I put on my coat and was not prepared to see Kyle for the first time since we'd returned home. He literally took my breath away with his dark dress coat that rode on top of his stiffly pressed white dress shirt complete with gold cufflinks, red satin neck tie with a stylish large knot at the top, and his fresh-from-the-cleaners black dress pants. His impeccable grooming complemented the complete package. A fresh edge-up and goatee trim always made him look quite exquisite. I knew I had that dreamy smile on my face, so I regained my bearings and said, "Good evening, Mr. Thompson." I slipped on my gloves, grabbed my two accessories for the occasion, and shut and locked the door behind me, stepping close enough to catch a whiff of his cologne. There was no kiss greeting, but I could live with that for now.

His sparkling brown eyes managed to shine with excitement as he replied, "Good evening, Miss Andrews. Let me escort you to the car." As he normally did, he ushered me down the stairs and opened my door. The first thing I saw when he opened the door was a single, striking white and red orchid in the passenger's seat waiting for me. I gasped in astonishment before I asked him, "How did you know that orchids are my favorite flower?"

He grinned as he answered, "A flower that's rare, delicate, and exotic fits you. I didn't know, but I'm not surprised at all." With that, he shut the door and walked around the car to join me.

He pulled away from the house, and I hadn't even thought about the couple in the back seat. Loud enough for them to hear, I asked, "Kyle, who is the couple joining us tonight?" I know I was beaming. Kyle had started things off beautifully.

Kyle grinned and said, "Oh you know them. Those are my parents back there!" I turned to greet them and knew without a shadow of a doubt that all four of us would have a good time that night.

⌒

"Mr. and Mrs. Thompson, thank you so much for coming out with us tonight," I expressed sincerely. "It was wonderful spending time with you."

"We enjoyed you too, Avail," Mrs. Thompson responded. Mr. Thompson just sat there with his arm around his wife, smiling and nodding in agreement. "We'll have to do this again soon!" she added.

"Yes, ma'am," I managed to say before Kyle shut my door.

Kyle did it again. Everything was wonderful from my surprise orchid, to picking his parents to go on a date with us, to tickets to The Nutcracker, *to desserts and café drinks at a quaint place near the theater, to now.*

I especially enjoyed my time with Mrs. Thompson. She and I had managed to slip away in the lobby of the Benedum Theater and have a brief conversation about the Thompson men while they checked our coats.

"You know they're trying to compete against each other," Mrs. Thompson mentioned to me on the side.

I giggled and asked, "Compete for what?"

"Well," she began to confide, "I heard them earlier debating who was more romantic. I knew we were in for a night of feeling overly special!" Her eyes twinkled with first-love excitement.

"He knows that I like poinsettias during the holiday, but I haven't had a chance to get them for the house. While I was getting ready, he must have run to the florist and bought them out because when I came downstairs for the date, they were everywhere! He had set them on every other step on the stairway, and in the dining room and living room—literally, everywhere!" I grinned as she continued. "Then, as if that wasn't sweet enough, he had a small dinner for two prepared—candlelit, of course." She gushed like a high school girl. "He didn't cook, but he picked up my favorite meal from Three Rivers Bistro downtown." As I listened, I mused, *It's apparent that Kyle gets a large measure of his skills from his father.* Mrs. Thompson told me how she and Mr. Thompson finished a dance to their favorite song just as Kyle declared that it was time to go.

Complete with a Kool-Aid grin, I remarked, "That sounds lovely, Mrs. Thompson." Inwardly, I reminisced about Kyle's and my private homecoming dinner/dance, and I could only smile harder.

As for what Kyle has done during this romantic challenge, I think he's doing his best to uphold the three areas we consented to and honestly, that would take some getting used to. Regardless, when he pinned the orchid in my hair, I thought I would melt—and he must have planned it, because he had hairpins! I had to admit that tickets to *The Nutcracker* were a nice touch. He knows how much I love dance, but the ballet holds a special place in my affection for the performing arts. I enjoyed every single moment of the performance. There were times I would catch Kyle gazing at me instead of the artistry on the stage, and I imagine that he enjoyed the fact that I took pleasure in the whole evening.

As we stood on the steps of my house, I said warmly, "This has been a wonderful evening, Kyle. Thank you for everything."

"Well, we haven't done all that we're supposed to do yet," he mentioned as he rotated a gift bag from behind him, placing it between the two of us. When I saw the bag earlier, my curiosity had shot through the roof. Yes, I wanted to know what was in the bag just to see his mindset on the kind of gifts he'd get me. I hope he knew that he didn't have to spend tons and tons of money on me. Though I like nice things, I'm not that materialistic. As if he read my thoughts, he dangled the bag in front of me and said, "I know you want to know what I got you, but there are two conditions with this gift."

I looked at him like he was crazy and asked, "What two conditions?"

"First, you cannot open this until Christmas day. Can you do that?"

What? I love gifts, especially from my boyfriend, and he wants me to wait another three days?

I pondered his question and replied, "I guess I can..." but wanting to hear the other stipulation, I guided, "...and the other condition?"

Now, with this condition, he grinned as if he had a trick up his sleeve as he commanded, "I want you to put the bag on your nightstand or somewhere close to your bed every night until you open it."

I thought that request was strange; nevertheless, I reached out for the bag and asked, "Why?"

Before I even touched the strings of the gift bag, Kyle snatched it back and teased, "I need you to promise that you'll put it beside your bed every night before you open it!"

"Okay, okay! I'll put it on my nightstand or somewhere close to the bed." I laughed and said, "Now can I have my gift?"

He obliged, grabbing my hand tenderly and looping the bag handles around four of my fingers. "I hope you like it," he said, gazing into my eyes. Then, as if snapping out of his playful, romantic routine, he asked, "Do you have a gift for me?" Just as I reached to where I had his gift clutched under my arm, he added, "If you don't, it's okay. I'm really thankful to have the gift of your love in my life."

I froze for a moment and then just smiled. I pushed the neatly wrapped box toward him as I asked, "Do you want me to take this back? Because I can—I mean, if my love is enough!"

He almost snatched the box out of my hand and said, "That won't be necessary!" He began to unwrap it, but then he paused and said, "May I open it now?"

"No." I had planned on telling him that he could, but for some reason, no came out of my mouth. "Call me tonight when you get in, and you can open it then."

He held my gift to him in both hands, delicately. "I can do that." He took an intimate step toward me in full view of his parents and said, "I enjoyed myself tonight," punctuating the remark with a quick peck.

Playing with him, I countered, "So did I," ending the statement with another peck.

"I'm going to miss you, but you can call me."

"That's long distance, so it depends on if my family in Maryland has an unlimited plan on their home phone or if someone will...."

Kyle stopped me from finishing my statement by putting his uncovered right index finger to my lips as he said, "We'll be in touch; don't worry." Then, he stepped into my receptive lips anxious for a deeper kiss than earlier. I knew his parents had to be watching, but it didn't bother me at all. Similar to previous encounters, he rested his available hand on my left hip, continuing to show me how much he'd miss me through that one single kiss. Once we pulled away from each other, he concluded, "I'll call you later, okay? Good night." He glided down the steps and returned to the car.

I immediately took my keys out so that I could escape the cold night. I went straight to my room and placed my gift bag on the nightstand next to my bed, just as I was directed, anxiously awaiting Kyle's call.

Five

His Way

My father had no idea how much he fired me up by challenging me. I remained confident that I would win this silent test, especially since I'd been at this a little more than he had the past few months. I decided to head to our family florist to look for a flower a little more expressive than a typical red rose. Sure, roses have their place, but I wanted to show some effort, and I thought an exotic flower like an orchid or calla lily would do the trick.

"I heard about the bet," Jackson greeted as I walked in the door. "Your dad was just here, and I wanna see what you have up your sleeve."

I laughed because I could imagine my father bragging about how he was going to show me up when it came to romancing our ladies. Actually, I had to admit to myself that my father had that part of their relationship on lock. It was as if he spoke a language only my mother responded to. He understood her needs for constant affection, greeting her with a hug, surprising her with a kiss, offering her his hand to hold in public. With all that attention, Mom couldn't help but to respond. Only on special occasions like their anniversary or her birthday did I get the chance to see glimpses of him stepping up his game to make Mom's feet leave the earth with special dinners, rose petals, candles, and I imagine, some things no one wants to think about when it comes to their parents! "I'm sure he went above and beyond his typical order of a mixed bouquet of red and yellow roses. So what did he get this time?" I asked, trying to gain an advantage over my father.

Beginning with his hearty laugh that matched his stature, Jackson saw right through me and played it cool. "Oh, no! You're not getting me in the middle of this! Besides, your father swore me to secrecy. But I can tell you that he's doing it big!"

I joined him laughing while I realized that I could only go so far in what I did for Avail. My thinking was that my father would overdo me simply because he had to. My approach would have to be severely understated and carefully calculated. Though I knew I could do it big too, I decided to use strategy to make this night special. I said to Jackson, "Well, since he needs to go so big, I think I'll take the simple route." Remembering the two flowers I thought of earlier, I asked, "What's the possibility of getting an orchid?" Sure, I could have gone with a calla lily, but I wanted to do something with this flower more than just give it to her. I thought the orchid would look good pinned behind her ear, if she let me pin it there.

After telling me that I was basically asking for the impossible, Jackson returned from the back of his floral shop and presented me with a perfectly bloomed white and red orchid. Inside its plastic sales box, it looked ideal. I paid Jackson immediately, thanked him for his help, and headed for the ticket office to pick up our tickets, and then to the cleaners to pick up a few items my mom had dropped off before I came home from school.

After a spontaneous trip to the barbershop, I found myself walking by the display of a nearby jewelry store, and for reasons I couldn't explain, I went in. When the salesperson greeted me, I let her know that I was just doing a little window-shopping—actually, a little research to get ideas of what a wedding band set would cost. After I said those words, I stood there feeling a bit shocked simply because I couldn't believe that I wanted to price some rings. Did I just infer to myself that the rings I wanted to look at could one day be on Avail's fingers and mine? Nevertheless, I stood there among countless sparkly treasures, and the salesperson gave me a quick lesson on the symbolic nature of engagement and wedding rings and the four Cs of a diamond. I filed every piece of information in my mental rolodex.

I returned home in the evening looking for any major changes my father had made while I was gone. The house looked just as it did when I left, so I figured that he went somewhere to continue his personal quest to beat me in our romantic wager. I took the boxed orchid out from behind my back once I realized I was home by myself and immediately placed it in the refrigerator behind some items I didn't think anyone would move. I then ran up the stairs to my room to place the garments from the cleaners in the front part of my closet before pulling out the shoes I needed to shine. I figured that since there wasn't that much snow left over from the blizzard we'd had recently, there would be no reason why I couldn't just wear a pair of dress shoes.

I stopped for a moment and really had to thank God for the change in my relationship with Avail. I could see how these adjustments would help me honor her for who she was and help us reach marriage.

Yeah, I said it: marriage.

When I looked at wedding rings earlier in the day, it felt natural. I never had the desire to look at rings for anyone else in my life, not even Celeste. I never wanted to take such drastic steps in my relationship in order to please both God and the young lady. Avail had changed my way of thinking, and I loved it. It was crazy to think that I had known her for less than half a year, but I knew without a shadow of a doubt that I wanted to marry her.

One day, I will.

⌒

All the excitement from the preparations for to-night caused me to fall asleep early, but that helped me wake up early today. The same anxious-ness flung my eyelids open at around 6:00 a.m., the time I'd normally get up for my morning workout with Avail. Going through a checklist in my mind, I lingered in bed making sure that I had everything to-gether for the evening. I knew that I didn't have to worry about a meal since the production started so late, but I thought I would make reservations at a small coffeehouse afterward not that far from the theater. That way, I could stretch out our holiday a little longer before Avail went out of town. Missing her would be the hardest part of this season. I knew we wouldn't see each other every day during it, but from what I could gather, I probably wouldn't see much of her at all until we returned to college in January.

Eventually, I rolled over, grabbed the phone, and called my girlfriend. If she had her new phone from me already, I would just text her and wait for her to call me back.

Actions like that will just have to wait until after we ex-change our gifts.

It seemed like the phone rang forever before a fa-miliar, but rough voice answered, "Hello?"

After a few minutes of teasing banter, I prepared Avail for the kind of night we would be having, but I kept a bit of mystery about it because she loves surprises.

As we talked about the Christmas date, it occurred to me that by celebrating the birth of Jesus under our new stipulations, we would also be honoring Him by keeping our vow. So, in a very strange way, we were giving Him a gift by putting Him first in our relationship. We said our good-byes, and I went back to figuring out a way to out-do my father.

⟨————⟩

Reflections from the stage lights danced in Avail's eyes as she became mesmerized by all the action on the stage during the scenes from "The Land of Sweets." I knew this couldn't have been her first time seeing *The Nutcracker*, but she enjoyed it as if it were. As for me, I enjoyed how this whole evening had taken shape. When I arrived to pick her up, Avail didn't keep me waiting. The door seemed to have been on springs, and it revealed a classier version of Avail than I was accustomed to. Her pulled-back hairstyle showcased her glowing complexion and the simplicity of her effortless, natural makeup. Even with her coat on, it was obvious that her black form-fitting skirt and sparkling red V-neck sweater hugged the body that I missed holding. I'd done well with our restrictions, but it was a lot easier when I didn't see her.

I was so used to being free with how I greeted her, be it with a lingering kiss or a boyfriend-only hug, but I felt like this pledge was holding me back to a degree—and in a good way. I knew better than to pursue her physically even though that was mostly what I'd done in the past. The important thing is that the past is just that: the past. We're in a new day in our relationship, and there are things we can and can't do.

"Good evening, Mr. Thompson," she spoke with her perfectly glossed lips that I focused on intently. Honoring the three restrictions would be a challenge for me, and she was not making it any easier at all. Even with the intense desire I experienced at that moment, I withheld myself and walked in a level of self-control that I hoped would last.

Promptly, I replied, "Good evening, Miss Andrews." She locked the door to her house then turned to face me again, and her close proximity was overwhelming. The scent from her freshly cleansed hair mixed with her usual ritual of cocoa butter lotions and oils was intoxicating. Holding out my arm in the most honorable, chivalrous manner possible, I added, "Let me escort you to the car." We took each step carefully, especially since she rocked a pair of peep-toe patent leather black stilettos, the sexiest pair of shoes I could recall her ever wearing.

Before getting out of the car, I had placed Avail's boxed orchid in her seat. So when I opened her door for her, she instantly saw it and gasped with pleasure. "How did you know that orchids are my favorite flower?" I knew I had hit the jackpot going simple with Avail. In natural sight, no, my selection could not compare with how my father decorated the whole downstairs and every step of the stairway of the house with multi-colored poinsettias, Mom's favorite holiday decoration. In my instance, it was the quality of the gesture through the single, unique flower and not so much the grand quantity route that my father chose to present to his lady.

"A flower that's rare, delicate, and exotic fits you. I didn't know, but I'm not surprised at all." I watched for her reaction to my words as she fastened her seat belt, and she looked completely enraptured. When she asked about the couple in the back seat, surprise glowed from her inner being when I revealed, "Oh, you know them. Those are my parents back there!" I knew she appreciated that calculated move.

After I checked our coats at the theater, I took the flower she treasured in her hand and said, "If you would allow me, I'd like to pin this on you." She yielded romantically, expecting me, I imagine, to pin the orchid on her sweater. Instead, I slid behind her and pinned it in her hair with some hairpins I had borrowed from my mom at home and slipped into my pocket. I secured the stem of the flower around the base of her hair bun, ensuring that the flower was showcased Billie Holiday style. Mom's suggestion of this gesture gave Avail a dreamy, euphoric glow that made the flower pale in comparison. That glow remained as the lights dimmed and the performance began.

After the show, the four of us walked to a nearby café that served light appetizers, hot beverages, and delectable desserts. Unbeknownst to me, it was karaoke night, and of course, I couldn't ignore the possibilities of showing Avail a little love from behind the mic.

The waiter took our orders, and out of the corner of my eye, I saw my father whispering sweet nothings into my mother's ear, confirmed by a girlish giggle I had never heard from her before. I looked at Avail, who obviously was doing her best to give my parents their personal space, and I distracted her by asking, "Have you enjoyed your evening thus far?"

Avail gave me a closed-lip smile before she answered, "Every minute of it." Then, an awful sound from the stage caused her to wince in pain. A midtwenties guy was serenading a woman in the audience and completely embarrassing himself.

"Oh, wow," I commented. "He needs to sit down!" Really, the guy had no skills, and it amazed me how he missed words when they were clearly printed on the screen in front of him. All I could do was laugh.

Avail almost looked at me cross-eyed as she said, "It's not about his skills; it's about his willingness to let it all hang out there because of his love for his girl." She stopped, glanced down at her hot chocolate, then looked at me and said, "I think it's sweet." With that, she turned all of her attention to the interaction between the man on the stage and his muse.

I took that as my cue and slipped away from the table while Avail was distracted. Before I knew it, my father stood behind me, asking, "What's up, man? Having a few issues holding down your romance?" Trying to clown me wasn't working right now. I was on a mission to win the affections of Avail.

She thought dude put it all on the line for his girl. She hasn't seen anything yet.

I heard my father ask, "So are you going to sign up for karaoke?"

"Yes, sir," I said as I flipped through the song selection book. Since it was so close to Christmas, all they offered were Christmas songs. I wanted to find a romantic one as well, similar to what that guy had sung for his girl. I selected the perfect song, signed up, and returned to the table before Avail even knew I was gone.

Eventually, the crowd erupted in applause for the guy's efforts, and Avail clapped and cheered right along with them. That only got me more pumped for my soon-to-be performance. *She'll love it.*

⌒

*A*vail and my parents said their goodbyes, and I walked her to her door. I just stood there feeling a little sad that this would be the last time I'd see her during the holiday season.

For me, it was still a little unclear as to when she'd return, but at his moment, I don't want to dwell on that. I want her to take our last few moments together with her so she can remember what she's coming home to—a new and improved us.

Avail turned to me, grinning, and sang my karaoke version of Boys II Men's "Let It Snow," and I couldn't help but laugh. Thank goodness I demonstrated some vocal abilities, but I personalized it a couple of times, throwing Avail's name in it here and there. I even came down from the stage with the cordless microphone, grabbed her by the hand, and serenaded her while we slow danced in the middle of the floor. Of course, the crowd ate it up, but what mattered was that Avail loved it as evidenced by the Kool-Aid grin plastered on her face the whole time. After I escorted her back to her seat, I gave my father a "Now, top that," look, and he couldn't do anything but smile, shake his head, and give me my props, but I had to give him his, too. After seeing everything my father had gone out of his way to do for my mother that day, it was fair to call our challenge a tie.

As we took steps toward her door, Avail murmured, "This has been a wonderful evening, Kyle. Thank you for everything."

I knew she hadn't forgotten, but we hadn't exchanged gifts yet. Besides, I knew she hadn't seen the bag I'd hidden behind my back that I eventually wedged into the limited space between us. "Well, we haven't done all that we're supposed to do yet." If she wasn't fronting about not caring about the gift, she was doing a great job!

"I know you want to know what I got you, but there are two conditions with this gift." I punctuated the statement with a sly grin.

"What two conditions?"

Simply put, I said, "First, you cannot open this until Christmas day. Can you do that?"

I didn't know she had the capability to raise one eyebrow so high! After a brief moment, she consented. "I guess I can. And the other condition?"

I ordered, "I want you to put the bag on your nightstand or somewhere close to your bed every night until you open it." I didn't say the Christmas day stipulation here because, little did Avail know, I planned for her to open it tonight.

Avail rose to the challenge and asked, "Why?"

I was just about to put the bag strings on her antici-pating fingers when I snatched it back playfully and said, "I need you to promise that you'll put it beside your bed every night before you open it."

"Okay, okay! I'll put it on my night stand or some-where close to the bed." She giggled as she asked, "Now can I have my gift?"

I figured I had put her through enough torture when it came to her gift, so I obliged by hanging the strings of the gift bag around her delicate fingers and added softly, "I hope you like it." If I couldn't see her over the holiday, then at least we'd be able to talk, text, and video chat limitlessly. For a brief moment, I forgot that Avail had made a minor fuss about getting me a gift, so I had to ask, "Do you have a gift for me? If you don't, it's okay. I'm really thankful to have the gift of your love in my life." I meant that. There's nothing tangible that she could get me that could equate to her love for me, but I knew she'd gotten me something when she took a small package from under her arm that she'd clutched between her ribs and a small purse she carried for the evening.

Suddenly, she stopped moving and offered, "Do you want me to take this back, because I can!"

I couldn't control my excitement any longer. I snatched it out of her hand and said, "That won't be necessary!" I tore at the paper, but then I stopped. It wasn't actually Christmas day, so I asked her, "May I open it now?"

"No," she said bluntly. "Call me tonight when you get in, and you can open it then."

I wasn't expecting that answer, but she has no idea that her request for me to call her when I open the gift plays into her opening her gift tonight as well....

I looked at the now slightly tattered wrapping on the gift due to my brief tirade and remarked, "I can do that." I stepped closer to her and, before I gave her a simple kiss, I declared, "I enjoyed myself tonight."

"So did I," she said, and then she gave me a quick kiss too.

I stared into her eyes and said, "I'm going to miss you when you're gone, but you can call me."

"That's long distance, so it depends on if my family in Maryland has an unlimited plan on their home phone or if someone will...."

I didn't want her to worry. Just because this would be the first significant distance between us since we'd met and started dating, there was no need to be concerned with how we would keep in touch. Besides, my Christmas gift to her would help us stay in touch. I gently silenced her words with one of my index fingers and promised, "We'll be in touch; don't worry." I kissed her a little deeper than I did earlier, holding her this time, and cherishing our connection. Knowing I couldn't feel her up or do anything beyond hold her while I kissed her, I broke the rising physical intimacy between us and whispered, "I'll call you later, okay? Good night." I left immediately, refusing for this great night to end on a sad note dwelling on the fact that she would be leaving town tomorrow.

I didn't bother to watch her go in the door. I knew she'd make it in safely. When I got in the car, my parents had shifted themselves to the front seats. I slid into the seat behind my father, who assumed the chauffer role, and I began to relax a little. Before pulling off, Dad turned around and said, "Good job, man." He had no idea that my surprises weren't over yet. *I'll share it with him later.*

After looking at my mother, who had reclined her seat a little and closed her eyes to absorb and relish every aspect of the evening, I replied to my father, "You too, man."

Six

HER WAY

*I*finalized some packing details for our family trip by placing my suitcase next to the nightstand where my gift bag from Kyle rested. It had been a good measure of time since he'd gone home after our date, enough time for me to take a shower, wrap my hair, give my parents a brief summary of my double date with Kyle and his parents, and find the cordless phone so that when Kyle called, I could answer it immediately. I didn't understand what could be taking him so long.

I sat cross-legged on my bed contemplating if I should call Kyle just to ensure that he and his parents had made it home safely. Scenes of the evening flickered through my mind's moviemaker, such as when Kyle attempted to sing both the lead and the background when he did karaoke! He sang so sincerely but added just the right amount of humor to attract the attention of the audience. I could only grin at how special he made me feel by pinning my orchid in my hair in the middle of the theater's vestibule. He smoothed strands that had escaped my tightly formed hair bun and pinned the flower in a way that accentuated my face and hair. When I caught a glance of myself in the ladies' room mirror, I admired his display of affection and felt more special than ever.

I released a pleasant sigh and resolved that I'd just have to listen for the phone from the pillow. I was tired but happy, and soon I would succumb to my need for sleep.

I kept the cordless phone in my hand as I turned the lights off and crawled under my comforter. Briefly, I allowed my eyes to stay open, embracing the darkness of my room. When I couldn't hold them open any longer, my eyelids relaxed and closed. As if he knew that I had just submitted to sleeping, the cordless phone rang. I didn't bother to look at the caller ID, knowing that it was Kyle. "Hello," I murmured in a sleepy drawl laced with love in my voice.

"Hey, Avail, it's me, Kyle." He sounded just as drowsy as I did. "Did I call you too late?"

I smiled at his consideration as I replied, "I'm still up, but I'm in bed. I guess the excitement of tonight wore me out more than I thought." Considering how awake he sounded, I asked, "Are you getting ready for bed yet?" I figure that since it was close to midnight, he would be heading that way. He has yet to show me that he was much of a night owl except for when he and I studied into the wee hours of Saturday mornings.

"I'm sitting on the edge of my bed holding my gift from you. I was wondering if it was okay for me to open it now." Just for a brief moment, I panicked.

I'm not there with him as he opens this gift, and he could possibly fake his response to it. What if he thinks that I'm trying to be too deep with the whole cross thing? What if he sees no value in it? What if he already has one and has no reason to wear this one?

I sat up in the bed, eyes wide open, trying to figure out what to say before he opened my all-important first gift to him.

"Kyle—before you open it...." I paused for a moment but continued quickly enough for him not to interrupt me. "Please understand that when I purchased this gift, I bought it with our promise to one another in mind—you know, about our relationship." I swallowed hard before adding, "It's just a reminder to both of us." I didn't want to start babbling, so I just stopped talking.

Without a word, he ripped the paper off the box so noisily that I could hear it through the phone, as if what I said made him more curious about what the box contained. I guess I could take that as a good sign. Shortly thereafter, I heard the crinkle of the carefully placed tissue paper I had included in the box. Then, silence. Not a single word came out of Kyle's mouth, and I didn't know how to interpret his reaction over the phone.

I should have let him open it in front of me on my doorstep. If he really likes it, I would have loved to enjoy his reaction. I'll be sure not to do this to him or myself for his birthday.

"I love it," he practically whispered. "Thank you so much. This means so much to me."

I was so relieved! His sincerity was genuine; there was no denying how pleased he sounded by the tone in his voice. "I have one request," I shared. "I want you to wear it all the time. Never take it off unless you have to clean it or something like that. It's real gold, so it'll be able to handle your day-to-day grooming." Tears welled in my eyes from being so tickled about him liking his gift.

"Okay, hold on." I heard him place the phone down, and, I assumed that he was clasping the chain around his neck right. Once he returned to the phone, he quietly said, "It fits perfectly. The chain length is perfect. This gift is perfect. Thank you again."

"You're welcome, love."

I'm so glad he likes it!

I repositioned myself under the sheets complete with eyes shut again knowing that I had done a good thing getting him that cross pendant. I rolled over to my favorite sleeping position on my side facing the wall.

As if he had snapped out of his euphoria, Kyle asked, "Where is the gift I gave you?"

I smiled and said, "It's right here on my nightstand where you asked me to place it. I haven't looked in it or shaken it or done anything to it because you made me promise that I wouldn't open it until Christmas." I just felt like it was necessary to remind him that I remembered his request.

"Are your eyes open?" he asked teasingly.

That's a peculiar question, I thought, but all I said was, "No, not right now. I'm just enjoying the sound of your voice. Why?"

"Open them, and look at your gift."

I was so comfortable that I really didn't want to roll over. I defended, "Why? It's not like I can open my gift now because you said I have to wait! I'm comfortable. I don't want to roll over."

Pushing me a little, his calm voice encouraged, "C'mon, Avail. Just do it." I imagined that he had a slight smile on his face.

Reluctantly rolling over, I opened my eyes to see my gift bag just sitting there. "Okay, I'm looking at it. What now?" I had no idea what he was up to, but I had to admit: my curiosity was wide open!

"Okay, I'll call you back." *CLICK.*

"Hello? Kyle!" I looked at the phone in my hand and said, "What? Why did he hang up? He didn't even wait for my reply! What is up with him?"

I flung the cordless phone on the comforter and sat there for a moment with my head propped in my hand just staring at the bag in the darkness. Then, as if in some science fiction movie, the bag started shaking, but stopped just as fast as it started. It repeated that sequence at least twice before I couldn't take it anymore! I sat up immediately and uncovered my legs so that I could place my feet on the floor. At that moment, the tissue paper at the top of the bag illuminated. Carefully, I maneuvered the gift decoration and searched for the cause of all the shaking and lighting. My fingers made contact with a slender piece of plastic and metal that continued to vibrate and light up in my hand. Pulling it out immediately, I looked at the cell phone screen and saw the words, "The love of your life" above Kyle's cell number. I immediately pushed the answer key and said, "Kyle?"

A much richer laugh came from him this time as he said, "I thought I asked you not to open your gift until Christmas!" He chuckled again.

"You are so bad, Kyle! You're the one who told me to stare at the bag in the dark!" By this time, I realized that Kyle had concocted this scheme when he decided what to get me—a cell phone—an interesting choice.

"Do you like it?" Kyle asked with a timid tone in his voice.

"I do. Now I see how we'll keep in touch during my trip!" I grinned. "I'll be sure to take it with me."

"Please do, and don't forget your charger. The battery will only last so long." I smiled before Kyle mentioned, "We both have long days tomorrow, so let's get some rest. I love you, Avail. Sleep well."

I glowed as I murmured, "I love you too, Kyle. I'll call you before I leave. Good night."

"Good night."

Once I disconnected the call on my end, I just stared at the phone. The touchscreen had so many features that were unfamiliar to me. In a flash, the screen revealed that I had a text message, and since Kyle was the only one who had my number, I knew it had to be from him. I pushed the appropriate button and read what he had written: "Just wanted you to know that I really love my gift—I won't take it off. I'll miss you while you're gone, but I'll see you soon on a video chat. Love you!" After reading the text, I figured out where I had to go on the phone to initiate a video chat.

As soon as we make it to Hagerstown, I'll connect with Kyle that way.

For now, my connection with him was around his neck, reminding him of how serious we both need to be about our joint commitment to maintaining an extraordinary relationship without typical lusts. I reached up to the cross hanging around my neck, a focal point of mine when I feel like I need an extra boost from God, silently thanked Him, and resumed my restful posture for the evening.

Six

HIS WAY

After Mom and Dad had settled in for the evening, I thought it was imperative that I get in touch with Avail, especially since she said I couldn't open my gift until I called her tonight. I looked at both her gift to me and my phone sitting on my nightstand and decided that this was the moment. I hadn't even loosened my tie yet because I was still floating with happiness from spending some quality time with my parents and Avail.

It was a great evening, and I'm so thankful that we managed to maintain our standards. The future is looking even brighter from this moment on. I know God must be pleased with us.

I stared at the box that contained Avail's gift to me and tried to figure out what was in it. When I dated Celeste, I could always guess what she'd get me, and that had annoyed her to know end. Speaking of Celeste and Christmas, it was my first holiday without her in my social life in a little over six years. Honestly, I hoped she was making the best of her life as I was doing regardless of the past.

Though the relief from everything going so well tonight had turned into an insatiable drowsiness, I forced myself to cross my room to retrieve both my cell phone and my gift from Avail. Before I dialed her number, I decided that it would be best if I changed into my pajamas and returned my suit to my closet. After taking care of those details, I sat on the edge of my bed and called my girl. It was getting late, and I didn't know whether she would still be up. To my surprise, the phone barely rang once before her voice murmured drowsily, "Hello."

I guess we're both a little worn out. I matched her sleepiness when I greeted her. "Hey Avail, it's me, Kyle. Did I call you too late?"

"I'm still up, but I'm in bed. I guess the excitement of tonight wore me out more than I thought. Are you getting ready for bed yet?"

"I'm sitting on the edge of my bed holding my gift from you. I was wondering if it was okay for me to open it now," I spat out before I could control my urgent curiosity. I smacked my palm against my forehead for blurting out my true feelings. Though I could barely hold my eyes open, I didn't want to neglect the importance of this moment by saying just anything.

It was apparent that she'd put a large amount of consideration into this gift, maybe even more than I did with hers. She added, "It's just a reminder to both of us."

As if renewed by her words and the depth of thoughtfulness in her selection of the gift, my inner little boy Kyle kicked in as I ripped the box open to find a smaller box from a local jewelry store nested inside. I didn't know we were at that level of our relationship just yet, but I should have expected something like this from Avail. For lack of a better way of saying it, she was deep, thoughtful, and considerate—totally unlike anyone I had dated before. After taking the top off the box, for some reason, I slowly caressed the tissue paper as if it were Avail's delicate fingertips.

I get it now; this gift will symbolize who she is to me when she and I are away from each other, and that couldn't be more appropriate than right now before this family trip she's taking tomorrow.

Eventually, I lifted the tissue that concealed my gift, a just-right gold rope chain with a simple cross pendant. If it was possible, I mentally gasped before I draped the chain on my fingers, allowing the cross to dangle just short of my palm. I was a bit choked up because I instantly heard the words Avail said to me again right before I opened the gift. I figured with all this silence, I needed to let her know exactly how I felt about her attentive gesture. "I love it." My voice betrayed me again by showing just how much I appreciated the gift. "Thank you so much. This means so much to me." If I weren't trying to be so manly, I would've shed a tear or two.

She made the request that I always keep it on and I had already planned to do that. I whispered, "Okay, hold on." Immediately, I placed my phone on the bed next to me and removed the gift box from my lap. I undid the claw clasp and attached it around my neck. The cross pendant felt solid and real resting against my chest just beyond my collarbone. It was just the right length. I touched it as I picked up the phone and said, "It fits perfectly. The chain length is perfect. This gift is perfect." *Avail is perfect.* "Thank you again."

"You're welcome, love."

Basking in the high level of appreciation I had for Avail's gift, I almost forgot that she had not opened her gift from me yet. Immediately, I inquired, "Where is the gift I gave you?"

After she confirmed that the gift was right where I told her to place it, I had to act quick because I wanted some of what I was feeling to transfer to her through my gift, but a cell phone doesn't have the deep, intimate effect that my cross pendant had. *I'll just tie it to her trip and this being the way we can keep in touch.* "Are your eyes open?"

"No, not right now. Why?"

A sly grin curled on my lips as I commanded, "Open them, and look at your gift."

Sounding a bit irritated, which was probably because she was extremely sleepy, she demanded, "Why? I don't want to roll over."

I turned on my smooth, can't-resist-me voice and said, "C'mon, Avail. Just do it."

I heard a little rustling before Avail reported, "Okay, I'm looking at it. What now?"

Reverting to my original plan, I simply stated, "Okay, I'll call you back." I disconnected the phone call immediately.

I silently wondered if she would have a similar reaction to the gift I purchased for her, but I had to dismiss that thought. We weren't in competition to see whose gift would evoke the strongest reaction. Besides, both are touching in their own forthright ways. Ending the risk of Avail going to sleep, I called her cell phone number and let it ring. I could just imagine that she probably flipped out when the bag began to vibrate and light up from the call. I knew that I had placed the phone on vibrate, but what really made me grin in the midst of trying to envision Avail's reaction was the phrase that I had chosen to display along with my number in her phone: *the love of your life*. I knew that we were just that for one another, which explained why I'd given her number the exact same caller ID in my phone.

Just before the service sent the call to voice mail, I heard Avail answer, "Kyle?"

"I thought I asked you not to open your gift until Christmas!" I couldn't help it; I laughed uncontrollably.

"Hey, you're the one who told me to look at the bag," she reminded. Avail sounded pleased, but I had to make sure.

"Do you like it?"

"I do. Now I see how we'll keep in touch during my trip," her smile was evident through every word she said. "I'll be sure to take it with me!"

"Please do," I agreed, adding, "and don't forget your charger. The battery will only last so long."

I am the worst at keeping my phone charged, but I'll do much better now that Avail has a phone too.

Squelching a yawn, I offered, "We both have long days tomorrow, so let's get some rest. I love you, Avail. Sleep well."

As if on cue, Avail responded, "I love you too, Kyle. I'll call you before I leave. Good night."

"Good night." I disconnected the call and immediately, I sent her a text message that resassuring her about how much I loved her and my gift.

I placed the phone right next to me and turned to fluff one of my pillows just as a specific ringtone that I had programmed for Celeste blared from the phone. I hadn't seen her since that day we ran into each other at the church—and she hadn't want to be bothered with me, so I wondered why she was calling me now, and so late at night, too. I couldn't imagine what she had to say to me now. Though I wished her the best, I had to admit to myself that I really enjoyed life without her.

My knowledge of Celeste told me that if I didn't answer this call, she would hunt me down. I turned my body to face the phone again, closed my eyes tightly, and answered, "Hello."

"We need to talk."

"Celeste, I'm getting ready for bed, so not now…."

"We need to talk," she insisted. "Now!"

I had no idea what was so important that would require me to sacrifice sleep, but I replied, "Okay—talk." Aggravation was inflected in every syllable of my short response.

"Meet me at our spot," she demanded.

"Celeste," I began with a little more patience, "there is no more 'our spot.' Either talk to me now, or let it go." I didn't have time for this foolishness.

"Either meet me at our spot, or I'm coming to your house. It's that simple."

I can't have that. Celeste will wake my parents, and I don't even want to think about the possibility of that happening.

I was stuck. There was nothing I could do. "Give me twenty minutes."

Seven

His Way

"Okay, I'm here. What is so important?" I asked as I spoke to Celeste's back where she sat on the all-too-familiar park bench on Mt. Washington that Celeste and I had designated as our special spot after I asked her to be my girlfriend when we were in eighth grade.

I'm in no mood to reminisce about our past, but something tells me that we're not out here to take a walk down memory lane.

Without turning around, she quietly requested, "Can we sit in your car, if you don't mind?"

I walked around to face her and saw that she looked like she had been crying. "Sure," I said as I gestured toward my car. Being that she didn't have her driving license, and the port authority buses had stopped running hours ago, I could not understand how she'd made it there in record time. Mt. Washington was at least a ten-minute drive from our neighborhood.

When she rose from the bench, I noticed her struggle. Because I am a natural gentleman, I gave assistance silently, offering my hand, but just as she made contact with it, she shooed me away. Though I didn't really have a chance to touch her, I knew something was bothering her physically. Her whole stature was different. Her swag appeared to be gone, and it had been replaced with a hand bracing her back and abbreviated steps in unusual-for-her comfortable-looking shoes. Celeste allowed me to open the door for her, and after I saw that she was seated comfortably, I walked briskly around the back of the car and took my place in the driver's seat.

The crisp evening air prompted me to start the engine so that we could have heat. I rubbed my hands together to warm them while I asked, "So what was so important to talk about that you couldn't say it over the phone?" I did my best not to sound irritated, but it was extremely difficult.

"Don't know where to start…." Celeste barely managed to whisper. She sounded shattered as though something had crushed her spirit, and her body language projected the same message. Although my level of concern and compassion rose with her statement, my patience thinned.

"How about start from the beginning," I pushed.

Detecting my rising irritation, Celeste snapped into her typical self and demanded, "When was the last time we had sex?"

"What?" I spewed.

Talking to me slowly as if I was slow to comprehend, she repeated, "When was the last time we had sex?"

I pondered in my mind before I stated, "It had to be before I left for Whitaker because we didn't do anything when you came up for homecoming or any of the times I came home." I paused and reemphasized, "Yeah, that was about four months ago." My mind reviewed the accomplishment; I really couldn't believe that I had gone four months without sex at all.

Before I could actually feel proud about that small feat, Celeste stated, "That's what I thought."

"Why?" I urged.

"You say it's been at least four months since the last time we had sex?"

"YES," I practically yelled and asked again, "why?" By this time, I didn't try to hide my frustration. I was ready to go back home and rest so that I could be ready for church the next day.

Fed up with me, she confessed, "Well, in five months you'll be a father."

⸺

A father.
I'll have a child on this earth in five months.

I had managed to break away from Celeste only to be connected to her for life through our child.

I'm going to be a father.

The stunning news numbed me so much that I had no idea how I drove Celeste home. I remember hearing everything she said before she said the word "father." Everything thereafter was a slurred version of everyday language. Being that she had been dealing with this reality for four months now, I was sure that Celeste's articulation did not alter to the point of weak verbalization. She didn't bother to cry; I guess she had shed enough tears. Perhaps my inability to hear came from the pulse of blood pounding in my ears. Without changing my clothes or conducting any of the grooming I usually do before bedtime, my body fell limp onto my waterbed and rode the waves I created.

How am I going to tell my parents?

My first child is on the way.

Did Celeste tell her mother yet? There's no way; I would have heard by now.

What about school?

Now I truly know how Raine and Reese feel.

What about my relationship with Avail?

I was reminded of Avail when my Christmas gift from her shifted around my neck. I grabbed the cross pendant and caressed it with my fingertips, wondering how a moment of passion four months earlier had caught up to me and now I was facing fatherhood. So much responsibility came with the new position. Not even twenty-four hours earlier, I had enjoyed the carefree company of my parents and Avail. The gravity of this turn of events pulled me deeper into my mattress.

I'd have to tell her sometime soon, but with her going out of town for the holiday, I just don't see that happening right now. On the other hand, her absence might give me the time and space to figure out what I'm going to do and how I'm going to tell her.

The juxtaposition of feelings within me made my head spin. On one hand, there was a level of unfamiliar positive anticipation. I had a son or daughter on the way, another human being who was half of me. Images of the many things my father did with me and for me flew through my mind, pumping excitement through my veins as I made mental lists of all the things I wanted to instill in my child. These animated ideas became tainted as I thought of raising this same child with Celeste while maintaining a relationship with Avail. Deep down, I wasn't completely convinced that Avail would want to be bothered with me after hearing this news. I think she could handle me having a child with another woman, but when I factored in the constant that the other woman was Celeste, I could not blame Avail for wanting to leave if she chose to.

But how could she be angry with me about the conception of a child before we even met? Avail is way too reasonable to blame me for this, to think that I would automatically run back to Celeste's arms just because she's carrying my firstborn. Plenty of people manage to raise their children jointly without being married. That's at least what I plan to do with Celeste. I no longer want to marry her.

I managed to let my eyes drift shut, but my mind raced so rapidly that I had to open them and just stare into the darkness. The ceiling became my focal point, and all I did was ask God over and over to forgive me. I hated thinking of my child as a mistake, but at the same time, if I hadn't participated in premarital sex with Celeste, then I would not be in this predicament.

I then realized that the act itself was the mistake, not the conception of my child.

Well, in five months, you'll be a father. Celeste's words echoed in my head incessantly. I tried to imagine how I would tell Avail, but no reasonable scenario appeared to me. I knew one thing: I definitely didn't want Celeste to tell Avail before I had a chance to. That would be a personal victory for Celeste. She would always have the coveted title of being the mother of my firstborn, and she would attempt to make Avail feel less than nothing, because she, Celeste, would have a direct, life-long connection with me through our child. This situation had the potential of getting uglier than I imagined.

Manning up, I whispered to myself, "I'll tell her tomorrow when I call her."

⁓

I discovered that I had failed to get any quality sleep when my parents called through the door to ask whether I was ready for church. I gave them some bogus reason for not being ready, and said they should leave without me. I hadn't stopped to think how I would tell them about the baby, but at this moment, I didn't want to face anyone. I'm sure that Pastor Johnson knew; that would explain the way Celeste treated me when I saw her on the church steps earlier in the week. It was only a matter of time before everyone knew, but at this moment, I wanted to be alone with my thoughts in a weakened attempt to strategize a plan to tell Avail. I closed my eyes, and soon I was lost in thought.

Seven

HER WAY

The repetitive thump of the road that culminated in a pavement-change bump woke me up right before my mother announced that we had finally made it to Hagerstown. Earlier that day, by the time we returned from church and I had recovered from the drama I felt from running into Donovan, my ex, and Candace, the chick he wanted to date while dating me, my father pushed that we needed to get on the road immediately. He had already taken care of placing our luggage in the trunk with all the gifts that would normally sit under our tree until Christmas morning. All Mom and I had to do was get in the car and go.

Rousing from my trip nap, I instantly grabbed my purse to check my phone for a missed call or text from Kyle. My parents made it clear to me before we left that we would stay until a day or two after Christmas so they could enjoy a brief amount of their vacation at home as well. That was fine with me, because I wanted to spend some vacation time with my man. It still stunned me that we were an exclusive couple and so in love.

To my dismay, I found no missed calls or texts. It was Sunday afternoon, and there was no telling what he had to do at church, so I could understand. Instead of waiting for him, I decided to text him. "Baby, I just wanted to let you know that we arrived in Hagerstown safely. I love and miss you. I'll be home by the end of the week!" My strongly embedded English skills wouldn't allow me to use text language! After saving the message as a draft, I took a moment to program Raine and Shea's numbers into my contacts list. When I had a chance, I would have to look up Grey's number from my email and save it in the phone as well.

I reread the text before hitting send, knowing that it would put a grin on Kyle's face. I loved his smile; I loved his sense of humor; I loved everything about him, *and that's why I'm convinced that he'll be my husband and the father of my children.* I remembered seeing how he interacted with the little kids in his family during Thanksgiving dinner, and I think it was then that I knew I wanted to be his wife and have his kids.

He's going to make a great daddy.

In the middle of the atrium and all the reuniting hugs and love going on between my parents and my mother's cousin, I stood back, feeling a little like an outsider, and took in my surroundings. The opulent two-story colonial-style five-bedroom house looked much larger on the inside than it did outside. The mahogany hardwood floors made the mint green walls trimmed with white crown molding pop with delicacy. Tastefully decorated with just-right accents that complemented the environment, I mentally dispelled the notion that this house was less like a museum and more like a home. An L-shaped staircase led to the second level that, from my vantage point, appeared to have more than just bedrooms.

We stepped farther into the home where a gourmet stainless steel and marble kitchen glittered as if it had never been used. The eat-in area of the room sat to the left of an obvious formal dining room where a beautifully decorated table was set for eight. On the other side of the dining room sat a grand living room with a wall completely filled with two-story windows that provided an unbelievable view of a mountainous horizon. A two-sided fireplace that provided a peek into another room that looked like an office only added to the warmth and charm of the ambiance.

"Avail, come over here and meet Bryan," my mom ordered, and I immediately obeyed. Being that he was so much older and my mother's cousin, I called him Uncle Bryan out of respect.

"Hello there, young lady," the slender man began. "I haven't seen you since you were just a baby!"

I smiled because whenever older relatives say that to me, I always wonder if they expect me to remember that specific time! "It's nice to see you again," I greeted as I stepped into a family hug with him. "You have a lovely home," I had to comment. It was a little difficult to believe that he lived there with twin young adults. Speaking of them, I said, "Mom told me that you have children my age."

"I do," he shared before he barked, "Dillard and Chrystina, get down here to meet some family!" After a yell like that, I could tell that we were related!

Promptly, we heard rapid footsteps from different ends of the second level of the house. My male cousin Dillard ran down the steps with no regard while Chrystina, his twin sister, glided down the steps with an unspoken grace. At first glance, if I had met Dillard on the street without knowing that he was a relative, I would have been fascinated with him. Though he was only average height, he looked model-gorgeous in a T-shirt, sweat pants, and a pair of socks. His longer-than-average-for-a-male hair rested against his scalp in neat cornrows tightly woven from the front to the back. The perimeter of his buttery brown irises flaunted upper and lower eyelashes that I'm sure Chrystina wished she had. His creamy-dreamy auburn complexion and nice body made him very easy on the eyes, and I had a feeling that he knew it, too.

Uncle Bryan introduced, "Avail, this is my son and your cousin Dillard."

I simply waved my hand, but Dillard commenced, "Oh naw, cuz! We're fam, so you need to give me a hug!" Before I knew it, I was in his arms, and he gave me a hug that resembled the ones my brothers give me when they haven't seen me in a while. "By the way, everyone in the family calls me Dill. Pops is the only one that calls me by my IRS name."

Laughing, I gently squeezed back and said, "It's nice to meet you, Dill."

As we came out of the hug, Uncle Bryan continued, "And this is my daughter, Dillard's twin sister Chrystina.

I turned toward Chrystina and noticed our similarity in style: cute, simplistic, and well put together. She looked like a slender female version of Dill without the eyelashes. She kept her hair in curly micro braids that stopped just short of her waist. We hugged as well, and just like her brother, she informed me, "Everyone in the family calls me Chrys. Daddy is the only one who calls me Chrystina."

"It's nice to meet you, Chrys."

In a flash, I saw Dill give Chrys one of those gestures that apparently only twins can understand before Dill offered, "Let me show you where you'll sleep." I looked back at my parents and Uncle Bryan and followed dutifully as my cousins swept my bag away to the second floor. Once in the privacy of a guest bedroom, Dill initiated a conversation by delving right in. "So, lil' cuz, tell us about yourself. Do you go to college now or are you still in high school?"

I choked on a laugh that I squelched as I began. "I'm a freshman in college; I just finished my first semester at a small school outside of Pittsburgh."

Dill kept staring at me as Chrys added, "Okay, that's good. That way, if Daddy gets us tickets to a concert in Baltimore that we want to go to on Christmas night, you might be able to go with us!" She spoke with such energy behind every word that I fed off her enthusiasm.

I sat on the bed and asked, "What concert are you talking about?"

"We're going to see Kindred the Family Soul and Anthony David in Baltimore on Christmas night. Pops told us we weren't allowed to buy our own tickets, but we seem to think that he got them for us as gifts," Dill added. "If we get them, are you down? We'll meet up with some friends of ours from our old neighborhood." Then Dill did that twin thing with Chrys before he added, "I think you'll enjoy yourself."

I looked back and forth between Chrys and Dill, trying to read their silent communication before replying, "I don't know, guys. That's a long ride, and I'm just used to chillin' around family on holidays. That would seem strange to me."

Really, it was a little peculiar. I can't imagine going to a concert of that magnitude on a holiday.

Chrys laughed before she said, "B'more is not that far away, and you'd still be chillin' around family because we're family, and the concert will be worth it." She paused, bit her bottom lip, and added, "Besides, our friends are crazy-fun to be around."

I couldn't form an argument against fun, so I nodded and said, "Okay, cool; I guess we'll see if your dad got you those tickets!" We went back and forth as I got to know my cousins and everything that made them tick. Both sophomores, Dill attended Morgan State University where he was studying hotel, restaurant, and hospitality management while Chrys went a little farther away to Howard University to study mass communications. Each wanted careers dealing with the entertainment business but had no desires to leave Maryland. I could tell from the little time I spent with them that they would make this holiday very interesting and fun!

⌒⟶

*B*efore settling for bed, I checked my cell phone to see if Kyle had called or texted me. There was nothing. I had no idea what could keep him from getting in touch with me, but I hoped everything at home was okay.

Since I'm out of town, there's no doubt that Celeste will try to take advantage of my absence.

After I texted Kyle again, I looked at my battery level and noticed it only had half its strength. There was only one problem: I had failed to put my charger in the bag before my father put my bag in the car! *Oh, no.* I checked with Dill and Chrys, and their chargers didn't fit my phone. In an effort to save some of the battery life, I turned off the phone and headed for bed praying that the battery would last at least until Christmas.

Part Two

Eight

His Way

" *I*n five months or so, I will have a child."

"Kyle, you can't be serious," my mother managed to say after my words knocked the wind out of her for a brief moment. Contrary to the pillar of strength that my father typically was, he looked floored as well. Mom continued, "You've only known Avail since the beginning of this semester. How could this have happened so quickly?" My father just shook his head and barely made eye contact with me.

I found myself shifting on the leather couch that served as the focal point in our living room. The hard part of telling them that I gotten someone pregnant was over; now I had to tell them, "Avail is not who I got pregnant. It's Celeste."

Their initial disappointment shifted to the epitome of being distraught as my father expressed, "I thought you and Celeste had been done with each other since

117

you met Avail. How could you do this to those girls?"
He had raised me to be a better man than the one I
showed myself to be right now, but I had failed.

"I didn't plan this, and I wasn't sleeping with both
of them at the same time...." I cut myself off when
my parents' expression changed to shock, I imagine,
from me inferring that I'd slept with Avail. I clarified,
"I haven't slept with Avail, and I don't plan to unless
we get married. I was serious when I told you that the
other night. The last time Celeste and I connected in
that way was shortly before I left for school. The timing lines up."

I gave my parents time to digest all that I had
shared with them. They were going to be grandparents to a child that I had created with a woman they
didn't like. I knew that they thought Celeste wasn't
right for me, and Avail was. My parents never said this,
but I could tell from the contrast between their feelings for Celeste and their feelings for Avail.

Mom dropped her head and massaged her left
temple. Dad finally made eye contact with me, and I
could see pain in his eyes when he asked, "Are you
sure the baby's yours? I hate to bring up the possibility,
but it's no secret that Celeste has had other guys in her
life, and there's no telling what she did with them."

To be honest, the thought had never crossed my
mind that the baby could be someone else's child. I
knew of her escapades with Evan, but I didn't know
about anyone else. Deciding not to bring up the other
possible men in Celeste's life, I said, "I'm pretty sure
that the baby's mine."

Still rubbing her head, Mom looked up and said, "Are you DNA sure that the baby she's carrying is yours?" I choked as she continued. "She has always had her hooks in you, seeking to do whatever she can to keep you. This may be another stunt."

"Mom, I don't think this is a stunt," I managed to say calmly. "Why would she go this far knowing that I would have to tell you about it? Why would she go through the humiliation of telling Pastor Johnson if she wasn't absolutely sure that I am the father?"

My mother's frustration broke her voice when she said, "You sound like you want this child to be yours! Kyle, you don't have to make up for the child she decided to abort on her own. That was not your fault."

I dropped my head in shame just as my father said, "You have to get a paternity test, son. Before you get attached to the idea of having a child, you should know if you're the biological father."

As much as it pained me, I was already attached.

⌣

I think the news of my baby killed the holiday spirit we normally had in our house during Christmas. The poinsettias were still vibrant and gorgeous, and I couldn't recall the Christmas tree looking better, but I had stunned my parents with news of my baby on the eve of the holiday.

In turn, they had stunned me with the idea that the baby wasn't mine. Yes, I might have had my other women, and Celeste might have had her other men, but there was no way whatsoever that the baby she carried was anyone else's but mine. I just refused to think that she would go through the dramatics of telling me something like that without knowing for sure.

Speaking of knowing, my girlfriend had no idea what I'd been going through since she left for her holiday in Hagerstown. I wanted to tell her face to face and be a man about it, not tell her over the phone, but really, I had no choice. I stared at my cell phone on my nightstand and decided that I needed to tell her now regardless of how it might ruin her holiday. I needed to know how she'd react. I needed to know how she'd take the news. I needed to know if she would still be a part of my life.

I picked up my phone and speed-dialed Avail's cell. Almost immediately, a recorded statement popped on stating that the person I tried to reach was not available and that I could leave a message. Her phone was probably turned off.

She must not have played with the phone enough to set up her voicemail.

Regardless, after the beep, I left her a message, trying not to sound broken: "Avail, this is Kyle. I need to talk to you. It's really important, so please call me back as soon as you can. Avail," I paused, "I love you. Talk to you soon." I held the phone tightly after I disconnected the call. Somehow, it made me feel as if I was holding a small piece of her and the love we shared.

With a child on the way, I had to figure out how I'd take care of him or her. The expense of a child was way above my nonexistent income. Basically, all the money I got came from my parents, and I wouldn't dare ask them to assume my responsibility.

The only possible solution is for me to get a job here in Pittsburgh and drop out of Whitaker, which would put distance between Avail and me.

I mentally shouted as I stood up and paced the floor. I looked down on the floor next to a dresser in my room and noticed a letter from Whitaker that my parents must have placed in my room within the past few days. After passing it one or two times, I stopped my walking rant, bent down to pick up the letter, and ripped open the envelope. Almost immediately, the word, "Congratulations," jumped off the page. It continued, "You have been selected to participate in the Introduction to Entrepreneurial Studies Grant Competition, which entails enrolling in this year's Intersession course and possibly earning the coveted Young Entrepreneur of the Year Grant that allows you to put your business vision into action, all expenses covered...."

I had completely forgotten that one of my professors had nominated me for the award when I'd spoken to him about the possibility of creating my own radio station.

Now, I'm accepted and have to figure out a way to manage both the preparation for my child and my education. I can't afford to let this opportunity slip away.

Eight

HER WAY

"Avail, what in the world are you doing?" Chrys asked as she walked into the kitchen. When staying in an unfamiliar place, I can never sleep as comfortably as I sleep at home. So when my eyes popped open a little before 6:00 a.m., I decided to try my skills in Uncle Bryan's culinary castle. The holiday wouldn't be complete without a Christmas Eve breakfast that I could hook up for the whole family. "Girl, you are going to make Dill and me look really bad!" Chrys said with a laugh as she took in the scope of my work in progress.

I laughed as I gestured to her to pass me the eggs I'd placed on the kitchen island just moments before she'd come into the kitchen. Since we were family, I didn't see a reason to wake Uncle Bryan to ask permission to start a meal. Besides, he probably would have refused, and I would have been stuck with sitting in my bed staring at the wall.

My menu was simple: scrambled eggs, sausage, bacon, scratch biscuits, and cheese grits. Cracking two eggshells at a time and dropping the contents into a large glass bowl, I giggled before I replied, "What do you mean, Chrys? Don't tell me that you don't take advantage of this wonderful kitchen! I love to cook, and I couldn't resist." I smiled.

Holding back a yawn, Chrys declared, "Daddy is always getting on us, saying that we should cook more when we're home, but I don't bother." By this time, Chrys had fallen into my natural culinary flow, looking over the biscuits in the oven and checking on the sizzling bacon and sausage patties in different cast iron skillets. Flipping the meats over, she included, "It's not like we don't know how to cook. Mama began teaching both of us when we were young."

After disposing of some eggshells, I noticed that a reflective look covered Chrys's face, and I had to ask, "You miss her, don't you?" I could only imagine how hard it was to lose your mother at a young age.

She beamed a brave smile and simply nodded.

Since we had just met, I didn't want to get all touchy-feely, so I quickly changed the subject by asking, "Do Uncle Bryan, Dill, or you drink coffee? We need to put some on, and just like the commercial says, it'll get everyone out of bed!"

"I absolutely LOVE that commercial," Chrys shared, and we both laughed. Ever since I began watching television when I was younger, I'd always thought that commercials entertained better than the actual shows. "I'll take care of making the coffee because there's a certain way Daddy likes it. I think your parents will enjoy it too."

On the way to the coffeepot, she hit a button and music began to play out of speakers encased in the walls. Old R&B Christmas songs filled the atmosphere, and I imagined that our actions would rouse our family members out of their slumber. Dill ran down the stairs and immediately asked, "What are y'all doing this early in the morning?" Suddenly, as if the popping of the butter in the electric skillet had caught his attention, he stopped short of entering the kitchen, inhaled the delectable aromas, and insisted, "Whatever it is, keep doing it because I like it!" All three of us laughed, and then Dill returned upstairs to prepare for the day.

"*A*vail, Chrystina, you did not have to make us breakfast! I had planned for us to go to a pancake house not that far from here," Uncle Bryan said after clearing his second plate of everything. "But this was a nice, unexpected surprise, and simply delicious." My parents and Uncle Bryan sat back in their house robes, relaxed and satisfied. "And Avail, however you managed to get Chrystina out of bed early to cook, you'll have to tell me. Keep rubbing off on her!"

His tentative laugh made Chrys defend herself by saying, "Daddy, it's not like I can't cook—I just don't!

But cooking with Avail was fun. It's nice to have another girl in the house." She grinned and we both began taking the serving bowls and plates off the table and to the kitchen.

Yelling at our backs, Uncle Bryan encouraged, "Well, Avail, you should consider coming back over the summer!"

Chrys and I laughed about it, but Chrys asked me seriously, "So, do you have anything lined up for the summer?"

"Anything like what?" I said while I made the dishwater.

"Like internships or anything like that. Last year, Dill and I did internships at Morgan; we helped their student activities director line up social events for the year. We were fortunate enough to learn how to contact agents and manage a six-figure budget to cover all the events."

I hadn't thought far enough into the future to figure out what I wanted to do during the summer, but this really caught my attention. Though it was not in my field, it sounded interesting. Chrys probed, "So what do you want to do once you graduate?"

I took a deep breath and shared, "After I teach for a few years on the secondary level, I want to earn my terminal degree while teaching on the college level." Water splashed here and there as I continued. "I want to train teachers, because there are not enough good quality teachers in the profession now." I looked at my cousin who stood there with an amazed look on her face.

"Wow, Avail. That's awesome! I know we can find you an internship at Morgan…." she stated, and she let her voice drift off. "That is, if you want one." She almost sounded a little sad at the possibility of me refusing her offer.

I couldn't give her an answer right then, but I assured her that I would seriously think about it. Dill came into the kitchen stating that Uncle Bryan had told him to take my place at the sink. He insisted that he and Chrys would take care of the dishes. I took my leave, retreating to my room immediately, liking the possibility of spending the summer in Hagerstown and Baltimore with my cousins. Needless to say, I had to consider whether Whitaker would accept the internship for credit and whether Kyle could handle my being away for the whole summer.

Not that I was making any major decisions at that moment, but I just wanted to see what he thought, and since it was on my mind, I turned on my phone to call him. On the welcome screen, it showed that I had one new message, and I knew it had to be from Kyle. My heart began to beat a little faster because it seemed like we hadn't talked in ages even though it had only been a little more than thirty-six hours.

Immediately, I pushed the voicemail button, put in the pin number that Kyle had recorded in the owner's manual, and heard my love's deep voice: "Avail, this is Kyle. I need to talk to you. It's really important, so please call me back as soon as you can. Avail, I love you. Talk to you soon." That wasn't exactly the message I had hoped to hear from him. Essentially, nothing was wrong with it, but he sounded troubled, like he did when he called me from the infirmary after he hurt his knee at the football game earlier this year. There was an unsettled undertone in his voice, and I didn't like it. *My boo is in a snag.*

I almost broke the phone dialing his number. When he answered, I could hear that tortured tone permeating his greeting.

"Hey love, I got your message," I began. "Are you okay? Because you sounded like something was bothering you."

Sounding completely unsure of himself, he said, "Ugh, yeah, I'm okay. I just have tons on my mind." He paused for a moment then said, "So how's your visit with your family going?"

I could tell that he had changed the subject on purpose, but I went along with it anyway. "I'm having a great time. My cousins are cool, and we cooked for our family this morning." I babbled on a little more, but eventually, I stopped because I knew he really wasn't listening. Just to test him, I said, "And afterward, we set the house on fire to stay warm. What do you think of that?"

"That's good…that's real good…."

Actually, it's not good, I thought, but I said, "Kyle, what's wrong? You're not acting like yourself."

After an overly long pause, he asked, "Can I call you back?" I didn't bother to say anything, but as if I did, he stated, "Okay, Avail, I'll call you back later." *CLICK.*

There's definitely something wrong, and I can guess that it mostly has something to do with Celeste. I wonder what she's done. Whatever it is, I know she's up to no good.

"Hello?"

After calling Kyle three more times and getting no response, I decided to let him have his space. It was obvious he did not want to be bothered with my calls. I'm sure he knew when it was me calling because my name or something referring to me popped on his phone screen every time I called. I reviewed the events of the past few days to see if he had any justifiable reason to be upset with me, and I concluded that the mood he marinated in had nothing to do with me. But his silence toward me bothered me to no end, especially since I was out of town and unable to talk to him in person.

Since I had pulled Grey's number from my email on Dill's computer and I didn't know if I would have enough battery power to call him during the holiday, I thought I'd give him a call before Christmas. "May I speak to Grey please," I requested of the unfamiliar male voice.

"Sure, hold on for a minute." I heard conversation on the other end, which included the phone answerer saying to Grey, "I have no idea who it is. The caller ID said that the call was from the 412 area. Isn't that where your school is? It's a girl, man! Just get on the phone!" I had to giggle because I could only imagine the questions Grey had asked this guy, who I assumed was a younger brother or cousin.

It took very little time for Grey to clear his throat and greet me by saying hello in a deep, come-on voice as if he was trying to mack me over the phone.

There's no way he could have known it was me.

"Hey Grey, it's Avail. How are you?" I tried not to sound flattered at his tone.

"What's up, girl?" His tone didn't change.

He knew it was me, and his tone didn't change.

He continued, "Merry Christmas! It's good to hear from you." He even sounded sexy wishing me a happy holiday.

Trying to control my growing excitement at his re-action to my call, I tried to be as cool as I possibly could convey in my voice by stating, "I'm good. I'm really enjoying my vacation so far." After a slight pause, I had to ask, "Who answered the phone?"

He chuckled a bit before stating, "Oh, that was Brady, a little neighborhood boy who chills with my younger brother. I try to spend a little time with him since he has no positive male role model in his life."

"I'm NOT a little boy," I heard Brady yell in the background, quickly followed by a muffled sound that could have been Brady hitting Grey in the face with a pillow or something like that. I giggled privately at the cute interaction between the two of them.

As if trying to brush off Brady's actions, Grey probed, "So what have you been up to?"

"We made it to Hagerstown and we're having a great time…" I drifted away for a moment before I continued, "…and the number on your caller ID is my cell number."

There's no need for him to know that Kyle gave me the phone as my Christmas gift. Since Kyle doesn't have time to talk to me, I'll talk to someone who wants to talk to me!

"Hagerstown," he almost groaned. "I think I told you in my email that you're not that far away from Baltimore."

Dismissing the fact that I researched it myself, I added, "That's what my cousins told me, too. They're talking about taking me on a side trip to Baltimore before we head back to Pittsburgh." I knew it would impossible for me to see him or Frick for that matter, so I didn't feel like I should even suggest it.

"Well, if you get a chance, and since I know you like seafood, you may want to go to the harbor. That's a great place for a first-time visitor to this area to go." He paused as if he was deciding what to say next, and then he said it. "Then, if you come back, maybe I can show you the real B'more."

I smiled because I liked the idea of coming back, both during the summer internship program at Morgan and spending some time with Grey. A part of me felt bad having these thoughts, being that Kyle and I now dated, but something had changed. He wouldn't even take my calls. Attempting to reduce any possibility of a flirtatious undertone, I replied blandly, "I may have to take you up on that. My cousins want me to come back for the summer, but it depends on whether I'll go to summer school at Whitaker or if I'll work at home."

"Why would you go to summer school at Whitaker?" Grey asked. "Most students from Whitaker get credits from somewhere else or they get some type of field experience with their major. Some schools in the Baltimore area offer great summer school classes and cool internships, and depending on where you go, the credits will transfer fully." His smooth tone melted away and his brotherly ways surfaced, dishing out his usual serving of valuable advice.

Instead of letting him know that I was already in the process of considering an internship at Morgan, I simply added, "Well, I may have to look into it."

"If you need any connections to schools here for a summer experience, let me know."

Did he just invite me to basically spend the summer in Baltimore with him?

I just grinned. It was nice to hear such encouragement when I was sure that Kyle would do nothing but tell me that we should spend the summer together in Pittsburgh. Not that it would be a bad thing, but I hated the possibility of missing out on a truly unique opportunity.

"Thanks," I said, "but enough about me. How is your vacation going so far?" At my very core, I wanted to prolong this conversation as much as I could. I liked talking to Grey.

Grey made a sound that made me imagine him doing one of those stretch yawns that made him look extra tall before he responded by saying, "I haven't been doing too much. I still have to stay in seasonal condition because we have a tough string of games as soon as we get back."

"Yeah," I jumped in. "I can't wait until the Waynesburg game. Before we left, I saw in the school paper that in the games before break, you were always one or two stats away from having a triple-double. I totally expect you to get one against them!" I was so pumped that I didn't realize that I'd revealed my keen observance of his skills.

"Wow, Avail! I didn't know you cared so much."

"Oh, I do," slipped out of my mouth before I could alter the undertone of my statement. Once again, attempting to divert any subconscious meaning behind my reply, I followed up by saying, "I like sports. I'm not a big NBA fan, but high school and college basketball is played with so much passion. Pickup games on the street have that hunger, that intensity that makes people want to watch."

"That's how I started playing the game, just for fun with the high school team. When the recruiter mentioned the possibility of playing at Whitaker, I decided that I couldn't go wrong attending the scouting camp to flaunt my skills. Honestly, I thought that after high school, I was done with the game in regards to playing with a team."

We continued chatting, and I sincerely enjoyed it. Grey went on a few moments, explaining his love for the game, and then he shared that he hoped to play throughout his senior year. He also shared with me that he signed up for an English literature course for intersession, so he kindly reminded me that he'd need my skills with his papers. After teasing him about leaning on a little freshman like me, we eventually ended our conversation with me promising to attend the Waynesburg game.

I just don't know how Kyle will take my cheering for Grey...I mean the team...

*J*ust so that Kyle couldn't claim that I was the one being distant, I attempted to call him one more time. I looked at my phone and noticed that the battery icon flashed red, showing that there was not much battery life left. The phone rang, and when I saw that it was Kyle, I knew something was up. He was keeping something from me that I should know.

"Hey love, I was just thinking about you. How are you?" He sounded normal, so maybe I was wrong. He could've been busy with all things holiday, but that wouldn't keep me from asking.

"I'm fine, but I'm more concerned about you." I took a moment to let my statement sink in so that he knew that I was genuinely concerned. "I haven't heard from you since I left town, and I called you three times before reaching you. Are you all right?"

"Sure, I'm great! I have some great news," he announced with his usual energy. He sounded more and more like himself. I was the one trippin'.

"Oh, what's that?" I inquired.

"I got a letter from Whitaker's Entrepreneurial Studies Department stating that I have been selected to participate in the intercession course, and that if I present my proposal well enough, I may have a chance to have an alumni finance the whole project!"

So this is what has consumed his thoughts the past few days.

I totally understood how he could become preoccupied with this. Kyle was very conscientious about his studies, and when it came to the possibility of seeing his dream become tangible, I understood our brief break in communication.

As excited as I could convey over the phone, I expressed, "Congratulations, Kyle! I know how much you really love working at the radio station at school, so this is a phenomenal opportunity for you!" Instantly thinking about the possibility of spending the summer with my cousins and wondering how Kyle would react, I admitted, "I have something I want to share with you too."

"What's that?"

I inhaled sharply before spilling it all. "My cousins told me about an internship program at Morgan State University where I may be able to work over the summer in their teacher education department." I stopped to take another breath, and then I continued. "I would stay with my cousins, and I'd be there most of the summer. What do you think about that?" Not totally sure how he would react, this time I took in an audible breath and waited for his response. I imagined that he wouldn't like it at all, and that I would have to search for an opportunity in Pittsburgh all in the name of keeping my relationship solid.

"That sounds just awesome, Avail. Have you applied yet?"

Part of me was thrilled that he didn't bother to push against my academic pursuits, but another part of me was a little disappointed as well. I don't think he realized what we would have to sacrifice for this. We would have to rise to a whole new level of trust. This was much larger than just taking a class with Camden or someone else who wanted to break us up. Answering his question, I said, "No, they just told me about it. They'll send me the link sometime in February." I did my best not to let my voice reveal my mixed emotions.

I opened my mouth to tell Kyle about the phone when he interjected. "Hold on for a minute; I have a call coming in." Before I could protest, he clicked over to answer the other call.

Taking the phone away from my face, I looked at the blinking battery icon hoping that it would hold out until Kyle clicked back over so that I could tell him that I had forgotten my charger. When I stayed on hold for over two minutes, I decided to disconnect the call and use what battery life I had left to text him. Frantically, I typed, "Kyle, the battery on my cell phone is almost dead, and I forgot my charger. If I don't answer the phone, that's why. Love you." I pulled up the menu to send the message, and just as I hit the appropriate button, the phone died. I had no idea if the text went through or not.

Nine

His Way

Avail's ringtone blared into the atmosphere and "The Love of My Life" flashed with urgency on the face of my cell phone. I still had not developed a way to tell her about Celeste and the baby, and I really didn't know what to say. I knew I had to answer the call, but what would we talk about? With no confidence at all, I pushed the answer button and said hello as if I didn't know who it was.

My sweet, normal-girl, drama-free Avail replied, "Hey love, I got your message. Are you okay? Because you sounded like something was bothering you." She detected that something was wrong, so I must not have done a good job leaving her a message.

I was almost to the point of being scared of what to say, so I stuttered, "Ugh, yeah, I'm okay. I just have tons on my mind." I patted myself in the face as if to wake myself up before I recovered by saying, "So, how's your visit with your family going?"

The light slaps didn't really work because my mind kept telling me to tell her about Celeste and the baby. I heard Avail talking into the phone, but my thoughts consumed my attention, preventing me from comprehending what she said. Imperative statements in my head encouraging me to confess stopped right before I heard a questioning inflection in Avail's voice. To play it off as if I was still listening, I said vaguely, "That's good…that's real good…."

"Kyle, what's wrong? You're not acting like yourself." Avail sounded angry, so that meant I hadn't said the right thing. Now she knew that I wasn't paying attention.

Still not knowing what to say and afraid that I would just blurt out the information, I requested, "Can I call you back?" Without waiting for her reply, I said, "Okay Avail, I'll call you back later." I hung up quickly, glad that I had managed to conceal the critical information. I knew it wasn't right to leave Avail in the dark, but my original idea of telling her over the phone just didn't feel right at the time, especially with it being Christmas Eve.

No—I'll wait until she gets back home.

ours later, Avail's ring tone sang at least three more times without a response from me. I couldn't face her yet because I hadn't developed a plan to tell her in the most informed, unemotional way. I resolved that telling her over the phone would not work. *That means I won't have to tell her tomorrow with it being Christmas, and I have two days after that before she returns. I know I probably won't be able to avoid her much longer, so I'll just have to divert the conversation to something else.*

While I was strategizing, her ring tone captured my attention yet again.

Let me see if I can take control of this call from the beginning.

I pushed the answer button and said, "Hey love, I was just thinking about you. How are you?" I was a good actor when I needed to be.

Her tone told me that she wasn't buying it at all, but she didn't challenge it when she hastily replied, "I'm fine, but I'm more concerned about you. I hadn't heard from you since I left and I called you three times before reaching you. Are you all right?" If she only knew what happened right after we exchanged gifts over the phone, but I couldn't dwell on that. I had to be present in this conversation to offer her a little assurance.

Putting on the largest front I had ever done with Avail, I said, "Sure I'm great! I have some great news," *along with some earth-shattering news as well. Of course, I only planned on sharing one of the two.*

"Oh, what's that?" She sounded perkier. My diversion worked.

"I got a letter from Whitaker's Entrepreneurial Studies Department stating that I have been selected to participate in the intercession course, and that if I present my proposal well enough, I may have a chance to have an alumni finance the whole project!"

I was excited about the possibility of starting and operating my own radio station. It would be a dream come true.

Joy poured out of Avail when she remarked, "Congratulations, Kyle. I know how much you really love working on the radio station at school, so this is a phenomenal opportunity for you." I believed she was genuinely happy for me, but I doubt she was thinking about the possibility that if I won, I would have to take classes online while setting up the radio station in Pittsburgh. "I have something I want to share with you too," she added.

It was my turn to ask, "What's that?"

"My cousins told me about an internship program at Morgan State University where I may be able to work over the summer in their teacher education department." She stopped abruptly, as if she wasn't totally sure how I would take the news of her prospect. Tentatively, she added, "I would stay with my cousins, and I'd be there most of the summer. What do you think about that?" It sounded as if she took a sharp breath and held it in, waiting for my response.

With Celeste due in late May, Avail taking an internship out of town would really work to my advantage. That way, I could concentrate on my child without having to maintain a day-to-day relationship with her.

Once I tell her about the pregnancy, my opinion won't matter anyway, and she'll run to Morgan and other opportunities as fast as she can.

She remained so supportive of my pursuits and exhibited so much excitement when I told her about the entrepreneurial contest that I would have been foolish not to give her my full support, especially since it was an academic endeavor. "That sounds just as awesome, Avail. Have you applied yet?"

"No, they just told me about it. They'll send me the application link sometime in February." She sounded relieved that I didn't shoot down the entire idea.

An abrupt beep signaled that I had an incoming call. Celeste's name blinked frantically on the screen, and immediately, I told Avail, "Hold on for a minute; I have a call coming in." I clicked over and greeted Celeste.

"I told my mother. Have you told your parents yet?" She got straight to the point as usual.

"I told them earlier. Naturally, they're not happy about this at all."

Celeste snickered before saying, "Yeah right, like my mom is! Dang, sometimes y'all can act so stuck up, like you're better than everyone else...." I tuned out the remainder of her tirade because I couldn't stand how she naturally assumed that we looked down our noses at her just because my parents were still together and we lived in a bigger house.

"Celeste, hold on for a minute," I demanded before I hit the button to get back to Avail on the other line. "Avail, I'll have to call you back."

"This isn't Avail; you didn't click over," Celeste proclaimed. "Have you told her yet? Or are you waiting for me to do it for you?"

Trying to keep the lid on my simmering anger, I stated, "I haven't told her yet, and no, I don't want you to tell her a thing. I'll handle it."

"You better, because Pittsburgh's not all that big, and it's not as if we wouldn't casually run into each other by chance." The last part of her evilly laced statement flashed me back to the incident Avail told me about when she ran into Celeste at the mall before Christmas. Now that Celeste was noticeably showing, I could only imagine how she would exploit the whole situation.

Unbeknownst to me, I gave her vital information when I said, "Avail is out of town now, but it doesn't matter. I will handle it. Don't you dare say a word or try to approach her about this. How and when I tell her is none of your business."

"None of my business?" Celeste shrieked. "We are having a baby together. Anything dealing with my baby or my baby's father IS my business!"

"Let's get one thing straight," I hissed. "The only reason we are having this conversation right now is because of the baby. The only reason I will talk to you is when the subject matter deals with the baby. Aside from the fact that you are my child's mother, I have very little concern for you. What I do independently of our child should have very little concern in your regard." In an attempt to put an end to any possibilities floating in her head, I daggered, "We will not get back

together just because of our child. Understand that."
I knew that everything I said was harsh, but she took
me there.

She's a big girl now; she can handle it.

"Kyle, let's get another thing straight," she whispered. "My concern *is* for the baby. I'm not trying
to tie you down. I just expect you to be here for him
or her—that's it. Stop trying to turn this into some
type of after-school TV sitcom, and look at reality. In
five months, we'll be parents." Then she screamed,
"PARENTS! I just expect you to do right by your child.
That's all!"

"Like I won't!" I practically yelled. "Let me take you
back to when you aborted my child without any consent from me...."

"I don't want to talk about this," Celeste interrupted with a humble tone in her voice.

"Good, because all I want you to do is listen." She
remained silent for once. "I was prepared to do anything and everything for our child. I wasn't going to
walk away. I had no plans of denying my child or anything like that. When you told me you were pregnant,
I immediately started planning what type of father
I'd be. Then, the abortion took away my hopes and
dreams of that in an instant. This pregnancy will not
end the same way. I will be an active, vital part of this
pregnancy. You will pull no stunts that might endan-
ger my child. You will remain healthy; you will watch
what you eat; you will take care of yourself; and you
will carry my baby to full term." Swallowing back man-
tears, I proclaimed, "This child will live and have a

happy, stable childhood, but all this starts now, with us understanding where we stand. We cannot change the past, but we can focus on the present." I stopped, lowered my voice to a calm volume, and continued. "This is not negotiable. You take care of the child in you by taking care of yourself, and we will start on a good foot. Can you handle that?"

I had stunned Celeste, and her momentary silence proved it. I heard her exhale before she said, "I can handle that." There was a long pause before she carefully added, "Kyle, Mom wants to see you tomorrow to talk about the baby."

Really? On Christmas Day? This talk couldn't wait one more day?

Instead of immediately saying no, I asked, "What time?"

"Any time after your family dinner will be fine."

I totally forgot about Avail being on the other line until my screen showed that she had disconnected her end of the call.

Nine

HER WAY

Christmas Day proved to be a joy with the exception of one thing: I did not hear from Kyle. I thought about calling him on one of my cousin's phones, but Kyle doesn't answer his phone unless he recognizes the phone number, so that plan was out. Kyle rarely checked his email, so I figured I wouldn't hear from him until I returned home.

As we did with Pittsburgh family, everyone exchanged gifts. I was a little shocked when Chrys gave me a pair of gold hoop earrings. I promised to wear them to the concert to which Chrys, Dill, and I received tickets from Uncle Bryan. With the ticket being a gift from Uncle Bryan and Mom and Dad encouraging me to hang out with Dill and Chrys, I could not back out.

Shortly after a five-star dinner that Uncle Bryan put together himself, Chrys and I began getting ready for the concert, trying to figure out what we should wear and how to do our hair—girlie stuff. I could feel an instant bond between us, like we were sisters instead of second cousins. After many switches and suggestions, I decided to wear a baby yellow sleeveless turtleneck under a black jean jacket. A pair of pale yellow ankle dress boots set off the skinny jeans that coordinated with the jacket. With my hair slicked back in a sophisticated ponytail that allowed me to showcase Chrys's gift to me, I walked down the staircase to find Dill on the phone jabbering away with someone. Once he saw me, he gave his closing remarks, ended his conversation, and instantly launched into teasing me.

"Baby cuz," he began placing his hands on my shoulders, "you're fam and all, but you're going to have to take that color combination off before we go to the show." He was referring to the fact that I had on my Pittsburgh Steelers team colors. "You'll be in the Ravens' Nest—B'more, Baby. Purple and black is the only way to go, Boo." In his oversized Ravens replica jersey coordinated with a black, long-sleeved Under Armor shirt, baggy black jeans, and just polished black Tims, I knew he was being playfully serious! I shook my head and we both laughed.

Soon after, Chrys joined us in her hot purple jumpsuit with a cropped black jean jacket over it. Instead of boots, she opted for black platform suede four-inch pumps that enhanced every curve she worked. She knew she had it going on!

Uncle Bryan, Mom, and Dad walked us to the garage while giving us the "call if something happens" speech. Before we got in the car, Chrys asked my mom to take a few pictures. We did every silly pose cousins could do before we took our respective seats, mine in the back, and headed for the concert.

As we cruised along debating the merits of the Washington Wizards and deciding who was best in the Steelers-Ravens rivalry, I asked, "Why does the concert start so late?" Thinking about the commute back, I know we wouldn't return to Hagerstown until daylight tomorrow.

Dill replied in his true, southern-country-ghetto drawl, "This ain't no huge concert in an arena or anything like that. We're goin' to a hole-in-the-wall type of joint that happens to have a stage, tables, low lights, and the bombest chicken wings and jumbo fried shrimp you'll ever taste"

"Don't worry about it, lil' cuz," Chrys chimed in. "You're going to have a good time!" Then Dill and Chrys did that twin thing again that I grew tired of trying to decode.

I know that Anthony David and Kindred the Family Soul will be worth it, but if I see a roach crawling on the floor, I'm going back to the car.

⟨⁓⟩

*O*nce seated at the table very close to the stage, I actually was impressed with the intimate atmosphere of Candy's. Tucked away from the general population of the attendants, the smoking section had a hazy cloud over it, but the remainder of the environment was pleasant and clean. After ordering my standard Pepsi with a lemon twist and my cousins keeping it clean as well, I took a moment just to think about Grey and Frick.

I'm in their city, chilling with my cousins, but I can't even call them since the battery on my cell phone died and their numbers are in my phone. And that's a real shame, because it amazes me how cool I became with them over the fall semester.

My first impression of Frick was that he was a player, just someone who wanted to get with as many females as he possibly could. I don't think I was really wrong in that impression, but maybe Shea introduced him to love and made him want to drop out of the game. After getting to know Grey a little better, I became more impressed with his character than anything else about him. In my brief dating life, I'd discovered that most men approached me and didn't care whether I had a man in my life. Grey confessed to me during last semester's snowball fight that he had feelings for me.

I wonder how deep those feelings run and if they're still there.

Our comfortable conversation yesterday had put a grin on my face. He didn't hit on me, but he was so sweet.

I'm sure he'd make a great boyfriend, and that's what I don't understand about that Chelsea chick he used to date. Unless he is totally different now, I don't understand how any female could treat him the way she did. I have an idea of how I'd treat him.

Still lost in my thoughts, I took a sip of my Pepsi when Chrys practically yelled, "Avail, we want you to meet our friends!"

I blinked my eyes several times to bring myself back to reality just in time to hear Dill greeting the two people standing behind me who were joining us. Though the background music muffled what they said, I would recognize those voices anywhere. "Frick? Grey?" I whispered to myself.

Just as I turned around with a surprised smile, Chrys introduced, "Frick and Grey, this is our little cousin from Pennsylvania, Avail." I rose from my chair in almost total shock. I was a step away from having some very interesting thoughts about Grey...*and now he's standing in front of my face.*

Frick, still in the process of greeting Chrys, explained our coincidental meeting in amazement. "Man, I don't believe this! Avail is the lil' cuz you told us about on the phone?" Dill and Chrys verified it by nodding their heads, and Frick clarified, "Avail goes to Whitaker with us. We're already cool!"

I stood up and gave Frick a hug. "What's up?" I whispered in his ear.

"Nothin', but it's good to see you," he responded as he gave me his customary brotherly squeeze. "I have to tell you something, but I can't tell you right now," Frick added.

I pulled away to make eye contact with him when his facial expression told me that now was not the time to ask for further explanation. That prompted me to turn my attention to Grey. If physically possible, I could have busted with glee just from the chance of seeing him right now. I never would have thought in a million years that my cousins were talking about Frick and Grey when they told me that we'd meet up with some of their old friends from Baltimore. The city is so large, and I didn't want to chance looking goofy by asking them if they knew the two of them.

Eventually, I forced myself to make eye contact with Grey, who at this time, looked just as stunned as I felt. Snapping out of it, he smiled that pretty, white-teeth grin of his and gave me a hug. "Hey girl, what a surprise," he said near my ear.

"I hope a good one," I heard myself saying as we pulled away from the embrace. My last remark didn't come off as flirtatious, even though, I had to admit, I wouldn't mind a little something jumping off between Grey and me. Besides, in my last conversation with Kyle, he had acted strange like he was hiding something, and I had no idea where his head was. He had not been the same since we exchanged Christmas gifts.

I'm enjoying my vacation, and Grey is right here, right now. There's no harm in that!

Then, something did jump off between us. When he pulled away from me, Grey looked me over in a way I couldn't recall him doing at school, and he said, "Indeed," and left it at that.

He turned to greet my cousins and apparently, it had been awhile since they had seen each other because all four of them caught up on everything that happened after the death of Dill and Chrys's mother. I sat there as a spectator until Dill asked me, "So, you know these knuckleheads from school?"

I laughed as I answered, "Yeah, I met both of them pretty early in the semester. We've been cool since then."

"Well, that's great," Chrys chimed in, "because this is who Dill was talking about, Grey." My eyes instantly flew over to Grey to see what Chrys meant by *who* Dill was talking about, but Grey refused to make eye contact with me. I wanted to know what was going on, but just as I opened my mouth to ask, a waitress stopped by the table to get appetizer orders from all of us and drink orders from Frick and Grey.

I wanted to get back to my urgent question when Dill, Chrys, and Grey excused themselves from the table to greet some friends from across the room. When I looked up at Frick, he looked as if he was trying to suppress a boiling laugh, and I had to know why.

In my investigative tone, I demanded, "What's going on here, Frick? I get the impression that something's up that I didn't know anything about." I wanted answers!

Frick smiled and said, "Avail, it's not that serious, so calm down. Your cousins just think a lot of you, that's all. They're impressed."

"Stop trying to be overly complimentary and just tell me. What do you mean?" There was no telling how long the three of them would be away from the table, so this conversation called for quick, direct comments.

"Well," Frick slowly dragged, "since you just met your cousins and all, when they talked to Grey about coming to the concert tonight, first he said he wasn't coming because he couldn't find a date for his extra ticket. You know I didn't need one because I'm not trying to play your girl at all." I was glad to hear that because I couldn't tell if Frick wanted to get closer to Chrys or if they were just good friends.

Plus, this affirms the fact that he's all about Shea. That's a good thing.

He continued, "Chrys thought it would be a good idea if Grey met you because she described you as pretty, smart, and just what he needed to get over Chelsea."

"Oh," was all I could say.

"Apparently, the description that Dill also gave of you was enough to make Grey want to come, in addition to all of us getting a chance to get together."

I wanted details. "What did Dill say about me?"

"What most guys say about you," was all that Frick had a chance to say before the three of them rejoined us just as the waitress brought our chicken wings, loaded french fries, nachos, jumbo fried shrimp, baby back ribs, and cheese sticks—a complete anti-holiday menu.

Everyone began chomping down on the variety of snacks laid out before us as band members took their places on the stage and the host for the evening greeted the crowd. "Good evening, everyone, and Merry Christmas! Welcome to Candy's and to this special concert where we are fortunate enough to book both Anthony David and Kindred the Family Soul!" Applause, cheers, and whistles filled the air while the announcer proclaimed, "So without further ado, let's welcome Anthony David!"

An eruption of clapping began just when the drummer began the heavy drum line of the first song while Anthony David took the stage and commanded it from the first note. As the other instruments and background singers began, I scanned my memory to see if I recognized the song. I don't own any of his music, but I knew I'd heard this song before. Eventually, Anthony David began singing, "Now, how can it be, that a love carved out of caring…."

Grey, who took a seat between Frick and me, looked like he knew the song, so I leaned over and said to him in his ear, "I've heard this song before. Is this a remake?"

Grey put down the shrimp he planned to devour at that moment and replied, "Yes, it's an old song called "Something about You" from a group named Level 42." He then popped the shrimp in his mouth, took a quick sip of his water, and looked at me in a way that I knew that if I kept eye contact with him, I'd blush.

Grabbing my attention, I heard Anthony David croon, "…that there is something about you, baby, so right, I wouldn't be without you, baby, tonight…."

As I allowed myself to enjoy the song, I wondered about this setup that my cousins had created between Grey and me, and the possibilities within it.

Ten

His Way

My steps grew heavier as I walked the plank toward the unusually brightly lit house to meet with Celeste and her mother. I insisted that my parents stay home because I wanted them to stay saved—something about the way Celeste's mother "discussed" matters brought out the ugliness in them. Besides, I got myself into this mess; it was up to me to face this as one of the many consequences of my actions.

Before I even sat down on the sofa comfortably, Ms. Miller interrogated, "So what do you plan on doing about this baby?" Her audible tone was only missing the physical ghetto evidence of sponge rollers under a hair scarf and a cigarette in her hand while rolling her neck. Putting on a front as if she really cared, she emphasized, "There ain't no way she's going to have another abortion!" Celeste just sat there with her arms folded across her slightly noticeable baby bump and rolled her head as if she agreed with every word falling out of her mother's mouth.

I wasn't going to let them gang up on me, but at the same time, I had to stay focused while sharing my view. Directing my reply to Celeste's mother, I said, "Ms. Miller, I know I have a responsibility to my child, and I have begun to develop a plan to…."

"I hope that plan includes coming back home," Celeste blurted out.

My look could have cut her, but I said as calmly as I could, "I have thought about that, but right now, that's not for the best."

The argument I knew was coming began. Ms. Miller shouted, "What do you mean that's not for the best? The best for who?"

"The best for you?" Celeste exclaimed loudly, her voice rising to a new pitch. "You want to continue your precious private school education and still have your on-campus girlfriend while I stay home with a baby! I didn't make this baby by myself, and I'm darn sure not going to raise this child by myself!"

"No one said that you have to raise *our* baby by yourself." I tried not to yell. "But I'll be no good to my child if I stop going to Whitaker. I just found out about a great opportunity where I may be able to start my own business. That will help in this situation."

Ms. Miller's mouth tightened as Celeste walked over to the sofa, stood over me, and demanded, "So what am I supposed to do—give up my educational pursuits? Just throw my dream of becoming an attorney to the side now?" Celeste shook her head and turned away from me adding, "You can be so selfish."

"I don't know why you even bothered with him," Ms. Miller punctuated.

By this time, my defense mechanisms went into overdrive when I commented, "You know, Ms. Miller, I wonder that same thing myself. With all the guys in Celeste's life, I have to wonder…." I dropped the statement before I completed it because I didn't want to get into the fact that my parents wanted me to take a paternity test.

"What?" they shrieked in unison.

Celeste turned back toward me and said, "Are you wondering if this is your baby?" Her voice was oozing the false hurt that she always pulled out to shine the victim spotlight on herself.

"You are, aren't you?" Ms. Miller then stood with the immediate strength that I imagined any single mother had to exhibit and joined her daughter at her side, both standing over me now. She added, "If you are insinuating that my daughter may have slept with another guy, got pregnant by him, and tried to pin it on you, you can leave my house right now. I won't have anyone calling my daughter a slut and expect me to take it."

I cut my eyes over to Celeste, who apparently had never told her mother about Evan, and I stared at her with quiet intensity. Aware of the proximity between us, I rose from the couch and announced, "I think it's time for me to go," while staring into a pair of eyes that used to have a soul, or so I thought.

"Yeah, you better go. Get on out my house right now!" Ms. Miller yelled and continued her tirade to my back. My stroll out the door climaxed with me almost ripping the door off its hinges when I slammed it behind me. I pulled out my keys and began my descent down the steps.

As if following a movie script, Celeste came running out the door, pleading, "Kyle, wait!"

I stopped and spoke into the empty space in front of me. "You set me up to look like the bad guy. Your mom has no idea about Evan or anyone else, does she?" When the proper amount of silence had passed, I turned and demanded, "Does she?"

"Keep your voice down," she whispered. Celeste approached me carefully, and I could tell that she was thinking of what to say. Her defending statement would tell me tons about the relationship that I thought we'd had. "There was no one else—at least around the time the doctors say I got pregnant."

"So you did sleep with other guys!" I stage screamed. "I can't believe you!"

"Wait just a second, Mr. Self-Righteous Saint. You act like you didn't sleep with anyone else. I know for a fact that you did. You didn't have to tell me—I knew. So I just gave you a taste of your own medicine." She tilted her head to one side and inquired, "Now, how do you like that?" She punctuated the statement by folding her arms and putting all of her weight on one leg while stretching the other one out at a defiant angle.

"That's not the point," was all I could say. "Your mom thinks I'm the only one who slept with you, but

I know better." I paused to look directly into her eyes, and then I said, "I want a paternity test."

"No."

"What do you mean 'no'?"

"No, your PARENTS want the paternity test."

"So what if they do? They are just doing the same thing your mother is doing—looking out for their child."

After rolling her eyes, Celeste bounced back by saying, "No, your parents don't like me, and they're hoping this baby isn't genetically connected to you." She stopped for a minute, rubbed her belly, and continued. "But I don't need any test to verify what I already know. This is your baby," she confirmed softly.

Then she did something I wasn't completely prepared for: Stepping toward me, she took my ungloved right hand and placed it between her belly and both her hands. The conception of the baby had been real to her since day one, I'd imagine, but at that moment, my baby became real to me. I didn't feel a shift in the baby's movements or anything like that, but I did experience an incredible sense of connection to my child growing inside of Celeste. I stared at our point of contact, feeling a little lightheaded from the energy surging through my body.

Lifting up my chin with one of her hands to initiate eye contact, she changed her proclamation to, "This is *our* baby."

Our foreheads met before our lips did.

Ten

HER WAY

"Thank you," Anthony David offered as thunderous applause and whistles lifted from the crowd. I sat there totally thrilled with the performance when he announced, "I have one more song I want to do before I get out of here, and I want to dedicate this song to every brotha' out there trying to spit his best game." Before I knew it, guys were leading their girls out to the dance floor just as a guitar line reminiscent of Eric Clapton captivated my ears. With my total attention on the stage, I was almost aggravated when Grey tapped me on my arm.

"Avail, would you like to dance?" He extended his hand to my accommodating fingers that unconsciously indicated a definite yes. I floated to the dance floor after catching interesting looks from everyone at the table.

Just at the right time, I returned my focus to Grey and his capable dance skills. Since I had only slow danced with him once or twice at a party earlier in the semester, I had no idea if he could get his jam on to a mid-tempo joint like the one Anthony David belted out for our enjoyment. Anthony sang, "I can walk on air, I can walk on fire, I'd do anything to get you, baby…." Grey started a sweet, swayed dip that coerced my body to follow. I had both of my hands in the air, snapping my fingers while he rested both of his hands on my hips lightly, guiding them with every rock. "Give you what you need, and what you desire, I'll make your every waking thought about me, yeah…." When I got bored with that move, he instinctively took one of my hands and half-pirouetted me to where my back molded against his chest, and continued the rhythm. My thumbs found a resting place right at the pockets of his jeans and stayed there while my fingers patted the beat to the song. I dropped my head slightly when the bridge of his nose snuggled against the nape of my neck. If I didn't know better, I would have thought that Grey was trying to make a move on me. Instead of debating the issue, I decided to enjoy this moment for what it was: two friends dancing… *two friends who are attracted to each other dancing… two friends who are attracted to each other dancing rather suggestively.*

We returned to the table just as the host thanked Anthony David and introduced Kindred the Family Soul. I anticipated someone at the table saying something about the two of us dancing the way we did, and Chrys did not let me down. "Avail," she began, "it looks like you're enjoying yourself! Aren't you glad you came after all?" She gave me a smile that proved that her question had a hidden connotation.

Before I even opened my mouth, Grey said, "You weren't going to come?" His dark brown eyes almost looked concerned.

I was floored by his distress just over the thought of me not coming to the concert, especially since he hadn't known that I was the woman my cousins had told him about. "I just thought about staying back at the house. I didn't know if the concert would be worth the trip."

That was an honest answer and simple enough.

"Are you glad you came?" Grey asked, and then he added, "Because I am."

I felt the need to pick with him. Our table audience was burning holes in the side of my head, so I asked, "Glad that you came, glad that I came, or both?"

Goodness, sometimes I'm such a flirt. I need to get that under control!

"Both." I guess that was enough for Dill, Chrys, and Frick to leave with Chrys and Frick taking the dance floor and Dill going over to another table to chat with some friends. Grey laughed before replying, "You know what all three of them are trying to do, don't you?"

Really, yeah, I knew, but I wanted to see what was going on in his head, so, before taking a sip of my Pepsi, I said, "No. What are they up to?"

"Avail, it's rather obvious; your cousins and Frick are trying to hook us up." Maintaining eye contact, he asked, "Do your cousins know about Kyle?"

And there's the name I didn't want to hear right at this moment. Grey had no idea that Kyle and I really hadn't been in touch with each other in the past few days, a fact that bothered me to no end. At this moment, I really didn't feel like talking about him, so I said, "I haven't talked about him much, so Chrys and Dill don't really know." I didn't feel like going into detail because I could just imagine how convenient it would be for us to be feeling the way we were now with the lack of communication in my relationship at home. In an attempt to get Kyle out of the conversation, I asked, "Isn't it a trip that all three of them would think that we'd make a cute couple?"

Did I just say cute couple? Ugh, that's so high school!

In times past, Grey had never taken advantage of anything goofy I might have said around him, and his next reply maintained his stand. "Yeah, it is rather interesting."

That's it? He doesn't have anything else to say besides interesting?

I needed to settle down because the very thing I admired about him—his character and sense of being honorable—was working against me here.

I want him to flirt with me in a more obvious way so that I can be really sure that he likes me. But the only thing he says is that it's interesting that Dill, Chyrs, and Frick think we'd be good together. Wait—why do I want him to be more obvious?

$\mathcal{W}$e raced the sunrise returning to Uncle Bryan's house, barely making it to our respective bedrooms before dawn. With Chyrs in the driver's seat, I shifted to the front passenger's seat while Dill stretched out in the back. Waiting until we hit a stretch on I-70 outside of Baltimore, Chrys placed the car in cruise control and inquired, "So, what do you think of Grey?"

I immediately dropped my chin to my chest and grinned to myself. My cheeks warmed with a slight blush that I knew Chrys could not see in the dark, but I felt it, just like I felt Grey. I had developed some type of sentiment for him, and it hadn't just started this evening. It felt so foreign to me; it wasn't like what I felt for Kyle or Donovan. I couldn't put it into words, but it dug deeper than any other attraction I'd had for other guys. Answering Chrys, I grinned as I said, "I think he's a great guy."

"I do, too," she added. "I kept telling Dill that the two of you would be a good mix." So, that at least revealed a bit of that silent communication code they shared.

I felt compelled to ask, "Well, if you think so highly of him, why don't you go after him?"

I thought I'd shocked her until she came back with the reply, "That's the same tall, lanky boy I used to run around Baltimore with as a tomboy. I don't see him that way." Clearing her throat, she emphasized, "I acknowledge what he has become, but…."

"You mean the tall, dark, handsome young man with tons of potential and a great wealth of wisdom for someone his age?" I questioned, knowing she would second my motion.

"Yes, exactly, but his personality matches or even exceeds his outer handsomeness. He's just a great person to be around." I couldn't have agreed more. It was just a little despairing that I couldn't get to know him better in a more private way. Sure, we were close friends, but I could not fathom describing my sort-of feelings for him *to* him. I think that would be friendship suicide, and I wanted to keep him as a friend, even if that meant denying myself of a potential, long-lasting romance with him.

Knowing that I could get a different perspective on a mystery, I probed, "But that's why I don't really understand why Chelsea left him. I mean, Grey told me that other men played a role in their breakup, but if he's all that, then why did she leave him?" My comments sounded as if I was challenging Grey's reputation, but I wasn't. Chelsea just had to be crazy.

Chrys took a deep breath before she shared, "Grey is a thinker and a planner. When you combine those two attributes in a man, there are depths that the typical woman is not prepared to delve into."

And all this time, Shea, Raine, and I thought that Reese was the deep one.

"There were things he required of a relationship that Chelsea didn't…."

"Like what? Sex?" I blurted out before I could catch myself.

"No!" Chrys rebutted. "I'd never feed you off to someone like that." That clarity made me feel a little better. "It was quite the contrary. He insisted that they maintain a sex-free relationship until...."

Hanging on to her every word, I demanded, "Until when?"

"...Until they married. You see, in his mind, Chelsea was the one he was going to marry. In fact, he planned to marry her right after graduation a year and a half from now. But she couldn't handle waiting."

"Yeah, so that's how she was involved with other guys—sexually?"

"Yep, one of his teammates on the basketball team was just one of the many. He never saw Chelsea the same way, but he was having a hard time letting her go..." Chrys let the phrase hang in the air as she glanced over at me, and then she said, "...until you."

"Until me?" I asked in shock. "Until tonight, he had no idea that you were talking about me." The comment rippled within me, and I found it hard to imagine that I would be the one who could break him of this Chelsea stronghold.

"Well, now that I put two and two together...." Chrys drifted.

"Put what two and two together? What are you talking about?"

Even in the predawn dark, I saw a twinkle flutter across Chrys's eyes when she said, "You must be the one that Frick told us about, the one that Grey denied having feelings for...." She pondered then added, "Yeah, it all makes sense now with you going to Whitaker with them."

Her statement proved that there had been man talk about me last semester in Frick and Grey's confining dorm room. That wasn't necessarily a bad thing, especially since Raine, Shea, and I needed to catch up.

I have plenty of girl talk to share with them.

Eleven

HER WAY

As soon as I returned to campus in January, I called Raine and Shea to see if they had made it back safely. Before I knew it, they knocked on my door, greeting me with a bag of tortilla chips and a jar of Raine's homemade salsa. Since Shea and I had talked quite a bit over the break, I knew she had spoken with Frick about seeing me in Baltimore. Neither Shea nor I had much communication with Raine with the exception of an email here or there letting us know that she was okay and planned to return to Whitaker. I hugged my friends who had quickly developed into being the sisters I never had, and I invited them in.

Raine immediately inquired, "What grand event did Kyle do for you over Christmas break? I know he went above and beyond because now you two are a couple."

Though I was still in a fog as to why I hadn't heard from Kyle since the day my phone died, I couldn't do anything but smile as I reflected on our double date with his parents to see *The Nutcracker*, and the competition between his father and him. I would always have special memories of the tenderness with which he had placed an orchid in my hair, and the symbolism behind my gift to him. I gave Raine and Shea a rundown with all the bells and whistles, including the ugliness of my cell phone dying and Kyle's fading communication thereafter.

Raine said, "So Kyle hasn't called or attempted to be with you since before Christmas?"

"Nope, but I don't mind." I lied, and then I lied again in my next sentence. "We talked here and there, and every time we did, it was as if something came up. He's a busy guy, so I understand." I hoped I sounded convincing.

"Enough about that—girl, I can't believe you saw Frick and Grey over break in Baltimore!" Shea squealed. "I know that was a surprise!"

I smiled, but I was laughing inwardly when I said, "Yes, it was quite a shock that my cousins knew them."

Raine tore into the chips and salsa. "So you had no idea that your cousins were trying to set you up with Grey?" She added a smirk before saying, "Sounds like you didn't mind it! How does Kyle feel about all of this?"

I knew that my face revealed my true feelings behind my earlier statement, despite how casual I tried to sound. The truth was that I had begun to notice things, like Kyle dropping the "I" from his "I love you" declarations and seeming as if he was always distracted by something else. I couldn't explain it. He told me that he wasn't upset when I left my phone charger in Pittsburgh, but I could tell there was something bothering him, and he gave me no clue as to what it could be. It had to go beyond our restrictions, especially since he was the one who established them. I realized that I hadn't answered Raine's question when I covered by saying, "There is no 'this'. Grey and I are just friends."

"There is no way you guys are just friends," Raine insisted. "Avail, be real with us. We're your girls! Everything we talk about stays between us. What's up?" Shea adopted the same look of curiosity that Raine had, and even though they were my dearest friends, I felt a little cornered because I didn't know what to say.

So I diverted the conversation. "This is such a little thing to talk about, especially when Shea and I have a niece or nephew on the way."

Raine's playful banter did a reality check, and she placed the chips and salsa on my desk and lightly placed one of her hands on her abdomen. Shea stood up and placed her hands on Raine's shoulders, and I captured her other hand in both of mine. Immediately, I added, "Sweetheart, we are concerned about you. We didn't hear much from you over break, and we didn't know what we could do to help."

"We already told you that we have your back. It doesn't matter what you need. We're here for you and Reese, so let us know what we can do," Shea suggested tenderly.

Raine didn't move. Her eyes failed to blink while they stared straight through the wall, and her breath became shallow before she proclaimed, "I'm still shocked…" and then she snapped back into her normal conversational tone and added, "…not so much at the fact that we're having a child, but what I wanted to do about it."

Shea and I connected with our eyes but said nothing. We knew what Raine meant.

⟨⟩

*M*y knock on the door conveyed the authority of the campus law enforcement. I was beyond tired of this distance between Kyle and me. In their normal and loving way, Raine and Shea had managed to pump me up to confront Kyle face to face. I wanted answers about what was going on with him, and I wanted them immediately.

"Who is it?" the muffled husky voice asked.

"It's Avail."

As if the door understood my thoughts, it popped open with John, Kyle's roommate, greeting me. Any other day, John wouldn't be near the room, and I always wondered where he spent most of his time, but at that moment, he stood in front of me practically blocking me from coming into a room that I considered my second home on campus.

Trying to peer around his big frame, I said, "Hey John. Is Kyle in there?"

John closed the door behind him as he stepped into the hallway with me. Usually, John looked confident, as if nothing and no one bothered him. His behavior looked like I had busted up something he didn't want me to know about, as if my inquiry disturbed a flow he had going on before I banged on the door. I apologized for interrupting, but he cut me off with an audible sigh and said, "Avail, this isn't a good time right now. I'm sorta in the middle of something...." His voice trailed off while he dropped his head to the left, sending his eyes upward, looking like one of my brothers did when I walked in on his girlfriend and him.

John's mystery girlfriend must be in there.

Completely embarrassed, I stammered, "Oh...oh, I'm sorry!" I blushed before asking, "Can you let Kyle know that I stopped by? I haven't seen him since a few days before Christmas, and I just wanted to check on him. Tell him to hit me up on my cell."

Only glancing at me for a moment, John said, "Okay," as he backed into the room and quickly shut the door, locking it with authority. Maybe I had embarrassed him because he knew that I had caught on to what he might have been doing. A slick smile appeared on my face as I headed for the stairwell and the back door that was closest to their room.

Once I descended the steps and began walking across the courtyard, the sounds coming from the men's dormitory were the usual background noise with the exception of a someone saying, "Man, you can't ask me to do that again. You need to keep me out of this and handle your business with Avail." I turned sharply and found John correcting Kyle in front of their open window.

So Kyle was there and avoiding me.

I witnessed with my own eyes Kyle explaining to John, "I know, man, but I'm not ready to see her. I just can't—not yet." What in the world had happened that would make Kyle have John cover for him and keep this distance between us? I was totally puzzled, and I couldn't wait to hear John's comeback.

Unfortunately, his statement became inaudible when Kyle closed the window, most likely to keep the cold air from coming in. I stood there for a moment totally confused and a bit hurt. Why didn't Kyle want to see me? Last semester, we were inseparable. Before I left for Hagerstown, he spent time with me and gave me a cell phone for Christmas in order for us to keep in touch. Then, all of a sudden, there was nothing: no phone calls, no dates, and no visit to my room once we returned to campus.

This is completely unlike Kyle. Whatever is going on, it must be huge.

No matter how much I tried to understand, I couldn't help but feel hurt and a little mad. I was not accustomed to being shut out of the life of a person who claimed to love me. Puzzling as it seemed, I would do my best to remain calm, rational, and reasonable until I heard from Kyle. I was sure he had a good explanation for all of this.

Eleven

HIS WAY

"You have got to be kidding me." John flopped down in his rarely used study chair with a look of shock on his face. "Celeste is pregnant?"

"Yeah," was all I could manage to say after recounting the events of my Christmas break. "When I realized that I was going to be a father, everything else about life really didn't matter. I almost didn't come back to Whitaker."

"Really?

After placing my last piece of luggage at the bottom of my closet, I took a seat in my study chair, placed my elbows on my thighs, and leaned forward to look directly at John. "Yeah. My very first thought was to quit school and find a job to start saving for the baby's arrival. I didn't think I had another choice but to do...."

Cutting me off, John insisted, "Man that would have been the wrong choice. It'll be hard in the beginning, but you'll do better for your child if you have a college degree."

"My thoughts exactly, especially after I received word that I've been accepted into an entrepreneurial program where if my proposal ends up number one, I can win the financial backing from an alumni to start my own business."

"Now that's what I'm talking about! That isn't the type of opportunity you'll have if you drop out of Whitaker! And you'll be able to start something stable for you and the little man...."

"Or little woman! I don't know what Celeste is having yet." After a pause, I added, "I just pray the baby is healthy. I don't care if it's a boy or a girl—just healthy and happy."

After taking a moment to ponder his comeback, John asked, "Well, how did Avail handle the news?"

I dropped my head in shame. I hadn't said a decent word to Avail since she returned from her family trip, and I definitely had not told her a thing about Celeste being pregnant with my child. I was too afraid that one of the many things that Celeste and I had discussed about the preparation would fall out of my mouth in casual conversation, so I didn't trust myself to call Avail or even accept her calls. I wanted to tell her everything, but being that we had just started officially dating at the end of last semester, I just couldn't deal with the strong possibility that Avail would want to break up with me. *And let me not forget the kiss.*

"I haven't told her yet," I pushed out.

Just as I lifted my head to make eye contact, John threw both his arms in the air in frustration. "What in the world are you attempting to do—ruin the best thing that has happened to you?" He dropped is arms before continuing. "You wanted her, plotted to get her, now you got her, and now you're setting it up to lose her. You're crazy!"

"Yes, crazy to think that she's going to stay with me after I tell her that my ex-girl is pregnant with my child!"

"Are you sure it's yours?" John confronted.

"You and my parents, I tell ya…."

"Me and your parents what? It's a legit question. Have you so quickly forgotten that this is the same woman who had a man on the side who called her while she was here with you during homecoming? The same man that you contacted to make sure he would keep Celeste occupied after your breakup? You don't think he was hittin' that all this time? He could be the father!" John practically shouted.

"According to Celeste, the dates don't add up."

"And now you think she's capable of telling the complete and utter truth? Did you fall down and hit your head over the break? Celeste WANTS you to be the father so she can keep you, but you need DNA proof!"

"There you go again sounding like my parents."

"They have sense—perhaps the sense you used to have. You need to get a paternity test."

I shouted, "I don't need a test! It's my baby!"

Out of nowhere, there was an authoritative knock on the door. I figured it was one of our neighbors complaining about our argument so I blared out, "Who is it?"

"It's Avail."

I stood up and paced the floor in a panic because I had nowhere to hide from her, and I still no good excuse for the distance I'd created between us. I shifted my eyes over to John when he asked, "So what are you going to do now?"

I desperately looked at him and proclaimed, "I need your help...."

"No, no, NO, I am not getting in the middle of this," John said as he slung his backpack over one shoulder and headed for the door.

I jumped in front of him, blocking his pursuit and practically begged in a loud whisper, "Please, really, I just need you to answer the door, tell her anything, but don't tell her I'm here!" John looked as if he was going to say no, so I added, "C'mon, man. I'll owe you big!"

John stared at me eyeball to eyeball and said, "I don't like this, but since we boys, I'll do it—just this once. After this, you're on your own." John threw his backpack down by his desk and directed me to go around the corner and stand by the closet.

"Hey, John. Is Kyle in there?" She had the most beautiful voice, and I longed to see her, but I couldn't face her yet. How could I...?

The door closing behind John ripped me out of my personal thoughts and made me consider another possibility.

Sure, Avail will be upset, but what if she is up for the challenge of dating me despite the fact that Celeste is pregnant? She could rise to the occasion. After all, she loves me. Surely, she could love my child. It's not like it's impossible for a man to date someone other than the mother of his child. Even within this surge of new possibility, I knew my chances of staying with Avail during this time were slim to none.

I heard John quietly come back into the room and lock the door behind him. He looked straight at me and said, "I didn't lie. I wasn't going to lie because I think Avail deserves the truth, but that truth should come from you and only you. You need to tell her."

"What did you tell her?"

"I told her that I was in the middle of something, and that something is trying to convince you to do the right thing by her. It's not right that other people know about your situation, but she doesn't. She wanted me to let you know that she stopped by, and to tell you to call her on her cell."

"Okay," was all I managed to say.

"Man, you can't ask me to do that again. You need to keep me out of this and handle your business with Avail." I knew he was right, but I just didn't know how I was going to do it. I needed a plan that would work to my advantage, where I could raise my child and still have Avail in my life.

"I know, man, but I'm not ready to see her. I just can't—not yet." The information I had to share with her was too time sensitive because she could very well run into Celeste anywhere in Pittsburgh.

John continued protesting my actions as he shut the window, but I didn't hear a word he said. My mind was racing with the requirements of my class, doing my best to win the Young Entrepreneur Award, and maintaining my relationships with Avail and Celeste.

There will be doctor's appointments that Celeste will not want me to miss, and I'll have to explain to Avail why I'm going home so much. I don't know if this can work, but if I can just hold off from telling her until the end of intercession, maybe I can develop a good way of breaking this news to her in a way that she can accept it and possibly still want me in her life.

Twelve

Her Way

The trek to the performing fine arts building was quiet and calm the first day of class. Being that it was still my first year in college, I had not really learned the concept of picking late classes in order to sleep in. First Time Orchestra, a class designed for students who had never played a brass or woodwind instrument, fulfilled a fine arts requirement in my schedule and provided a fun time for my intercession class. I figured that learning how to play an instrument as a neophyte should be a great experience and a nice way to connect with people who normally didn't travel in my present circle of classmates.

When I received my email notification that my registration for the class was approved, it suggested that I contact the recommended music store to rent my instrument of choice, the flute, to avoid any lapses in learning how to play. We would meet as a complete orchestra every day, Monday through Friday, from 8:00 a.m. to 11:30 a.m. Our sections would meet for ninety-minute sessions after lunch at our leisure. In the electronic copy of our syllabus, Dr. Taylor made it clear that we needed more practice time outside of class than what was outlined for class meetings. Since I had no other activities going on in the month of January, practice time should not be a problem.

As I walked into the assigned room for our class, I wondered if I had the wrong starting time, because people were already in seats and experimenting with their instruments. I shook my head and reminded myself that being on time was not good enough at Whitaker; ten minutes early was on time. On time was considered late.

"And your name is?" a young lady who was a grad student assistant, I imagined, asked me from the registration table.

"I'm Avail Andrews. I signed up to play the flute."

The class roster was in alphabetical order, so it wasn't hard for her to find my name at all. She highlighted it immediately and handed me a small rectangular case that contained my rented flute from the local music store and copies of the music we would learn. "If you look at the seating arrangement," the grad student added, "you'll see that we're divided into sections based on our instruments. Find the flutes and you'll find where you are supposed to be."

I looked around and saw one young lady attempting to put her flute together by following the directions she'd found inside the case, and I headed to that section. Immediately, I noticed that there were only three seats, but someone had his or her materials in one seat. Attempting to overcome my jitters that had developed after feeling like I was late, I said, "Hi, I'm Avail. Is this seat taken?"

Her green eyes and strawberry blond hair met my gaze, breaking her solid concentration on the assembly of her flute, and she greeted, "Well, I guess you complete our section! I asked and they told me there are only three people attempting to play the flute. The other student went to the restroom or something." She paused as if she forgot something then added, "By the way, my name is Stephanie. It's good to meet you, Avail."

"I see you're putting together your flute."

"Yeah, I figured it would be a good idea if I had it in one piece before class started. Do you need help putting yours together?"

Being that I was industrious enough to fix small jobs around the house, I doubted that I needed Stephanie's help. However, since she offered and appeared to be further ahead than I would be within the five minutes we had left before our professor was expected to appear, I took her up on her offer. Connecting the crown piece to the barrel and foot joint required little skill, so we decided to jump into our instructional book in order to look at all the parts and finger combinations to create the notes we would form. I attempted to blow a note and produced a funny-sounding squawk. Stephanie and I shared a comfortable laugh.

We traded small talk in an attempt to get to know one another, and she seemed to have a great personality. She was a senior and just noticed that she had this one last core requirement to take before she completed an internship within her major second semester. Stephanie quickly assured me that she was willing to do whatever was necessary to keep our section strong, but because of her commitment to keeping statistics for the women's basketball team, she would most likely not meet with me and the other student in our section.

"Hey, now that I think about it," Stephanie said, "you may know the other student in our section."

"Who is she?

"It's a he—and a fine-looking one at that."

A familiar voice behind me said, "Yeah, I'm most definitely a 'he', Avail!"

I turned around with a grin and sighed. "Grey. Now this is a surprise!"

***

"*I* could have sworn you told me that you were taking an English course during intercession," I fussed over lunch. "Why didn't you tell me that you switched your class?" I did my best not to beam my inner excitement over being in the same class with Grey for a whole month, but I was sure he felt my joy. Matter of fact, I knew that he did as evidenced by his trademark grin. "And you chose to play the flute. This is almost too much of a coincidence."

A sparkle flickered across his eyes as he explained, "By the time I registered, my first choice was filled up.

I already have my fine arts requirement completed, and nothing else piqued my interest. As for my choice of instrument, a few people who have played instruments told me that the flute would be a good instrument to learn, so I went with their recommendation." He took a few bites of food, washed them down with a small glass of water, and added, "Besides, it fits with my basketball schedule."

"Oh, goodness, the Waynesburg game is Wednesday, right?"

"It is," he stated in an approving way, as if he was happy that I remembered.

"In case you don't recall, I'm expecting you to get a triple-double this game. You've been keeping your complete game in shape, but if you want to be strong on paper, you need to boost all of your stat averages into the double digits. Your points are no problem with you being a low-post player, but when it comes to your defense, I think you might want to up your blocked shots. Your arms are long enough to prevent a shot before being called for goal tending, so there's no need for you to avoid blocking shots. Your assists, rebounds, and steals need a little attention too. Any combination of those will help your triple-double factor." For a moment, I felt like I was babbling, but I think I impressed him with my knowledge about basketball.

"Avail, trust me; I haven't forgotten. After we talked, I seriously evaluated my game and mentally noted some things I can do to improve."

As he returned to his lunch, I shared, "Well, just so you know, I'll be in the stands making my own notes.

I'll give you a full report after the game." I couldn't be-lieve that I was that wide open with Grey, but I didn't have anything to hide. He was a good friend, extreme-ly respectful, and just an all-around great guy. *I know that my Freudian Slips regarding my feelings toward him can skid out any moment, but he never acknowledges them, which reveals to me that he's handling them just as they are: light admiration for his great attributes.*

"I look forward to it," Grey accepted.

I don't want to think this, but maybe that was a little ap-preciation toward me.

I must have drifted in my own personal thoughts when Grey reminded me, "Avail, Stephanie said that we'll meet in classroom two of the fine arts building around two. Will I see you there?"

Flirting just a little, I echoed his words with a smile. "I look forward to it."

Twelve

His Way

"Welcome to Introduction to Entrepreneurship. My name is Dr. John Delta, and I will be your point of contact for the next four weeks. You will think of me, dream about me, and have nightmares about me because you had the audacity to be in my class. All of you must be out of your God-given minds being that this intercession course combines the following semester-long courses: The Principles of Business, Marketing 101, and Business Ethics. If you pass this class with a B or higher, not only will you get credit for this course, but you'll be exempt from the other three." He paused before he added, "But only *if* you pass."

After hearing an introduction like that, I wasn't totally sure that I wanted to stay in the class, but I decided to absorb everything Dr. Delta had to say. "Some of you crazy people signed up for the challenge." With a lift of an eyebrow while he scanned the entire class population, Dr. Delta proclaimed, "The remainder of you received nominations from your previous professors based on who knows what." For dramatic effect, Dr. Delta stopped pacing, slammed down his Hugo Boss-clad foot, and stated, "I really could not care less which way you got into this class, but I will say this: All of you have the opportunity to compete for the prestigious Young Entrepreneurs Award, which will provide you with grassroots funding to start your own business."

It seemed that every student in the class sat erect in his or her seat at the mention of the award, proving everyone's true motivation for being there. The possibility of having the capital to start one's own business as an undergraduate had attracted everyone here. What student wouldn't want to put theory into practice and prove that his or her idea was worthy of unlimited resources? The award really appealed to me, especially with my child coming into the world within the next five months. Dr. Delta cut into my personal thoughts as he explained, "If your project requires relocation or cannot be established in Whitaker County, relocation costs might be paid as well, depending on what the business school alumni decide."

An overly eager student raised his hand, and after Dr. Delta acknowledged him, the student asked, "What happens to our status as Whitaker students if we set up our business elsewhere?'"

Trying to exercise first-day patience with my fellow freshman classmate, Dr. Delta inhaled deeply and removed the irritation from his voice that now showed on his face as he answered, "The winner or winners will become full-time online students, maintaining no less than a 3.5 grade point average in business classes and any core electives required for the program." I could understand why Dr. Delta appeared frustrated. If my classmate had read the packet that we had all received in the mail, he would have seen that printed in the terms and conditions for entering the class.

Once again, the same classmate raised his hand, and without waiting for Dr. Delta to acknowledge him, he immediately remarked, "You just said winner or winners. Does that mean that there will be more than one winner?"

This time, Dr. Delta snapped at him in a reasonably professional tone and said, "There is only one award. There can be winners if you decide to team up with another classmate or classmates." He emphasized the words winners and classmates. He stopped and surveyed the room again before saying with a touch of sarcasm, "Now, if no one else has any questions, I can get back to my traditional monologue before we delve into work." I looked around the room for a possible partner, someone who could share the load in creating this dream of building a radio station from the ground up. A few of my teammates caught my attention, but there was no telling what they had in mind. Though the zealous question asker appeared to be a little annoying, I imagined that he would be a hard worker and willing to research any background information we needed to know.

Too bad Mike, my cohost for our Friday night R&B show on the campus radio station, didn't enroll in this course. He would be the perfect partner.

A few rows behind me over my left shoulder, I saw Camden and knew that she had the work ethic and the wherewithal, but our history together outside the academic realm was the exact opposite. Just her presence bothered Avail to no end, and I knew that if I chose Camden to be my partner, that would only add more strain to our relationship.

Strain that Avail isn't totally aware of just yet, because at this point, I'm not even sure we have a relationship. I've avoided every single call she's made because I'm just not ready to face her about the pregnancy. We arrived on campus yesterday, I didn't visit with her when she came back from her trip, and I barely said a decent word to her when I saw her last night. Even if she could tolerate the news, intentionally partnering with Camden for another class project would bother her to no end. There's no way I could do that to her again.

⟨⁓⟩

Dr. Delta gave us the charge of developing our first business and marketing plan for our projects, and immediately, I began brainstorming ideas. The more I thought about it, the more I realized that I didn't need to look at this as an assignment. I needed to look at this as the first step toward owning a radio station that I built from the ground up. I decided to go solo and do this on my own so there would be no legal snags when it came to running and operating the station.

Dr. Delta said that after completing the template on which we were to list various aspects of our business plan, we were free to go since this first class was primarily an informational session. As a few of us walked out of the classroom, the questioner from class got my attention by asking, "Hey, you're Kyle Thompson, right?"

I looked at him and simply replied, "Yes, I am. And you are…?" I wasn't trying to blow him off; I was just deep in thought.

"Oh, I'm sorry," he apologized while sticking out his hand. "My name is Devin. I was in the same English class with you and Avail last semester."

I shook his hand and said, "Good to meet you, man. How can I help you?"

It couldn't hurt to take a moment to feel him out and check out the competition.

Getting straight to the point, he said, "I remember you being a pretty good student in Dr. Brown's class. I was just wondering what your idea was for the competition and if you already have a partner." He was doing the same thing—checking out the competition—but he was a little more forthcoming than I was.

"I don't have a partner just yet, and that would be the only person in class I'd tell my idea to," I disclosed honestly. "What did you have in mind?" I really didn't expect him to share too much because, if he were strategizing like me, it would be smart of him to keep his ideas under wraps as well.

"To be honest, I don't have an idea. My father is a trustee here at the school and alumnus of the school of business. I imagine that he had something to do with me getting in the class. I'm a premed concentration, and he feels like I'll need some business background to open some grand clinic when all I want to do is work with the Red Cross or some organization like that."

That's admirable enough, and he's a legacy student with connections. Maybe I should consider partnering with him.

As we headed for a late lunch in the Commons, he shared more about his desire to help underserved communities. In an attempt to get him to develop his own idea, I asked, "Why don't you complete a business plan for a clinic? That could offer tons of help to people who can't afford decent health care."

Chewing obnoxiously on some random tasteless food he'd thrown on his tray, he said, "What's so entrepreneurial about that? There are plenty of clinics all over the country. What would set mine apart from all the others? What would make mine so good that the benefactors would want to fund my project totally and completely?"

Whether he knew it or not, Devin had revamped my thinking. Sure, I wanted to start a radio station, but what would make my station stand out from the crowd? How was I going to prove that my idea was the best? I meditated on that while I took a few bites, and then had an unexpected interruption.

"Kyle!" Camden practically sang while she placed her hands on my shoulders. "What time do you want to get together to work on our business plan?"

Looking a little hurt, Devin said pointedly, "I thought you didn't have a partner."

I turned my torso and burned a look right into Camden's eyes while replying to Devin, "I don't. Camden seems to be mistaken."

"Oh, come on!" Camden wheedled in an overly dramatic fashion. "We worked so well together in baby bio. I just figured that we'd team together again." And with a not-so-hidden message in her words, she added seductively, "You know we make a good pair."

I looked at Devin and said, "See, I told you that I don't have a partner."

He laughed and glanced between Camden and me. "Well, I see the two of you have some things you need to straighten out. Kyle, I'll check you later." He did his best to give me a cool handshake before he departed.

I turned my attention back to my food while Camden took unrequested liberties by sitting in the chair across from me. Before she could open her mouth, I immediately asked, "So, what do you know about starting a radio station?"

She grinned with anticipation.

I guess I've done it now.

Thirteen

Her Way

"Okay," Stephanie began, "the first page of our book states that we need to establish our embouchure...."

"And what in God's name is an embouchure?" Grey questioned as if Stephanie didn't know what she walking about.

I giggled before reading verbatim, "According to our text, the embouchure is the use of facial muscles and the shaping of the lips to the mouthpiece of woodwind instruments or the mouthpiece of the brass instruments." I stopped to comprehend the definition before adding, "So, I guess it's how we shape our mouth in order to blow air through the instrument to produce sound."

"Thank you for clarifying that for me," Grey said. "Let me try it." What followed would only get him an A for effort. Stephanie and I plugged our ears in agony and begged Grey to stop. Eventually, he did and asked, "What was wrong with that?"

"There are too many things to list, so let's get back to the point," Stephanie barely got out between chuckles.

After I stopped laughing, I said, "Okay, Grey, the book says that the best way to establish our embouchure is to remove the crown piece, place it between our palms with the mouthpiece facing us, plugging the opening of the crown piece, and then to experiment with sound by blowing into the mouthpiece, adjusting our mouth muscles and wind direction as needed." We attempted the exercise repeatedly, making minor adjustments, and eventually, Stephanie and I managed to produce a decent sound. Grey, however, approached the whole exercise as if he was trying to blow up a balloon.

After glancing at the clock, Stephanie said, "I had no idea it was this late!" An hour had passed, and none of us thought that it would take us this long to get our mouths prepared to play. "I'm late for practice. Coach likes for me to keep stats at practices before the game so the players will know what they need to work on."

"Okay," Grey managed to say, looking totally defeated.

"Don't forget that by tomorrow, we need to know our notes and scales. I'll be ready," Stephanie assured us. With that, she packed her flute, tucked her music and book under her arm, and dashed to the practice gym.

I looked at Grey who, at the time, looked like he wanted to throw the crown piece of his flute against the wall. "Are you okay?"

"I'm starting to think that I picked the wrong instrument."

"Grey, it's only the first day...."

"So if it's *only* the first day, why did you and Stephanie make a sound so quickly and I didn't?" The overachiever in him took a blow and needed some help.

"I don't know why, but I did notice something in your attempts."

Grey leaned in and inquired, "What's that?"

A little intimidated by his physical proximity, I shifted my eye contact to his lips and told him, "You're blowing into the mouthpiece like it's a bowl of hot soup!" He looked a little confused when I asked, "May I?" He nodded his head indicating his approval as I lifted my fingertips to the muscles around his mouth before I instructed him. "Put your mouthpiece down and blow like you did when you were trying to make a sound." He did, and I immediately noticed the lack of tension in the right areas of his mouth. I suggested, "If you pull your top lip over your bottom lip and blow down softly instead of projecting both lips forward like you're about to kiss someone and blow out, you should be able to produce a decent sound. Just relax."

Heeding my guidance, he closed his eyes and allowed my fingers to mold his mouth into its proper position. I joined his deep breathing as I studied his features, admiring them a little more than usual because my fingers enjoyed how they felt. My thumbs caught the breeze coming through the small opening of his adjusted lips and warmth shot through my body. "Just like that," I whispered as if we were in a more intimate situation.

When Grey's eyelids fluttered open, I pulled back my fingers in an attempt to diffuse any miscommunication. Grey asked, "Do you think I should try it in your mouthpiece?" Correcting himself, he then said, "I meant in the flute's mouthpiece…."

I had to look away from him because after touching him and shaping his lips, I wanted to kiss those lips. He felt something too, but I couldn't encourage it because of the limbo I was in with Kyle. Knowing what Chrys had shared with me, Grey wouldn't place himself in another situation where his heart could possibly get hurt. *I couldn't blame him for that.*

Putting an end to any romantic energy brewing between us, I picked up the crown piece to his flute and gave it to him.

And he created a sweet sound.

⌣

*G*rey left for basketball practice shortly after we mastered all the notes and scales that we needed to know for the next day's class, and bypassing an early dinner, I headed straight for my dorm room. I needed the quiet time to think some things through.

What in the world was I doing playing with Grey's lips? Wait, that doesn't sound right. It was perfectly innocent. All

I was doing was helping a fellow classmate with his embou-
chure. Did it require me touching him? Probably not, but I
couldn't help myself, and that alone is a problem.

Yes, I felt a trace of curious affection for the statu-
esque Grevarian last semester, but recently, our paths
continued to cross, first at the concert in Baltimore,
and now taking the same intersession course. All this
contact only kindled my curiosity, which was not a
good thing because of everything my cousin told me
and because of my dysfunctional relationship with my
boyfriend.

I saw Kyle more when he was pursuing me than I do
as his girlfriend. I understood the whole idea that we
needed to maintain restrictions in order for the two of
us to keep our vow of abstinence, but I didn't understand why he had stopped calling or texting me. If I
thought he'd return my emails, I'd try that route, but
that was unnecessary. Whitaker wasn't that big, and he
knew that he could get in touch with me at any time.
Last night when he had no idea I was listening, John
alluded to the fact that Kyle was keeping something
from me, and after a whole day's worth of activity, Kyle
still hadn't shared whatever it was. How was I supposed
to take this?

With this small campus, someone is bound to know some-
thing, and I'm going to find out what it is.

After reaching for my keys and coming out of
my thoughts, my gaze landed on two figures that resembled Kyle and Camden. Knowing how I feel about
Camden, I didn't understand why he would even be
around her, but I tried not to be the jealous, insecure

type. Camden knew what was up; she knew we were a couple. I could only hope that there was a shred of decency in her and she would keep in mind that Kyle was off limits.

Wait a minute; did she just place her hand on his chest? Friends of the opposite sex don't just place their hands in the middle of someone's chest! What kind of mess is this?

Instead of walking up on them, I wanted to try something just to see where Kyle's head might be. I ducked out of sight behind a tree and called Kyle on his cell phone. As I kept my eyes on them, it seemed like it took forever for his phone to ring. Eventually, I heard his phone ringing on my end and watched Kyle pull out his phone to acknowledge the call. The next thing he did blew me away. Instead of ending his conversation with Camden immediately, he must have pushed the ignore button to send my call to voicemail. I disconnected the call in a completely confused state of mind. I didn't get it. If he didn't want to be bothered with me or if he felt like what I was asking of him was too much, that's all he needed to say.

Unaware that I was technically spying on Kyle—something I normally would not do—I headed for the seclusion of my room.

Thirteen

His Way

"Hey, I'm glad you called me. I think we can do some big things together!" Devin said with excitement. "And what exactly do you bring to the table, Miss...."

"Camden is my name, and I bring plenty to the table; don't worry about that. I plan not only to do my fair share..." she paused while she directed her comment to me, "...but I'll go above and beyond the call of duty." Looking back at Devin, she asked, "Does that answer your question?"

The meeting room in the back corner of the library seemed the perfect place to begin drawing out the diagram for our business plan, but this project was so much more to me than just a requirement for a class. It embodied my dream. It provided a possible way for me to take care of my unborn child. It became a way out of all my issues.

"Okay, you two, settle down," I said, taking a leadership role. "If we're going to be a team, we must be united. Unity requires a specific vision that we all feel passionate about." I took a presidential pause before continuing. "Both of you already know that I want to start a radio station, but that in and of itself is nothing inventive. What in your backgrounds can contribute to the establishment of this radio station? Let's brainstorm." I pushed the button on a digital recorder that would document all of our discussions.

Devin offered, "First and foremost, where are you talking about having this radio station? That's a big factor."

"I haven't looked into a specific place, but since all three of us are from the Pittsburgh area, Pittsburgh is a natural choice. We know its basic demographics and needs."

"Excellent choice," Camden chimed in just to make sure she was an active part of the discussion.

"That puts a whole new spin on it. That works, but let me ask," Devin probed. "What is the purpose of this radio station? Will it just play music? What type of music? How will it serve the community? What kind of people will we recruit to work there? Are we looking for experience or passion for music, or both?"

"Wow, Devin, you're giving us a lot to think about," Camden said. "Regarding the purpose of the radio station, that will be something that we wrap into the mission for our company. What do you think, Kyle?"

Camden was more pleasant to be around when she stayed focused on the task at hand instead of trying to flirt with me. "I couldn't agree more," I confirmed. "The format of the radio station can be a mixture of any and everything we want. For example, Devin, you're in the premed program, so we need to make sure we incorporate that somehow, maybe through a talk show."

"The same can be done with my education background. If they listen to the shows, they can get tons of information in a parent-friendly format." Camden smiled at the thought and added, "Then both Devin and I will stay sharp on the specifics within our major while working at the station."

"Wow, Camden, you sound as if we have already won." Her enthusiasm got me pumped, and the sparkle in her eyes ignited my passion for the project.

"Oh, I thought you knew: I play to win."

⌒

*D*evin, Camden, and I stayed in that study room until we finished the business plan due the next day. It was a good session, and in our opinion, we had a winning proposal.

Our radio station would be an outreach to inner city boys at risk of dropping out of school in that we would expose them to a possible career field that would entice them to stay in school. The workforce would be future graduates of Whitaker and hopefully students who would enroll in the mass communications program, which we planned to propose to the president as a possible career curriculum at Whitaker. As for our format, it would include a little of everything from talk radio to music, but being that Pittsburgh no longer had a prominent radio station that served the African-American community, it was an easy choice to focus on that neglected demographic. With our joint excitement, the excellent notes we took, and our discussion thoroughly documented on my digital recorder, I didn't see how we could lose.

Our marathon session drained Devin of all his energy, but he insisted on going to dinner straight from the library in order to get a good night's rest on a full stomach. Camden and I walked toward her dorm reviewing everything we'd discussed.

"I love the fact that we'll use the inner city boys as interns to our employees. You know, if I write the curriculum the right way, we might be able to get Pittsburgh Public Schools to give them some type of academic credit beyond what they earn in school."

"Camden, that's a wonderful idea, and as soon as you get to your room, you need to write that down. That will add strength to our proposal. Think about the possibilities of the boys performing research for the talk shows so that they learn the importance of research. There's so much they could do with this!" The more we talked about it, the more I became motivated.

When we reached the outside door of her dorm, Camden changed her tone, and I wasn't sure that I wanted to hear what she had to say. "Kyle, if I may ask, what's going on with you and Avail?"

Her questioning was a little different this time; instead of being flirtatious, it revealed her concern. I still found it hard to admit the whole truth, however. "Nothing is wrong with us," I said, striking an overly casual tone. "We're still together. I just have some issues I have to deal with." I didn't want to go too far because the last person I needed to confide in was Camden. As John had said, it was bad enough that other people, including him, knew about the baby, but Avail didn't.

"I can tell something's not right. You're not your usual self—I mean, your drive for schoolwork has tripled. What's that all about?"

"That's because we're working on starting a radio station from the ground up in the first years of our college careers. Who wouldn't be motivated?"

Camden quieted me by putting her gloved hand against my chest inside my unzipped jacket where my heart was beating at a fast pace, giving away my true feelings. "It's more than that, and I know it. I hope you know that you can talk to me about anything, and I do mean anything. We're friends, and when we win, we'll be business partners."

I gently removed her hand and shared, "Thank you, but it's nothing I can't handle. I appreciate your concern though."

I had planned on walking away immediately, but my cell phone vibrated in my pocket, catching my attention. I looked at the screen and saw *The Love of My Life* blinking urgently. I must have shown some type of reaction, because Camden immediately asked, "Is it Avail?"

I just shook my head and hit the ignore button. "I can talk to her later. I want to review our notes before

I get on the phone." I gave her a brave smile and ended with, "I'll see you in class tomorrow."

"Okay, good night."

My steps grew heavier and heavier during my trek toward my dorm room. There was no way of avoiding the inevitable anymore. The secret was eating at me from the inside out, and I might lose Avail if I didn't connect with her soon. I needed to tell her about the baby tonight.

Fourteen

HER WAY

"Lord," I began, "I thank You for this day and all that You placed in it, its ups and downs. Thank you for guiding me to this school, for all the friends I have met here, and for opening doors that only You could." I paused a moment because I felt like my routine evening prayer was becoming a little stale, like I wasn't sharing my true concerns with God. I approached the remainder of my prayer carefully.

"God, I'm really worried about Raine. She's pregnant during her freshman year in college, and essentially has the rest of her life in front of her, and somewhere deep within me, I think she might try to terminate the pregnancy. I know that the baby has purpose, and though You aren't pleased with the premarital act that created the baby, all things work together for good for those who love You. I know she loves You, so I have to believe this is working for her good, no matter how unexpected or unplanned this pregnancy is. I believe that with all my heart. Show me how to encourage her throughout this."

Feeling as if I was on a roll, I added, "So that brings me to my relationship with Kyle." I sighed hard enough for my shoulders to rise and fall, shaking my head while my prayer-clasped hands barricaded my mouth for a moment. "I know You have forgiven me for almost giving in to my personal desires after the wreck, and I'm not tied up in guilt about that, but I thought my relationship with Kyle would get better and stronger when he insisted on these stipulations he put in place. Kyle and I are so far apart now. He doesn't call me as much as he used to; we don't hang out like we used to. I'm at a loss because he doesn't seem to be mad at me, but he doesn't to want to be around me, either. When I went to see him, he had John cover for him. Kyle is keeping something from me, and I need to know what it is! I don't know how much more of this I can take."

Then I just started going off! "It doesn't help that I have class all month with Grey, and it's no secret to You how I'm sorta feeling for him. God, I just need help. Maybe I don't need to date right now. Maybe I'm blowing up nothing—I don't know! I promise You this: if You show me what to do, I'll do it."

I stayed on my knees next to my bed and remained completely quiet for a few moments, hoping to hear some type of direction from God when my phone rang. I could somehow sense an unusual urgency in the ring. The tone itself was no different from usual, but the timing of the call startled me. I rolled back onto the balls of my feet and took tentative steps toward the phone, disregarding the caller ID and answering it with my customary, "Hello."

Background screams and cries from the receiver swallowed my greeting while Shea attempted to explain. "Avail, can you get over here now? When I came back to the room after dinner, I found Raine on the floor near the bathroom in a small pool of blood. I called the ambulance."

I hung up the phone immediately and grabbed a jacket before I headed for the door. If Kyle had been anyone else, I would have run him over. He stood there with a bag of food in his left arm and his right fist in the air as if I'd caught him getting ready to knock on my door. *His timing couldn't be worse.*

"Avail, what's wrong? Where are you going in such a hurry? You almost ran into me!"

"Shea just called; something happened to Raine. An ambulance is on the way."

As I ran down the steps, I faintly heard him say, "But...okay...."

⌁

"*C*all me or text me with updates about Raine. I'll be up until I hear from you," a text read from Kyle on my cell phone, reemphasizing what I imagined he said to my back as I ran down the back stairwell. Raine had been admitted to the hospital, and according to the doctors, she had lost so much blood that they needed to replenish her with a couple of pints. That was the only information they shared with us. I sat in an uncomfortable visitor's chair while Shea blotted Raine's forehead with a moistened cloth in an attempt to make her more comfortable while she slept.

We hadn't heard anything, and since we weren't immediate family, the doctors would not share details with us. From the brief moments that Raine was conscious, she told us to call Reese and not to worry because she was fine.

"Shea," I whispered quietly as if I was afraid my question would wake up Raine. "Did you notice how Raine didn't mention anything about the baby when she told us that she would be fine?" I felt guilty for analyzing Raine's statement when I knew she wasn't fully herself at the time.

Shea just slowly nodded her head, eventually adding, "Yes." She continued caring for Raine as if she couldn't talk to me and check on her at the same time. Once she felt satisfied that Raine was sleeping comfortably, she turned to me and said, "In the deepest part of my heart, I'm positive that Raine didn't do anything to herself. There was no evidence of an attempted suicide or a self-induced abortion; just blood and her complaining about having cramps that wouldn't let up." She cleared her throat and continued. "I haven't known Raine long, but it's just not in her nature. She started making plans with Reese over break about what they were both going to do when it came to attending school and raising their child. They had picked up some apartment booklets to find off-campus housing for the three of them, and they'd found a great day care. They've done all kinds of other stuff to get ready. I think she was getting excited about the possibilities of being a family."

At the end of her statement, Reese pushed Raine's hospital room door open wide enough for him to enter followed by Frick and Grey. All three looked like they'd come straight from the gym. He demanded, "What happened?"

"I don't really know," Shea said. "I came back to the room after dinner, and as I was unlocking the door, I could hear Raine screaming like she was in the worst pain."

Frick walked over and hugged Shea, whispering in her ear, "Are you okay, love?"

"A little shaken, but I'm okay," Shea confirmed.

Reese moved closer to the bed and began talking directly into Raine's ear, and Grey crossed the room to ask me, "Avail, are you all right?"

"Me? I'm fine. I'm worried about Raine. I hope she's okay." I was holding back tears and trying not to show it.

"It's perfectly natural to be shaken by this. You don't have to be brave for anyone."

Forcing my lower eyelids to become like dams, I said, "Really, I'm okay." Then I turned away to wipe some tears that escaped. When I turned around, I found myself in a comforting embrace that welcomed every bit of the confusion, anxiety, and fear I was feeling. My arms fell loosely around Grey's hips as I buried one side of my face into his chest and released more tears and a small pent-up sob. I felt Grey remove one arm from around me to adjust a swoop bang above my eyes so that he could gently peck me on my forehead. His other hand maintained a soothing stroke on the small of my back.

"It's okay, Avail. It's okay to let it go."

And I did.

"What's everybody crying about?" Raine managed to ask loud enough for Frick, Shea, Grey, and me to hear. Reese held her hand with a tentative grin on his face.

At that moment, Shea and I showered lots of love toward Raine, showing her how thankful we were that she seemed to be her usual self while the guys gave us our space, congregating in a corner to themselves. Reading the questions in our eyes, Raine explained, "I went back to the room after my class because I wasn't feeling well. I thought I could sleep it off before dinner, so I lay down for a nap. About an hour into it, I woke up cramping and noticed that the bed was soaked with something. I crawled to the bathroom in an attempt to see what was going on, but I never made it all the way. That's when Shea found me." Everyone stared at Raine for more information when she said, "You should know everything, Reese, because I told the doctor to tell you."

"Tell me what?" We held our collective breath.

Raine grabbed Reese's hand, looked him directly in the eyes, and declared, "I had a miscarriage. We are no longer having a child."

The drive from the hospital was just short enough to catch a small nap in the back seat of Frick's late-model SUV that all five of us piled into once the nurses told us that we needed to leave so that Raine could get her rest. Frick and Shea sat in the front seats while Reese stretched across the middle row. Grey sat close enough to me to where his shoulder became my pillow and his arm enveloped me with warmth. The guys made sure that Reese was okay before he returned to his room. Shea and I both decided not to disturb them, figuring that Reese needed the company of his boys at a time like this. Since our dorms were next to each other, we would walk together to the merge spot and then head our separate ways.

After Reese walked away, Frick yelled to our backs, "Hey, where in the world are y'all going?"

"To our rooms," I called out.

"It's one o'clock in the morning. There's no telling who might be out here and what they might want to do to either of you," Grey contributed. "We're walking you back to your rooms."

I turned to say, "That's really not necessary," but Shea accepted the invitation by snuggling under her man's arm.

"I'll see you after class so we can go visit Raine," Shea said before Frick and she disappeared.

Grey stood there with his hands stuffed in the kangaroo pocket of his basketball hoodie and stared at me. "It doesn't matter what you say, Avail. I'm walking you back to your room. It's late; let's go."

We started walking toward my dorm when I quietly said, "Thank you."

"You're welcome…." Grey said, but his voice trailed off as if he wanted to say more. He was quiet a moment, and then he added, "Why is it so hard for you to accept stuff, Avail? I mean, like when we were in the hospital, you fought your emotions and my attempt to help you with them. I had to basically force you to let me walk you back to your room at this hour before you accepted it. What's with that?" He looked down at me with a curious look on his face.

"I don't know," I attempted to explain. "At this stage in my life, I'm trying to learn how to be independent and strong instead of dependent and weak."

"The strongest people depend on someone or something; it's a form of stability. Take your relationship with God; you depend on Him a lot, don't you?"

His example threw me for a loop, but I replied, "Yeah, and…?"

"Well, He puts people in your life for a reason. We all need help, and at this time, I can help you."

I imagined how he could help me, and I liked some of the images I saw, but I snapped out of it and asked, "Help me how?"

He grinned as if he knew what I was imagining. "Like walking you to your room to make sure you're safe. Like practicing together to make sure we both know what we're doing with the flute!" Thankfully, his statements didn't reflect my thoughts. We shared a mutual laugh with him adding, "Like all the help you gave me last semester. We need each other."

I think the weight of his last statement hit him a little heavier than he expected because he changed the direction of his gaze from me to my approaching dorm. In an attempt to ease what he might be feeling, I told him, "Well, you know that I'm here for you if you need me. If I can help you in any way, just let me know." I took out my keys and unlocked the security door. He held the door for me to walk all the way in and stepped in as well. A bit confused, I said, "You walked me to my dorm, and you can see that I'm safe, so I'm good from here."

Grey smiled again, showing his teeth that seemed to gleam this time, and stated, "I told you that I would walk you to your room, and I am, Avail. So go on up the stairs!"

I laughed before I said, "I guess this is what you mean by me accepting stuff, huh?"

"Exactly. Now, you get it!"

We walked up the three flights of steps quickly while he continued to pick on me about not knowing how to take assistance. When we reached the security door of my suite, I insisted, "Okay, really, from here, I'm okay! Thank you for walking me all the way back to my room, Grey." I reached up to give him a hug, and he received it just fine.

Before walking away, he said, "You're welcome, and I'll see you in class in a few hours."

Yes, you will, Grey.

Fourteen

His Way

I couldn't wait any longer. It was time for Avail to know about Celeste and the baby. I didn't know how I would break the news to her, but I figured that food would be a good buffer, a way to wiggle my way back into her world since it had been days since we'd spent time together alone. Unfortunately, I'd be breaking one of our relationship rules, but I thought this was a worthy exception.

I rehearsed several different scenarios of how Avail would take the news, everything from throwing things at me and throwing me out of her room to being mysteriously calm to the point that I might need a witness or some type of evidence. I thought about bringing my digital recorder to document the incident just in case she killed me in a fit of temporary insanity. I wouldn't want her to get time in jail for a crime of passion. After coming to the conclusion that she was nothing like Celeste, I decided against it.

Once the delivery guy had dropped off a special order from one of our favorite restaurants in town, I started out the door and began my trek across the courtyard. I ran into John along the way, who was heading to our dorm room. As always, we gave each other our traditional handshake and greeting with John adding, "Are you going where I think you're going?"

After building up my confidence with a strong inhale, I said, "Yeah, it's time; it's beyond time." I held up the bag of food and said, "But first, I have to apologize for not seeing her or talking to her since she got back from her family trip. That's what this will help me do."

Sniffing the air, John said, "It smells good, but the food is only going to go so far. You know Avail better than I do, but being that you have a bomb like a pregnancy to drop on her, accepting your apology for not hookin' up lately will be the least of your issues."

"Who's pregnant?"

The voice came out of nowhere, and as protected as I kept my business, I couldn't believe that my private conversation in an open courtyard was picked up by…

"Camden, what's up?" John attempted to divert her curiosity. "I haven't seen you since last year. Happy New Year!"

"You too, John," she said, "but is it going to be a happy one for Kyle?" She aimed her glare toward me and shot an accusation along with it. "You didn't strap that up before you and Avail got down?"

"John, I'll holler at you later," I said, dismissing him after grabbing Camden by the arm and steering her in another direction. I tore into her with barely controlled fury. "Avail's not pregnant, and I don't want you to say a word to her or anyone else about what you think you heard!" I heard the paranoid tone in my voice and almost didn't recognize myself. I just had to manage the situation as calmly as possible and make sure Camden would keep her mouth shut.

Yanking her elbow out of my grasp, she replied, "You act like I'm just going to run all over campus telling people something about a pregnancy that I don't have all the facts on! I know how to keep my mouth shut. As your business partner, you have to understand that."

She provided the perfect segue for me to divert her attention. "Have you started outlining a possible internship curriculum for the boys in our program? Since this is only a month-long class and a competition, we need to be ten steps ahead of everyone else."

"Actually, that's what I was coming over to discuss with you." Camden then pulled out a notebook that showed an outline of how our program could align with established curriculum for the boys' four years in high school. "So, as you can see, I really don't have to come up with a curriculum. The schools should be willing to offer an independent study credit that might give them an honors credit as well."

Amazed at what she had accomplished in a few hours, I had to compliment her. "Good job! This is exciting." Remembering the task at hand, I shared, "Camden, I gotta go. Thanks for your hard work, and please keep what you heard to yourself. As business partners, I'd appreciate it." I had to pull every card that I could. Since she had established the relationship between us, I used that phrase to remind her how important confidentiality was between us.

"Don't worry; your secret is safe with me," she said, and I could tell she meant it.

I turned away immediately and headed for Avail's room with a little more pep in my step. Camden may not have known who was pregnant, but she knew there was a pregnancy and could probably infer that I was the father. If any of this got to Avail before I told her, there was no hope for us trying to work things out.

Slipping into the back door that led to the laundry room, I took the back steps two-by-two and reached Avail's room door just inside the cracked security door. I straightened out the jogging suit I had changed into, placed the bag of food in my left hand, and raised my right fist to knock on the door.

Instantly, as if she knew I was standing there, Avail's door popped open, but the urgency in her exit showed me that her actions had nothing to do with me. I moved out of the way before asking, "Avail, what's wrong? Where are you going?"

"Shea just called me; something happened to Raine. An ambulance is on the way," was all I heard before she ran down the steps.

"But...is there anything I can do?" I mumbled, but I got no response. "Okay, call me and let me know what's going on," I said, but I felt as if I was talking to myself because Avail was long gone down the stairs.

I had no clue whether I should follow her or not, but Avail had left her room door wide open, so I walked in and sat on the bed feeling a little bewildered. I had pumped myself up to tell Avail about the baby, but Raine's crisis occupied her right now. *I hope Raine is okay... but when am I going to tell Avail about the baby?*

I opened the bag of food. Since I had missed dinner and I had to figure out how I would tell her in a different way, I chomped down on the bag's contents, drowning my sorrows in some of our favorite sandwiches and fries.

———

I sent Avail a text to check on Raine's condition, but she didn't reply. I knew her phone wasn't in her room because I didn't hear it when I sent the text. After an hour of waiting, I decided that it was time for me to make my way to the hospital. I had more concern grew for Raine than I had realized at first; after all, Raine was like a sister to me, and I had no idea what was going on. I didn't know if it had to do with the baby, or if it was something else totally unrelated.

University Hospital wasn't that far from campus, and a few side streets allowed me to get there within fifteen minutes on foot. I had to believe that since Avail hadn't called, Raine was in stable condition, but the brother in me wanted to see for myself.

The secretary at the registration desk in the main lobby told me the room number Raine was in and let me know that there were only a few minutes remaining for visiting hours. Raine's room appeared to be on the labor and delivery floor, and that sent my mind in a whirlwind. First, I thought about the possibility of her developing complications in her first trimester and what that could mean. Then my mind flashed to Celeste, and I wondered how she was doing at the beginning of her second trimester. My thoughts became consumed with my child and whether Celeste was taking care of herself and eating right, and what appointments we had coming up. I found it interesting that I had not heard from her. *I'll have to check on her once I make sure Raine, Shea, and Avail are okay.*

The elevator door opened, and I followed the directions on the wall signs until I found Raine's room. I took a moment to gather myself just in case I walked in on bad news. The door was slightly cracked, but I could not hear any sounds coming from anyone in the room. I released a deep breath as I opened the door and saw Reese kneeling next to the bed, Frick cuddle-holding Shea, who looked a little upset, and...

Grey...

Grey holding my girlfriend...shifting the hair on her forehead...

Grey holding Avail...Grey consoling my girlfriend...

Grey...KISSING MY GIRLFRIEND....

I backed out of the room undetected and hot as fire. Grey had taken advantage of Avail in a weak moment and kissed her! The kiss was on her forehead, but it was still a kiss. He rubbed the small of her back with a seductive vigor that looked like her clothes didn't exist to him, and his lips lingered on her forehead a little too long. *Man, his lips had no business being on her at all.* The hallway spun around me as I walked to the elevator and waited for the door to open.

How could she willingly accept that kiss from him? Why didn't she pull back? *In fact, I think I saw her lean into it!* When the bell chimed announcing the elevator's arrival, I stumbled into it and barely hit the button for the lobby. A small part of me wanted to cry, but a larger part of me wanted to confront Grey and Avail and find out what was going on.

And I will do just that. It's a good thing I left Avail's door unlocked. I'll start with her.

Fifteen

Her Way

"How's Raine?"

I couldn't recall ever hearing Kyle's voice so dark and ridged, but before I turned on the lights in my room, I knew it was him. I had failed to lock the door before running to Shea's room and figured that he would be waiting for me here for news, especially since I hadn't texted him with any.

I flipped the switch on my desk lamp and stretched to relieve the tension my body had absorbed within the past few hours. After setting my keys down, I looked over toward my bed and expected to see Kyle fully reclined, but that wasn't the case. He sat on the edge of the bed, impatiently wringing his hands while his left leg twitched rapidly. He stared at me hard, almost as hard as he spoke to me, and his demeanor was ice cold.

"She's stable," I took a few steps toward him but felt the need to stop before I told him, "She lost the baby."

His eyes revealed an inner sadness that chipped at his present façade. He dropped his head before stating, "I was afraid of that. Is she okay?"

"Yes, at least she appears to be. I won't really know until she's discharged. That may happen tomorrow."

"Did anything else happen?"

I thought the question was strange for the occasion, but I answered, "No, but they gave her a couple of pints of blood. She had lost that much."

"No, I don't mean with her. Did anything else happen with you?"

For some strange reason, I felt an argument coming, and being that I didn't have my verbal filter up and ready, I sputtered, "Besides not seeing you or really talking to you since I got back from Maryland, no, I can't say anything else has happened to me."

"It's funny that you bring up Maryland. Isn't that where Grey is from?" Kyle questioned with very little inflection.

"Yes and why do you ask?"

"I just heard his voice in the hallway. So he's walking you to your door now?"

I snapped, "It's one o'clock in the morning! He didn't want me to walk back to my room by myself. Is that a crime?" I was tired, had class later that morning, and didn't have time for anything but some sleep action. Why did he stay to pick an argument? Did he come over with those intentions?

"It becomes a crime when you start hiding things from me in regards to him. You're holding something back, and you just need to be honest with me," Kyle demanded.

He adjusted his tone in such a way that made me feel as if he'd found out about Frick and Grey being at the concert in Baltimore. I knew people around here ran their mouths, but the only people I had told were Raine and Shea. *They wouldn't dare tell Kyle about that!* It's a possibility that Grey or Frick mentioned it to someone, and then that someone took it upon himself or herself to tell Kyle. *I can't stand it when people run their mouths!*

Instead of directly addressing the issue in my head, I counter-attacked him by saying, "Is this what all this distance between us has been about? Is that why I haven't heard a decent word from you since I got back in town *and* since we got back on campus? At first, I thought it was just about the fact that I didn't call you because my cell phone died and I didn't have the charger with me. But if you're talking about what happened in Baltimore and you're trippin' like this, you need to get a grip! It was nothing!" *Oh no— I let it slip.*

Kyle shook his head as if something was loose before he asked, "Wait—what happened in Baltimore?"

He wasn't talking about my seeing Grey in Baltimore. He didn't know, but now it was out there. How do I get around this? "I told you, it was nothing," was the best I could come up with.

"Nothing." Kyle stood up and paced back and forth in front of my bed. I figured that I should remain standing in order to have the best options for my reaction. "Nothing, you say," he emphasized. "Well, SOMEthing happened because you brought it up. Maybe," he whispered and paused his pacing at the same time, making direct eye contact with me, "that's when Grey kissed you the first time."

"Kissed me?" Confused, I attempted to clarify. "And what do you mean 'the first time'? What are you talking about? Grey has never kissed me!" I tried to control the volume of my voice because of the late hour, but it wasn't easy—not when Kyle was putting me on the defensive like this. "Grey wouldn't do that!"

"Oh, yeah?" Kyle pondered as he took deliberate steps toward me. Using the few inches he had to stand over me, he posed, "Well, what did I see him do in Raine's hospital room? Tell me that."

"I don't know what you saw, but you didn't see him kiss...." I stopped my words immediately. Kyle must have come to the hospital, opened Raine's door, and seen the moment when Grey pecked me on the forehead after I started crying. Instantly I winced at the thought of how Kyle must have felt, but at the same time, it was just a peck on the forehead. It wasn't like Grey caressed my cheek, gazed into my eyes, and planted a full-lipped French kiss on my mouth! That peck was all about trying to keep me calm, so I explained, "What you saw in the hospital room isn't what you think it was."

"Exactly what about Grey's lips making contact with you isn't a kiss?" Turning his sarcasm to its highest level, he grabbed the dictionary from the bottom of a pile of books on my desk and declared, "Let's see what *Webster's Dictionary* has to say about it," and turned the pages frantically to find the word *kiss*.

I reached for the dictionary and said, "Kyle, please, this isn't necessary. Let's talk about this. You don't understand what happened before you walked in."

My efforts met his back as he walked to the other side of the room and stood near the window. Once he found the definition, he read loudly, "Kiss, the verb, as defined by *Webster*, is to touch with the lips…" Following him, I reached for the dictionary again, and he avoided me again, continuing, "…ESPECIALLY as a mark of affection or greeting. Hmmm…I think I got it right. He kissed you, all right."

"I was upset about Raine and hoping the baby was okay because we didn't know yet, and Grey just checked on me." The words fell to the stretch of floor between us. "He saw that I was close to crying, so he gave me a hug."

"And a kiss," Kyle added hotly.

"Why are you making such a big deal out of this? It was on my forehead. It was more paternal than anything else."

Finally facing me, he slammed the dictionary onto the floor and yelled, "Well, since he wants to be your daddy, I think it's time the two of us had a talk, man to man." Kyle walked out of the door, and I stood there in disbelief.

And then I remembered that Grey couldn't be that far away since he had walked me to my room. I stared at my doorway wondering if I should follow Kyle.

Fifteen

HIS WAY

"You're welcome, and I'll see you in class in a few hours!" Grey's voice boomed through the wall and I knew instantly that Avail was on the other side of the door. I had turned out her lights hours ago and lain on her bed in an attempt to calm myself down, but it hadn't worked. I felt a rage building in me that I could only associate with my arguments with Celeste. An impulsive tic that made my left leg twitch had started at least an hour ago because all I could see over and over again in my mind was Grey smoothing Avail's hair out of the way and kissing her forehead with the tenderness of a lover. Since I'd left without being noticed, I had no idea what else happened. So, of course, my imagination went into overdrive and took me into a scenario that probably didn't happen: After the forehead peck, Avail probably looked up at him and questioned lightly, "Grey, what in the world –"

Gently placing an index finger on her lips, he stopped her from saying another word and boldly stated, "Avail, it's not like you don't know how I feel for you. I know the situation with you and Kyle, with y'all being together and all, but I'm here now, and he isn't when you need him the most." He then removed his finger from her lips enough to help part them and added, "And I know the kiss on the forehead probably went too far, but I couldn't hold myself back anymore."

Even in my imagination, I had to give Grey credit. It was no secret to me how he felt about Avail, but he managed to respect our relationship and keep his distance, even if it was just in what he said. My main concern stood with how Avail would react toward any advances from Grey. He shared desirable characteristics with Donovan, the boyfriend she had when she came to Whitaker. She appreciated the tall, dark, and handsome type, and with the additional factor that Grey played basketball, Avail's favorite type of male athlete, Grey could sweep her off her feet with all his honor, charm, and Avail-appeal without me having a second chance. I could just hear Avail saying, "Grey, I know you didn't mean any harm. You were just trying to make me feel better."

Grey slid out of the embrace that he initiated and declared, "Still, I went too far, and for that, I apologize."

An apology? I knew how apologies worked on Avail. The first day of classes, I had to apologize for picking with her in front of the whole class, and that's how we started dating! Grey was playing my game in my daydream!

Avail attempted to brush it off, and involvement from Frick, Shea, Reese, and Raine took over the imaginary scene, but the whole idea of the forehead kiss spoke volumes. He wanted her, and honorable or not, he was willing to slip into any gap I left open when it came to Avail.

The sound of Avail turning the knob and then realizing that the door was unlocked pulled me back to reality, and I began my second nervous tic, wringing my hands. I always did it when I tried to figure out what I was going to do in a sticky situation, and this scenario definitely qualified.

I confronted Avail to make her aware of my presence, but the tone of my voice revealed my irritation with all that I witnessed and imagined. "How's Raine?"

She confirmed my suspicion about Raine loosing the baby, and I wondered how Reese was doing. I knew that women have their way of dealing with the loss of a baby, but it's fair to state that men do too. I'm not as deep as Reese, so I know he must be taking it pretty hard. *I'll have to give him a call later.*

Though I grieved internally for what Reese and Raine had to deal with, I had to force myself to address the improper infraction Grey and Avail shared. I began my interrogation by asking, "Did anything else happen?" I wanted to see how much truth would she offer before revealing that I knew what happened.

Avail thought I was talking about Raine, so she gave me a quick overview of what the doctors did for her. I lost a little of my patience when I had to clarify,

"No, I don't mean with her. Did anything else happen with you?"

As if she was hiding something, Avail snapped, "Besides not seeing you or really talking to you since I got back from Maryland, no, I can't say anthing else has happened to me."

Her nasty attitude gave me permission to turn this mild discussion into a full-fledge argument. I connected Grey to her holiday trip and the fact that I just heard his voice outside the door. I tore into the fact that he walked her to her door, probably hoping that she would invite him in. When she asked me, "Is that a crime," I pushed her closer to the issue at hand.

"It becomes a crime when you start hiding things from me in regards to him. You're holding something back, and you just need to be honest with me." She was hiding this kiss from me; there's no telling what else she hid

Avail completely shook off what I said and explained what she felt like I misunderstood. Though I was highly aggravated by this time, she included, "But if you're talking about what happened in Baltimore and you're trippin' like this, you need to get a grip. It was nothing!"

I didn't even know she went to Baltimore. I thought her family was in Hagerstown. If that wasn't irritating enough, I remembered instantly who lived in Baltimore.

"HOLD UP! Wait—what happened in Baltimore?" I demanded. It looked as if she was hiding something from me, and I pierced her eyes with my stare and took a few steps toward her.

"I told you, it was nothing." She looked ashamed. I was time for me to uncover all of what she hid from me. *And to think that I thought I could trust her...*

When I asked about the kiss, immediately, Avail defended him. I'm her man; she should have been defending what we have by not even being in Grey's arms. She had no boundaries when it came to Grey and that's unacceptable. I adjusted the volume of my voice so I could make my point loudly.

"Nothing...nothing, you say. Well, SOMEthing happened because you brought it up. Maybe that's when Grey kissed you the first time."

"And what do you mean 'the first time'? What are you talking about? Grey has never kissed me!" *Now, she's lying. I saw it with my own eyes.*

"Oh, yeah? Well, what did I see him do in Raine's hospital room? Tell me that."

Avail began to mumble before she realized that I must have seen them in order to accuse them. She quickly proclaimed that I misunderstood the scene.

I went off. I ripped the dictionary off her desk before I asked, "Exactly what about Grey's lips making contact with you isn't a kiss?" "Let's see what *Webster's Dictionary* has to say about it."

I paced the perimeter of her room as I looked up the word. As she reached for the dictionary and followed me around the room, I strong-armed her and screamed the words, "Kiss, the verb, as defined by *Webster*, is to touch with the lips—ESPECIALLY as a mark of affection or greeting. Hmmm...I think I got it right. He kissed you, all right." I slammed the dictionary closed for emphasis.

I turned away from her. Never in the brief amount of time that Avail and I had been involved had I once thought that she would betray me. I knew that brothers out there wanted her, but I couldn't fathom the possibility of her falling for any of their game.

"Why are you making such a big deal out of this? It was on my forehead. It was more paternal than anything else." That was the last time I was going to let her defend him to my face. Grey needed to speak up for himself.

Completely peeved, I threw the dictionary to the floor hard enough to wake the neighbors downstairs, and then I faced Avail and stared her down for a moment. With as much sarcasm as I could muster, I said, "Well, since he wants to be your daddy, I think it's time the two of us had a talk, man to man." I left her standing there because I didn't want to hear another thing about how Grey didn't mean it, how Grey was just comforting her, or anything else about Grey. *I'm tired of Grey.*

I knew he couldn't be far away, and even so, I knew which dorm he lived in.

Sixteen

HIS WAY

"Dang, man, I thought you'd never get here. Frick got back from Shea's room at least twenty minutes ago."

I could tell that I startled Grey right before he put his key in the outside door of his dorm though his stature and demeanor didn't waiver from his everyday confidence and swag. If the tables were turned, I'd front just like he was doing right now, too, and I would wonder how he had managed to reach my dorm without me detecting his presence while I took the same extra ten-minute walk he had taken to return to his room. It was a nice night for January, a clear sky with all the stars shining brightly. It was the perfect setting for someone who needed a few quiet moments alone to think, and I guessed that was what he'd been doing on the way back from Avail's room.

"Do you need something, Kyle?" I can remember Grey being confrontational only on a few occasions last semester, but I couldn't recall him being this irritated, as if his recent actions didn't deserve my immediate attention. "I'm just getting back from the hospital, and I have class in a few hours, so…."

"That's nice," I interrupted as I rose from the bench outside, "but let me rewind your statement a little. Did you just say that you were coming back from the hospital? Are you all right?" A fist formed in my right hand just from the thought of wanting to put him in the hospital. "I thought I heard you outside of Avail's room." I started pacing and emphasized, "In fact, I KNOW I heard you outside of Avail's room. What's up with that?" My voice grew louder, and I knew it was just a matter of time before Frick ran down the stairs to see what was going on, especially since one of their windows just happened to be open.

"Dude, you're reading too much into that. I just walked her to the room to make sure she made it back safely and nothing happened to her. I imagine that you already know that she was at the hospital."

"Oh, yeah, I knew. I know more than you think I know." I stopped pacing and made undeniable eye contact with him.

After throwing his gaze toward the sky briefly, Grey sighed. "Okay, it's obvious that whatever chip you have on your shoulder, you're not going to let it go, so let me ask: What do you claim to know that you don't think I know you know?"

Unable to bear it anymore, I yelled, "I know you kissed my girl!"

"Who, Avail?"

"In the hospital room."

"You mean that peck on her forehead? She told you about that?"

"She didn't have time to. I saw the two of you. Were there others?"

"What?"

"Other kisses, man. Straight up! Have you and Avail crossed any lines that you shouldn't have?"

"Dude, you're paranoid."

When I heard what I presumed were Frick's footsteps running down the steps, I quieted my voice and suggested, "Stay away from my girl."

Almost nose to nose, Grey replied, "That's going to be hard being that she and I have the same intercession class." Shock appearing on my face prompted Grey to add, "I guess you didn't *know* that being that you haven't talked to her in a while." I backed off for a moment while he continued. "It's the curse of a small campus. Everyone knows everything that's going on with everyone." Without warning, Grey invaded my personal space again and simply said, "I told you last semester that if you didn't take care of her, someone else would. You were nowhere to be found when Avail was falling apart in Raine's hospital room. I may have been a substitute tonight, but if you keep acting like you are, I'll be full time in no time."

Combined with the fact that I didn't know that Avail and Grey were taking the same class, his last statement angered me enough to attempt a swing at him. I pulled my fist back right before Frick busted out the door and jumped between us, saying, "Aye, yo, man, really, I don't think you want to do that, not tonight, and not during this part of the year."

Just as I lunged to make contact with Grey, someone grabbed me from behind and said, "Kyle, what are you doing? You aren't thinking clearly. If you get into a fight or anything that requires disciplinary action, you'll disqualify for the Young Entrepreneurs Award." I shook Devin off before I realized it was him. His dorm happened to be directly across from Grey's.

Eyeballing Grey the whole time and leaving Frick and Devin spectating, I walked away because the deepest part of me knew that a fight would hurt both of us beyond any physical harm we could inflict on each other. With my anger still raging, I pulled out my cell phone with the intention of making two specific phone calls. The first was to Camden. When she answered, I directed, "I need to see you now; come downstairs."

Then I called Avail's room. When she didn't answer and her message service picked up, my message was simple: "Drop the class with Grey or we're through."

Sixteen

HER WAY

"Avail, what's wrong? Why are you crying?"

"Shea..." was all that I managed to say before I burst into tears again. Once I got myself together, I recapped everything that had happened with Kyle and added, "He just left to talk to Grey. None of this makes sense to me!"

"Well, Avail," Shea began, "I can see how Grey's kiss could bother him, but usually Kyle's a little more understanding, a little more calm. Do you think something else is up with him, like is his class stressing him out already?"

"I don't know because he hasn't talked to me since Christmas—not until this big fight, I mean. I wonder if I should go after him. I was thinking about heading to Grey's room to warn him, because Kyle seemed really mad when he left, but I don't see how that would help.

It would only make Kyle madder because it would look like I'm trying to stand up for Grey or something."

Shea sighed and suggested, "If you hold on, I can see what Frick knows." She clicked over immediately to initiate the three-way call, and within seconds, she had Frick on the line.

He immediately asked, "Avail, When did Grey leave your dorm?"

"Not too long ago. I thought he should have made it back by now."

"If I know m'boy, he's probably out taking the long route back. Shea, babe, I'll text you if anything happens down here, okay?"

"All right, love." Shea clicked him off and told me, "Kyle's not crazy. He wouldn't go down to their room this early in the morning and try to start something."

I shook my head in doubt as I flopped on my bed and said, "I don't know, Shea. I've never seen him like this. Even his voice sounded different. But it seemed like he was upset about more than just this; something else was bothering him too. I have no idea what's going on in his head because I haven't talked to him in weeks."

"Well, I don't know either, but I can tell this is going to be a long evening." Shea paused then said, "Frick just texted me. Kyle is down there starting some mess with Grey."

Going against my earlier hesitation, I declared, "I'm going down there."

"Not without me," confirmed Shea.

Consequences and Repercussions

By the time we both got dressed again and started walking toward Frick and Grey's dorm, everything was quiet and there was no sign of a disturbance. A few lights were burning in various windows, but most of the light came from the bright moon and stars. The closer we got, Shea became a little tenser about what we would see and what my presence there would say.

"Are you sure you want to go down there? Sometimes guys just have to handle this type of stuff on their own. You might not be able to help this situation." Shea was sincere, and I knew that she didn't want to see anything ugly go down between Grey and Kyle because she cared about both of them like they were big brothers. Furthermore, Frick would get involved if she got involved.

I halted my steps and took into serious consideration of what Shea said. It was a point that I hadn't considered before. Kyle felt like Grey was threatening our relationship, and no matter how much I said he wasn't, Kyle didn't believe it. So he had to hear it from Grey. I could understand that. It was a testosterone thing; no need to throw my estrogen into the mix. That would make things messier.

I looked at Shea and glanced down the path we had taken, saying, "You're right. I'm sorry I pulled you out here with me."

"Girl, you didn't pull me out here! I just wanted to make sure all of y'all were going to be okay!"

We turned and headed back to our dorms. After a few moments of walking in silence, I said, "This was definitely a misunderstanding, and if I know Grey as well as I think I do, he'll stand his ground, but he'll make everything crystal clear to Kyle."

I stopped talking when Shea began hitting me on my arm vigorously as she covered her mouth with her other hand as if to keep from screaming. She managed to point to a couple outside of Newman Hall, the dorm in front of Shea's dorm. At first, it was no big thing to me until I recognized the guy as Kyle leaning up on a wall very close to a woman who looked like Camden. Before I caught myself, I started walking toward the unsuspecting couple.

"Avail!" Shea shrieked in a loud stage whisper. "What are you about to do?"

With slow, deliberate steps, I whispered back, "I just want a better view. I saw the two of them out here together before, but I didn't think much of it at the time. After the way he treated me tonight, I just need a better view of this action." I crouched behind a large oak tree and Shea joined me.

Initially, it looked as if all they were doing was talking. Periodically, Kyle paced back and forth the way he normally did when he was discussing something important to him, but in the moments when he stopped, I felt like he stopped way too close to Camden. Adopting a defeated stance, he dropped his head and shoulders and let tears run down his face. Camden cupped his face with her hands, wiping away as many tears as she could with her thumbs, and then she said something that caused him to look into her eyes with an expression of renewed hope. He leaned into her body and found comfort in Camden's arms.

I never thought that Camden was one of his confidants. He probably told her everything that just happened. And he has the nerve to accuse me!

Shea looked at me with deep concern as I pondered what I should do next. I wondered if I should be upset about what I'd just seen. Was it a sign of intimacy between them, or was it as innocent as what happened between Grey and me?

Seventeen

HIS WAY

The outside door to Newman Hall swung open violently as Camden burst through it and started looking all over for me. With her medium-length hair tied under her scarf, her sweat suit and untied tennis shoes, she looked like she hadn't made it to bed for the evening yet. I couldn't really understand why I called Camden with the exception that I just needed someone to talk to—someone who would know the answers to my questions. Camden tended to know everything that was going on with everyone, and most of the time, she knew the truth. Tonight, I was willing to take my chances with her in order to satisfy my curiosity about Avail and Grey.

First and foremost, I needed to know what happened in Baltimore. I knew that Avail's family went to Hagerstown for the holidays, and I knew that Baltimore was not that far away. I also knew that both

Grey and Frick lived in Baltimore. Based on what Avail inferred during our argument, she went to Baltimore and possibly saw them. What was the context of their encounter, and why didn't she tell me about it? If she saw them, did she call them hoping to see them? Secondly, I knew that if anyone on this campus knew who liked whom, it was Camden. She could confirm who Grey had his eye on, even though I already knew it was Avail, and I knew Camden would know if anything had happened between the two of them. Last but not least, there was just so much running through my mind about Celeste, the baby, and the pressure to win the Young Entrepreneurs Award that I needed someone to talk to. The pressure had gotten to me. It showed through my actions earlier.

If I didn't have the overhead of the new responsibility of a baby on the way, I don't think I would have flipped out as hard as I did when I saw Grey kiss Avail on her forehead. Truth be told, I would have walked in immediately and flexed my role in Avail's life in his face. Avail would have left him standing there while running into my arms. I had to wonder though—was there a part of me pushing Avail away on purpose? I left that ugly message on her voicemail, giving her an ultimatum of dropping the class or facing a break-up between us. That's not even my style, but now I had to stand on what I said. I was tired of Grey practically leaping onto a white stallion and riding to Avail's rescue to make himself look more valiant to her. Having a month-long intensive class with her would be too much.

Nope—Grey has to go, so she has to drop the class—that's all there is to it.

"You know, Kyle, if I knew that this project was going to consume you to the point that you call your business partners to meet you in the middle of the night, I think I would have rethought being your partner," Camden said as she walked up to where I was leaning against the back of a bench.

"What I want to talk about has everything and nothing to do with our class. There's just so much on my mind, and I need some straight answers...." I drifted off, wondering for a slight second if I could trust Camden with all this inquiry. She already knew how important confidentiality was to me; it's just that I needed her help. "Do you have any idea what Grey did over Christmas break?"

"As far as I know, he just went home and chilled. There were no basketball tournaments for the team, but that's all I know."

Direct and to the point, I asked, "Do you know if he saw Avail over break?"

Suddenly looking interested, she revealed, "No, but I now remember hearing about him and Frick going to an Anthony David and Kindred the Family Soul concert. Do you know if she was there too?"

In a flash, I remembered seeing a ticket stub tacked to one of her bulletin boards in her room while I waited for her to return from the hospital. I had noted that it was a Christmas night concert in Baltimore, but really hadn't thought much of it. Since I didn't know the definitive answer to Camden's question, I kept

Avail covered by saying, "I'm not sure." After a slight pause, I asked, "Do you know if Grey is trying to get with Avail?"

"If he is, he's keeping it to himself!" She stopped to ponder my question. "Do you think that he's trying to break you and Avail up?"

I looked into Camden's eyes and said, "I don't think it's his style just to blatantly break up a couple to get what he wants, but I don't know what's going on."

When I looked at her as if I was asking her if I could trust her, she automatically answered, "I told you, as your business partner, you can trust me."

I sighed heavily. "It's just so much at one time. I know everyone knows about the accident we had. If it wasn't for us hitting the tree, I'm sure things would have been way worse than they were." I was careful with the next part when I explained, "Because of some things that did and didn't happen that evening, we came up with some rules for our relationship, and all was great until I got a phone call from Celeste…" I stumbled through the remainder of the story, using coughing techniques to mask the emotion brewing in my voice. I shared the news about the baby, and that I was contemplating whether I should break up with Avail. I told Camden I didn't know how to tell Avail the news, and how I'd almost quit Whitaker to get a job until I received the news about the Introduction to Entrepreneurship class with the competition. I started pacing back and forth while Camden leaned against the wall. Eventually I stopped right in front of her and claimed, "I saw it as a way to provide for my child and still be in school. We have to win this competition. It's the only way!" With a pound of my fist on the wall, I added, "And on top of it all, I had some beef with Grey tonight. He kissed Avail."

"Grey kissed Avail?" Camden repeated. "Now that really doesn't sound like him." *Not her defending him too!*

"It was on the forehead, but it was the principle behind it all. Anyway, all this is too much, and I'm close to flipping out. Everything around me is crumbling, and I can't seem to do anything about it." I propped my hand against the wall and hung my head while two small tears escaped from each eye. Without a thought, Camden cupped my face and wiped the tears away.

"Kyle, try not to worry. I'll do all I can to make sure you win this contest so that you can still go to school and make money for the baby. I have your back." She then hugged me and that instantly made me feel better.

It seemed as if Camden lingered a little too long in the embrace because she began caressing the nape of my hairline. Stepping out of the embrace, I said, "Thank you. I really needed someone to talk to. I knew you wouldn't let me down."

After yawning and cat stretching, she replied, "If I don't get to bed soon, I'll let you down in class later on! Don't we have to share our business plan with Dr. Delta in the morning?"

"You're right." I touched her shoulder as I said, "Thanks for everything. I appreciate it." *I really do.*

Seventeen

Her Way

"Since you didn't want to talk about it before class, tell me now. What happened last night when Kyle came to your dorm?"

Grey had been very tight-lipped the whole morning and a touch pensive beyond his normal self. Our fellow flutist even noticed how tense he was. When Grey claimed that he wanted to head to the gym early before his practice, I insisted that he get something to eat and get whatever was on his mind off it by talking to me. I had enough sense to know that it had something to do with Kyle's confrontation, but I still had no idea what went down.

"I don't want to talk about it," Grey said with a note of finality in his voice.

"That's not an option." I grabbed him by his elbow and stopped him just short of the exit doors for the fine arts building and reminded him, "Early this morning, you gave me this whole spiel about how I can't accept help. Well, you're showing me now that you can't. I just want to help, that's all—nothing more, nothing less."

Through a gesture, he led me toward a bench in the lobby area in front of the ticket box where we both sat down. He took a deep breath and said, "I'm furious with your boyfriend, but I'm not really sure why. I don't know if I'm mad about the fact that he had the balls to challenge me, or if I'm mad that I didn't knock him out, or if it's just the fact that he's your man." His last option of anger prompted a surprised look on my face, and he instantly remarked, "You said you wanted me to talk about this, so we're talking. Can you handle this conversation without thinking that I'm trying to come on to you?"

"Yes…."

"Okay, because it's not like I don't know you have a man. I know, and I'm doing my best to respect your relationship and him, but I just don't like him for you. The only thing that kept me from bruising my knuckles on his face was the fact that I knew I would get kicked off the basketball team if I did. I haven't wanted to hit a brother like that since I found out about the guys that messed with Chelsea behind my back. I won't be that guy, but Kyle is pushing it. I haven't done anything wrong…" Grey switched his gaze from me to the floor, "…unless you feel like that kiss I gave you on the forehead last night was inappropriate."

I knew the kiss was the main reason that Kyle had confronted Grey, but Grey said a multitude of things in his opening statement that caught my attention. I knew he wasn't the head cheerleader for Team Kyle—in fact, I remember him questioning me on it during homecoming—but I knew he wouldn't interfere with it either, at least not on purpose. Secondly, he still had issues with this Chelsea chick. Lastly, it was obvious that when he remembered what it was like kissing me on the forehead, he probably found himself thinking about it as much as I did when everyone finally managed to get some rest.

In an attempt to attract his eye again, I said, "I know you meant no harm by that kiss; you were just trying to comfort me in that tense situation."

"See, you don't get it either," he said, looking directly into my eyes. "I slipped; I let my guard down, and even though I did it because I wanted to comfort you, it felt too good to be the one—to be yours—for the moment. I even told Kyle that if he didn't step up, I would replace him, because really, Avail, I want to but I can't, and I'm slightly miserable for that reason."

Wow....

"Does being around me bother you that much?"

I didn't think my question would prompt a model-perfect smile on his face, but it did right before he said, "No, silly, I actually enjoy hanging around you. It's just that I have to know my boundaries and keep my guard up with you; that's all.

"And what about your interactions with Kyle? You can't be at this school wanting to beat him up for the next year and a half!" We both laughed.

"That's a matter of self-control and poise that I get from the basketball court. I never let the opponent see panic or anger in my eyes. I'm not going to let Kyle know that he got under my skin last night. He has no idea, I'm sure."

I cleared my throat before saying, "Just for the record, no, the kiss didn't bother me, but I can understand why it bothered Kyle, especially after what I saw early this morning after your run-in with him."

"What did you see?"

"I'll tell you on the way to lunch."

In our short trek to the Commons, I told him how Frick had texted Shea to let her know what was going on, and that Shea and I had planned to come down to their dorm to make sure everything was okay. Then I shared with him the scene that both Shea and I witnessed between Kyle and Camden without either of them knowing.

"See, it's stuff like that—I don't understand why you put up with it! Last semester, he had a girlfriend at home but he had you here. Now that y'all are legit, he's still acting the same way, just with a different female."

Once we placed our music and flute cases in our chairs, I asked him, "Are you sure that's not just a little hate showing up in you right now?" I smiled as I punched him in the arm.

He grabbed his firm muscle as if I hurt it and said, "No! It's something I want you to consider. Aren't you even mad about it?"

We stopped short of the line when I replied, "Getting mad about it isn't going to fix whatever is really going on. Seeing that scene last night made me realize how he felt when he saw you kiss me." As we began picking up food, I said, "Sure, it bothered me, but two hotheads will not work in this situation." I picked up a pudding cup and noticed that I must have been slamming my food down onto my tray without noticing because French fries were scattered all over it and the top bun of my chicken sandwich had completely fallen off the plate.

"Hey, don't take it out on the food!" Grey joked. "Seriously, you need to talk to Kyle about this and get it resolved. If y'all are as tight as you claim, you'll be fine."

Walking back to the table, I asked him, "How do you do that? How do you just flip the switch from telling me that you'd like to date me, but can't, to being annoying older brother who knows his little sister needs some guidance?"

He laughed before he said, "I got skills! I'm a philosophy and psychology double major, remember?"

I giggled, and then we sat, blessed our food, and dug in to it.

Eighteen

His Way

" *I* can't believe that we are the only group whose proposal was approved by Dr. Delta on the first round," Camden practically squealed as she walked to the Commons with Devin and me to grab lunch after class.

"I guess all that hard work from yesterday and following Dr. Delta's detailed requirements for the proposal really paid off," Devin contributed. They seemed to be waiting for me to say something, but I had lost interest in the conversation. We were on point when it came to our presentation and defending our proposal, but the moment we finished, my thoughts were consumed with the ultimatum I'd given Avail and the fact that she hadn't called me.

I had to wonder why. I knew Avail checked her answering machine religiously, and I knew that she had a cell phone now. Maybe she had made her decision, and truth be told, I didn't want her to make a decision about us based on that message. I was beyond angry when I left that message, and my malicious thoughts about Grey had consumed me. I still thought that she should consider how much time she spent around Grey, but it didn't have to be as dramatic as dropping her class just because he enrolled in it too. Class choice dealt with her education, and I would never ask her to compromise her course selection just because Grey took the same course. *I'm too confident to worry about that.*

Devin, Camden, and I grabbed cafeteria trays and selected our meals. As I thought about the approval that we had received from Dr. Delta today, my mind shifted to my main drive behind winning this competition: my unborn child. *It's only been two and a half weeks since I learned about my baby, but I've done a poor job of making sure Celeste is taking care of herself so we can have a healthy and happy baby.* Once we placed our trays at a table, I excused myself to call Celeste while she was on my mind.

"How are you feeling?" I asked as soon as she answered.

Sounding like she was squashing a yawn, Celeste answered, "I'm feeling pretty good. Your daughter is keeping me up in the middle of the night squirming here and there."

A daughter. The world around me started to spin as I thought about the idea of having a daughter, not just a baby. Then I wondered aloud, "Did you have an ultrasound and didn't tell me, and who's to say that I wanted to know the sex of the baby?" I smiled.

Celeste laughed before saying, "I know you pretty well, Kyle, and I know you'd want to know—and no, I haven't had an ultrasound, so I don't know the sex of the baby yet. I'll find out on Friday."

"What time is the appointment?" I asked automatically. My mind surveyed all that I needed to do on Friday, but if the appointment was late enough in the afternoon, I might be able to make it home. "You weren't going to call and tell me about it? I told you that I want to be an active part of my child's life, and that includes doctor's appointments, especially this ultrasound."

"Look at you, Mr. Thompson!" Celeste commented. "I had planned on calling you tonight. I know you're probably wrapped up in classwork."

"Celeste, I see I'll have to do a lot of putting you in place," I began. "There is absolutely nothing more important to me than this child. I'm only back in school in order to be my best for the baby!" I caught my voice getting louder and brought it back down. The last thing I wanted to do was upset Celeste, especially in her condition. "So, what time is the appointment? I want to be there when the doctor tells us about our daughter."

"At four in the afternoon, and you know it might be a boy. I was just taking a guess since my symptoms are tapering off now, which is sometimes a sign of carrying a girl."

Since class ended at noon every day, and I didn't foresee my group having a large amount of work to do Friday evening, I declared, "I'll be at your house at three to take you and the baby to the doctor."

"Thank you," Celeste stated in the meekest tone I had ever heard her use.

"No problem," I said before I ended the call. I stood facing the exit doors just taking a quick moment to think about how much I already loved my child. I didn't care if she ended up being a girl or if he ended up being a boy. My focus was on having a healthy child and raising him or her in a happy environment with plenty of love and support. I let a smile curl my lips as I turned around to go back to my table.

If I hadn't controlled my steps, I would have run right into Avail and probably knocked her right into the man I was tired of seeing everywhere I looked: Grey. I didn't feel like seeing either of them, but here they were, together, in my face, with Avail looking pale and Grey looking disgusted. Grey's reaction made my self-proclaimed righteous indignation surface before I said to Avail, "I guess you didn't get my message from last night, judging from the flute box in your hand, music under your arm, and your ever constant shadow behind you." *Why did I say that when I just told myself that she didn't have to drop the class?*

By the time I finished my statement, tears were filling Avail's eyes when she inquired, "Did the message have anything to do with your daughter?"

I couldn't believe that I had slipped again. The one person I should have told from the beginning had now overheard me on the phone, and there was no way to deny it. "So now you're listening to my private conversations?" I retaliated.

"A few weeks ago, we didn't have too many things between us that were private." She stood there too proud to cry. Then, Avail became quietly angry, being mindful that we were in a public place. "But private like a baby? Don't you think that's something—ugh, I mean *someone* I should know about?"

"You mean like what's going on between you and Grey? Don't you think that's something I should know about too?"

"You cannot equate a baby that I didn't know you were having to an imaginary relationship that you're paranoid about!"

I shifted my focus to Grey while addressing Avail by saying, "Paranoid? Now, the two of you are sharing vocabulary words. That's the very same word your man on the side used last night when he was trying to defend whatever is going on between the two of you."

Grey threw up his hands and said, "Man, I don't have anything to do with you having a child with someone other than your girlfriend."

Avail dropped her head, grabbed her stomach, and said, "I think I'm going to be sick."

Gritting my teeth, I looked at Avail and said flatly, "Well, since everyone will know soon anyway, I am expecting a child...."

Avail choked. "With Camden? I didn't expect this at all. I've seen y'all together a lot since we got back from break, but Camden? Really?"

"No," I clarified. Then I cleared my throat before saying, "Celeste is the mother."

Avail doubled over completely, dropping all of her materials, grasping her mouth as if to hold back everything that wanted to come out. Shea, who had just entered the cafeteria, and Grey began picking up her items from the floor as Avail's other hand left her stomach and snatched one thing off the floor.

"What's going on?" Shea demanded.

Though I was still mad at Avail, I couldn't ignore her pain and confusion. I attempted to help her back to standing fully on her feet as I said, "You don't know the whole story. Let's go somewhere and talk about this."

"Now you want to talk?" Avail spewed. "With your secret out in the open, NOW you want to talk? I can't do this…."

"Okay, we'll talk tonight," I reasoned.

Avail straightened herself out in such a way that it was almost as if nothing had just happened, like the situation had not caused her the worst heartache in her life. She looked at me coldly and said, "By this, I meant us." With that, she shoved the cell phone, the one item she grabbed from the floor, into my chest and walked away with Grey trailing her.

I couldn't make eye contact with Shea or return to my business partners, so I headed for the side door to escape the spotlight.

Eighteen

HER WAY

"As much as I would love to go somewhere and practice with you and Stephanie, I can't. I gotta get to the gym and run a few drills to get ready for the Waynesburg game on Wednesday night. Don't forget that you promised that you'd come to cheer us on," Grey reminded me. With all the drama that had ensued with Kyle and Raine losing the baby, it had almost slipped my mind.

We both picked up our trays and belongings as I confirmed, "I will be there, as usual, on the third row behind the scorer's table cheering you..." I paused, a little miffed at my blunder, before correcting myself, "...you and the team on." *I hope I covered enough for him not to question my Freudian slip.*

If he noticed, he let it slide as he stated, "Sounds good. If you want, we can practice later on. I can concentrate a little better now that you made me talk about what was on my mind." After a few steps toward the dirty tray conveyor belt by the exit, he added, "Thank you; I needed that."

I just smiled at him as I put my tray down. Ready to practice the flute with Stephanie, I turned my attention to the doors when I saw Kyle standing there with his back toward us, and I froze. After Grey put his tray down, I turned around as if I wanted to walk back into the cafeteria, and I murmured to Grey, "I don't feel like dealing with him right now."

Grey first looked at Kyle and then down at me. "Avail, eventually, you're going to have to come face to face with him." Then, oddly enough, he suggested, "Maybe I should go through the side door so I won't cause any unnecessary friction."

"If I'm going to say anything to him, I'll need you with me," I insisted. "Besides, Kyle's not the type to start a scene in public, and neither are you." He gave me a nod, and we both took tentative steps toward Kyle who was absorbed in his conversation with whoever was on the other end of the call.

As we approached, I heard Kyle express with a particular level of joy, "Did you have an ultrasound and didn't tell me, and who's to say that I wanted to know the sex of the baby?" I stood there for a moment, not really sure that I'd heard him correctly. *Who's having a baby? And why should he know about the sex?* I shook my head as if to clear my ears to hear better right before I heard him say, "I told you that I want to be an active part of my child's life, and that includes doctor's appointments, especially this ultrasound." I could feel my tear ducts swelling when I turned to observe any evidence of Grey gaining the same information I did, and then I heard Kyle say, "There is absolutely nothing more important to me than this child. I'm only back in school in order to be my best for the baby. So, what time is the appointment? I want to be there when the doctor tells us about our daughter." *Oh, my God, he said **our** daughter. Who did he get pregnant? Then my mind flashed back to the two times I'd seen him with Camden. She was carrying his child, so that explained why they had been around each other a lot and he had put some distance between us, barely speaking to me on the rare occasions that we had talked.* I felt the tears threatening to fall, but once he disconnected the call, I pulled all the power in me in order to regain my composure.

But how can I stay calm? Kyle, my boyfriend, just said he's having a baby, and not with me! I don't want to have his child now, but I do hold the coveted position of being his girlfriend. I was the one he claimed he loved. I was the one he said inspired him to obey God at a higher level by abstaining from sex. *I guess he just had to have it, and since I wasn't giving it up, Camden was happy to. I knew she wanted him, but I had no idea that she would stoop so low as to use sex to lure him away from me. I can't believe this.* The thought of Kyle having sex and creating a baby with Camden made my heart feel as if it had been ripped straight through my chest and both lungs had collapsed.

Before I could expect it, Kyle turned around and Grey made his strong presence known behind me by putting one of his hands on my right shoulder. Instantly, I felt all the color in my face drain and my stomach began a gymnastics floor routine. I searched Kyle's eyes for any level of truth in them, and they greeted me with a cold, unfamiliar annoyance.

"Celeste is the mother."

So, it wasn't Camden, but Celeste being the mother of his child is no better. Now I know I'm going to be sick! Celeste? CELESTE? This is the same chick that he insisted was no good for him! Obviously, she had something that was good to him, something he couldn't resist. I think I could have somewhat accepted Camden, but to think that he had gone back to Celeste behind my back and done this.

I remember feeling my knees buckle, and attempting to spread my feet far enough apart to keep my body from hitting the floor. Hunched over at my waist, I felt like I couldn't breathe, and the need for air kept me from screaming out in pain and anguish. One of my hands quieted a yelp that wanted to escape my mouth while the other hand attempted to calm my stomach by grabbing it. My tears showered down my cheeks and over my hand. Kyle had just broken my heart and ended a promising future between the two of us. *Things will never be the same.*

I dropped everything in my arms and saw Grey and someone else frantically pick up my stuff. The cell phone that Kyle gave me for a Christmas gift landed between my feet, and I snatched it before the other two could get a hold of it.

Kyle tried to explain himself, but, thinking back to the misunderstanding about Grey's kiss on my forehead, I didn't see a reason why I had to listen to a single word he had to say.

Adrenaline-fueled strength returned to my body as I stood confidently and proclaimed that I didn't need him as a boyfriend anymore. Breaking all ties with him, I threw the phone into his chest and walked purposefully to the exit, resolving in my mind that nothing like this would happen to me again.

Part Three

Nineteen

HER WAY

"Avail, Stephanie, I don't know if I would have made it through this class without you and all the practicing we did together around my crazy basketball schedule. It's been fun. Thank you so much, ladies." Grey was his usual pleasant and polite self as everyone who had taken our intersession class relaxed at the post-performance social.

Truth be told, I should have been thanking him. Grey was a large part of the reason I hadn't lost my mind since breaking up with Kyle three weeks ago. Grey kept me busy with extra flute practices that I knew he really didn't need. He brought food from the cafeteria to my room so that I would not possibly run into Kyle; and, most of all, he invited me to a Bible study on campus that ministered on real issues such as the feelings one experiences following a breakup. The pain of what happened with Kyle was still there, but

I was now refocused on my studies as I contemplated what God required of me. It would be hard to see Kyle around campus, but I couldn't avoid him forever, and at least the painful part of the healing process was lessening with every day that passed.

I finished the last bite of a quiche appetizer and said, "Stephanie, I thank you for helping with our section solos, and as for you, Grey, you were sweet to initiate rehearsals after tiring basketball practices."

"It's been one of my favorite intercessions here," Stephanie offered before adding, "and it was a great idea to suggest to our professor that we do a multimedia documentary on our journey of being flutists instead of writing that required ten-page paper! That was sheer genius, Avail, and I had a good time with the two of you!"

After gaining the attention of all the students, our professor directed, "Before you leave tonight, be sure to turn in your instrument if you rented it. I hope you will continue playing the instrument you learned how to play this January, and maybe one day you will join the Whitaker ensemble or the pep band! If not, have a great upcoming second semester, and enjoy the remaining refreshments. Have a good evening, everyone!"

We gave our professor a round of applause and immediately began returning rented instruments. Behind me, I heard Grey ask, "So what's next for you, Avail? The Benedum? Carnegie Hall, maybe?"

I turned to him with a grin on my face and said, "Not hardly. This was a great experience, but I don't think I will pursue playing the flute more than we did in this class. It takes a large amount of dedication to perfect the skill of playing an instrument."

After turning in his flute, he concluded, "I guess I will have to find something else that will occupy your free time."

Stephanie motioned to us from across the room, and the three of us said our farewells before Grey and I started the route we normally took to my dorm after a late rehearsal. Turning my attention back to Grey's statement, I said, "Grey, I don't want to be your personal community service project." Grey looked a little hurt before I added, "You have been a great friend during a tough time in my life, and honestly, I don't know what I would have done without you, but I know you have other things to attend to, like your studies and your basketball skills."

Slowing our pace a little, Grey assured, "You never have to worry about my basketball skills being on point...."

"But I do," I interrupted. "We're a few weeks away from our conference tournament, and the way it looks, we will meet Waynesburg in the finals. Sure, you guys beat them the last time, but they'll want blood in the finals. The team made careless mistakes overall, and we will not win again if you guys fail to play a near-perfect game."

"I see what you're saying, but let my coach take care of that," Grey said with a laugh. "If you'd like, I'll share your concern with him! Meanwhile, I don't look at you as a community service project, a charity case, or anything like that. You're a friend of mine that I care about, and I didn't like having to see you in pain. My job as your friend was to do all that I could to help you with it."

Unlocking the outside door to my dorm, I added, "By 'it' you are referring to the breakup with Kyle. You know, you can mention the incident and the guy's name. It bothers me less and less every day."

"Oh yeah?" Grey said as we started up the back stairwell.

"Yeah," I affirmed. "The sound of his name or talking about the breakup is okay. The good teachings at the Bible study and my private prayers about this have helped me tremendously."

Just as we reached my door he asked, "I am curious; has he called or emailed you?"

"Only a few times immediately after the breakup. He hasn't tried since then."

Grey leaned against the wall next to my door and asked, "Are you okay with that?"

"I'm okay. I've accepted that this is the way it should be." I pulled out my key, unlocked my suite security door and my room door, and then turned to Grey. "As always, thank you for walking me back to my room."

I stepped into my brotherly hug from him as he said, "No problem, Avail. I'll check... ugh, I mean, I'll call you tomorrow." His facial expression showed proof that he knew he had revealed that he was still thinking of me as a special project.

I laughed and said, "Good night, Grey." I shut the door behind me and heard Grey run down the back steps. After I took my coat off and placed my bag in the chair by my study desk, I began prepping for bed by brushing my teeth, washing my face, and wrapping my hair. I returned from the bathroom I shared with my suite-mates and pulled out a set of pajamas to change into. Before I started changing, I heard a faint knock at my door. *Grey must have left the security door open.* I put my pajama set on my bed and opened the door without asking who was there.

What I saw made me wish that I had ignored the knock.

Nineteen

His Way

With his typical strong demeanor, Dr. Delta stood behind the podium with an officially sealed envelope that held the names of the winners of the prestigious Young Entrepreneur Award, and I could not keep my anxiousness under control. Small beads of sweat developed on the edge of my brow. Devin's nervousness showed through a tic in his leg, and Camden refused to blink her eyes, which were fixed on the envelope. Since the first week of intercession, our classmates had proclaimed that our group was a sure win. We always completed our assignments with excellence and often were used by Dr. Delta as examples of how to complete this or that, but I knew we had competition that could possibly pull a string here or there. Even though I was sure about our team winning, I needed confirmation. I needed Dr. Delta to call our names and proclaim to our class and everyone who attended the ceremony that my team had won the Young Entrepreneurs Award.

The tie around my neck seemed to grow tighter as Dr. Delta explained how the recipients would still manage to take classes as they opened their own business according to the guidelines in their submitted business plans. Devin actually had the boldness to loosen his tie and unbutton his suit jacket just as Dr. Delta managed to explain how a panel, all business major alumni who had started their own businesses, agreed that there was only one clear winner in all the projects they reviewed. Camden, who had managed to blink a few times, shifted her nervousness to my hand by squeezing it. She inhaled and exhaled through her mouth as though running sprints.

"And now, ladies and gentlemen, let's find out who this year's winner of the prestigious Whitaker University Young Entrepreneurs Award is…" and time froze for me.

I shifted my eyes to find my parents in the crowd. When I called and told them that my partners and I were finalists, they insisted on attending the award ceremony. My father looked as if he was uttering some type of prayer under his breath, and my mother had adopted a prayer posture with her head bowed and her hands clinched. I explained to them how beneficial it would be to earn this opportunity with the baby due in early May. They agreed that the award was an answer to my prayers about staying in school and beginning a career in radio.

Sitting two rows behind my parents were Celeste and one of her cousins who drove her wherever she wanted to go. Since my breakup with Avail, Celeste and I had talked almost every day so that I could stay up to date on her health and the progress of the baby. I would be a fool not to acknowledge how close we had become. It had been a natural process, because all our focus was on our child. I had been to every doctor's appointment since finding out about the baby, and we had shopped together for things we knew we'd need for two nurseries, one at her mother's house, and one at my parents' home. Things were going well, but I would also be a fool not to admit how much I missed Avail.

At such an important moment in my academic career, I wished Avail was here, sharing this with me. Whether I won or not, she'd know the perfect thing to say and would keep me completely grounded. Her smile would affirm how proud she was of me, and her hug would assure me that I had a safe place in her arms, but I didn't have that anymore, and it was entirely my fault. When I saw Celeste expressing a level of anxiousness that, to me, was completely self-serving, I wished she were Avail without the pregnancy.

If anyone had to be pregnant, I wish it was Avail—strange, I know, but my mind has been in a strange place this past three weeks.

I turned my attention back to Dr. Delta just as he opened the envelope and announced, "The winner is the team of Kyle Thompson, Devin Stepp, and Camden Bloom. Congratulations!" A round of applause from the crowd echoed throughout the auditorium, and when silence resumed, Dr. Delta explained,

"If you look in your programs, you'll see that this team has come up with an innovative way to start a radio station while working with Pittsburgh Public School high school students who are interested in broadcasting. Kyle, Devin, and Camden, please step forward to receive your award!"

The three of us stood on our feet and shook the hands of the members of the committee who sat on the stage with the finalists. Keeping our composure, we then shook the hands of the other finalists and Dr. Delta as well. Then, we congratulated one another. I shook Devin's hand and patted him on the opposite shoulder while I asked him, "Are you ready for this?"

"I am, boss!"

Camden could not contain herself and interrupted us with a hug while she jumped up and down. I managed to pry the arm she had draped around my neck and asked her the same thing: "Camden, are you ready for this?"

"You best believe I am! When do we get started?"

"You have twenty-four hours," Dr. Delta interjected. "Your alumni benefactors believed in your project so much that they want to hit the ground running. You have a day to pack up your dorm rooms, register for online classes, and report to the designated office space that they secured for you."

"Dr. Delta, when will we meet the benefactors?" I asked.

"They will meet you in your office space in two days. It's a good thing that all of you are from Pittsburgh. You can move back in with your parents immediately unless you want to find your own living arrangements." Dr. Delta cleared his throat and said, "Now it's time to celebrate and take tons of photos!"

And that we did. The press and Whitaker historians took pictures of our team and each of us with our families before and after reporters conducted interviews. I don't know how, but Celeste found her way into my family shot and made sure she remained by my side for every photo op.

"How are you feeling? You've been on your feet for almost three hours and I know you get tired." Celeste looked worn out, but she was still presenting herself as if nothing was bothering her physically.

"I'm good, Kyle. Your daughter, however, is a little hungry for more than just the heavy hors d'oeuvres served here. I'm going to see if my cousin will take me somewhere to grab a bite to eat before we head back to Pittsburgh." A sonogram at the first doctor's appointment I attended with Celeste confirmed that we were having a little girl—*a little girl to whom I have the responsibility of being the first example of a man. Every time I think about her, I get choked up.* I nodded before she added, "I'm proud of you, Kyle. You're going to be great at this. Your daughter and I have all the confidence in the world in you."

"Thank you," I said as I gave her a small hug. "Be careful getting home." I watched Celeste and her cousin walk away, and in that moment, I believed that everything was going to be all right.

I turned to my parents and waited for them to say their typical, heartfelt congratulations, but my mother greeted me with, "Did you invite her up here?"

"No, Mom, I didn't, but she knew it was happening. I kept her informed throughout the whole process so that she would know what I was doing for the baby."

"Are you sure she's not thinking that you're doing it for her *and* the baby?" my father quizzed. "Have you said anything to her to make her think that you want to reunite with her?"

"No, Dad, I haven't, and I've made it crystal clear to her that when we talk, we need to focus on our daughter."

My mother gasped suddenly. "Did you say daughter?" Happy tears filled her eyes. "You're father and I are going to have a beautiful granddaughter?" It had not hit me until that moment that I had never told my parents the sex of the baby, because every time we talked about the baby, they had something negative to say about the whole situation and about the fact that I refused to get a paternity test. I had learned not to mention it as much as possible. I looked at my father, and even he looked excited.

I smiled as I said, "Yes, you will." I pulled out my wallet and asked, "Would you like to see the first ultrasound picture?" They both looked as if they wanted to burst with grandparent joy.

*had been sitting on the back steps of Avail's dorm for the past hour, trying to figure out what I would say to her. I hadn't seen her since the incident in the cafeteria, and I had no idea where her head was when it came to me. I tried emailing her, but she never responded. I called a couple of times, and again, no response. She needed her space, and I understood that, but she could not keep me out of her life forever, especially since she had no idea that the baby was conceived before I met her.

I couldn't build the strength just to knock on her door, but at the same time, my body couldn't stay still. A sense of relief mixed with anticipation had kicked up my adrenaline levels, and I was exhausted and energized at the same time. Yes, I had worked hard throughout intercession, grabbing sleep here and there between class sessions and outside meetings with Devin and Camden, but mentally, my thoughts constantly reviewed where things went wrong with Avail and me. Was it completely fair of me to blame everything on Grey's close presence in Avail's life, or did I push her away because I couldn't imagine how things would work with Avail as my girlfriend and Celeste as my daughter's mother?

None of that matters now; the reality is that I'm leaving campus tomorrow, and I must move on.

As had become a habit for me when I faced a tough issue, I touched the cross pendant hanging from the chain that Avail gave me, and I listened for guidance from God as to what I should do. Eventually, I stood, looked up the stairs, and decided to finish my last night on campus packing my things in my dorm room.

Twenty

HER WAY

"What? You're not going to invite me in?" Celeste asked with a smug look on her face, standing with a strong posture that allowed her back to support the slight bump she advertised by maternally placing her hands on it.

I could not believe that Celeste had come all the way up to Whitaker County to, no doubt, flaunt her pregnancy in my face, and start some mess. On the outside, I played it cool, but on the inside, I flipped out. I had a reaction that I didn't expect—a sudden desire to smash her face in. It was a rage that I had seen in other females going crazy about other girls in the lives of their boyfriends, but never in a thousand years would I have imagined being able to identify with girls who wanted to fight over a guy.

On top of everything, this chick was pregnant by my ex and still had the boldness to come to my door this late.

"No, you're not welcome here," I said, and I attempted to close the door.

Celeste blocked the door and said, "Wait a minute, Avail. We have some things to get out in the open."

I stared at her hard and asked, "What could we possibly have to say to one another? Kyle and I broke up; you're pregnant with his child. End of story." Again, I tried to shut the door, but Celeste blocked it.

"But that's *not* the end of the story!"

"Celeste, if you raise your voice at me one more time, I will call security."

Gesturing toward the window, she said in a lowered volume, "Call security. I got my own version of security outside." Curiosity prompted me to look out the window. I saw another woman looking up at my window. When she saw me, she reached into her pocket and pulled out a switchblade that glinted in the streetlights. "So, either we can talk like grown women, or my cousin can come up here and make sure this doesn't get ugly."

I turned back around in complete survival mode. I remembered the crazy things Kyle told me that Celeste had done in the past, but this was insane. *Threatening my life? Really? Over a man?* As civilly as I could, I looked at the couch and asked, "Would you like to have a seat?"

"Now that's more like it."

"Get to the point, Celeste. What do you want?"

Celeste didn't bother to take the seat I offered her. An evil grin appeared on her face as she said, "I want you to leave Kyle alone."

Playing with her a little, I stated, "Kyle is a grown man; he can be with whomever he wants."

"This is true..." Celeste said in a fake pleasant tone, and then she lowered her voice and warned, "... anyone but you."

As if she had low comprehension skills, I asked, "I'm sure you know that we're not together anymore, right? You just heard me say that, right?"

Before answering, she sucked her teeth. "Yes, I know that, for now, you are not going together; however, I know Kyle well, maybe a little better than he knows himself. When he realizes that he misses you, he'll be back pleading with you, asking for your forgiveness, and proclaiming that the two of you can work things out. I'm here to tell you that as long as I can help it, y'all aren't getting back together."

Looking out the window at her "security guard," I proclaimed, "If I want him back, I'll take him back."

Celeste looked at me ready to pull her trump card. Carefully, she added, "I read somewhere that the bond between a man and a woman grows very strong when they have a child." She rubbed her belly again as she eyeballed me. "It's a bond so strong that no one or nothing can get between them." Celeste then took a few steps closer to me and whispered, "Are you willing to deal with me for the rest of your life just for the sake of having Kyle? You need to think about that, because this is a bond I'm willing to protect by any means necessary."

Tired of Celeste's verbal attacks and the thought of her cousin downstairs with a knife, I simply asked, "Really? Do what you gotta do, Celeste, because if what you say is true, and Kyle decides to approach me again, and I forgive him, he's as good as mine forever. Even with the baby, you are not a factor." I let that soak in before I added, "But I want you to think about this: you won't be able to get rid of me either, because if I take him back, we *will* get married, and then I'll be your child's stepmother." I walked back to my room, but right before I shut my door, I turned to witness Celeste's growing rage. Adding insult to injury, I said, "And we'll all be a happy family."

"When you least expect it, I'm going to get you. I promise you, you better watch your back."

That threat met the slamming of my room door and the loud click of my lock. Celeste no longer fazed me.

Twenty

HIS WAY

John asked, "Are you totally sure that you want to leave campus without saying anything to Avail?" He sounded concerned, but I knew that he probably already had plans for the extra room he'd gain when I moved out, and he was just yanking my chain about my decision not to say a word to Avail before leaving campus. "I doubt she even knows that you've won the YEA. I'm sure she'd talk to you if she knew you were moving off campus permanently. That puts a different spin on things."

John's comment didn't keep me from packing various items of clothing in a suitcase. I had to admit that he made sense, but I shared, "I feel like we've hurt one another too much."

"How did Avail hurt you?" John practically yelled. "Is it because she wouldn't switch out of the class she had with Grey?" John shook his head as he added, "Dude, that's downright selfish of you."

"It's not just that," I protested. "I know in my gut that there's something going on between the two of them."

"If something was going on between Grey and Avail, as small as this campus is, we would know. You're just using them as a reason to walk away from Avail. It makes you feel justified."

I stopped packing and stared at John because, though I knew he spoke the truth, I didn't want to hear it at that moment. "It's best this way." I started packing again.

"Again, you're being selfish. It's best for you because you don't have to deal with the complications of raising a child from another woman and maintaining a relationship with a woman you love."

I threw down the shirt that was in my hand and shot a deadly glare in his direction. "Do I have to remind you of all the stuff that Celeste has done to other women who attempted to be my girlfriend? Celeste is not just crazy; she's crazy enough to carry out her threats. Her defenses are probably upped a thousand percent since she's pregnant, and now she probably feels like she has to protect not just our child, but also the father of her child." I stopped and admitted, "I'm trapped."

"You're only trapped if you allow yourself to be trapped. You're going to fall straight into living a life with a woman you don't want and always wondering what could have happened between you and Avail."

The gravity of the situation prompted me to sit down and face John. "Dude, I'm in no position to win here. Avail probably thinks that I slept with Celeste while I was dating her. She didn't give me an opportunity to explain. I'm not someone she wants to see right now."

As if he was trying to pump me up before a game, John pushed, "The fact that she doesn't know that the baby was conceived before you met her is why you need to talk to her now. You can't leave campus with this unresolved." He paused a moment before he added, "This single decision—right here, right now—can impact the remainder of your life."

I knew he was right, but my pride would not allow me to admit it. I stood up and resumed packing my belongings. John must have felt as if I was a lost cause because he didn't bother to say another word.

⌒⌒

I didn't close my eyes at all the whole time I attempted to sleep. I just stared into the darkness replaying everything John had said and every good time I'd had with Avail here at Whitaker. I knew I was going to miss her, but my heart ached with the thought of not seeing her one last time before I began this new chapter in my life. I became restless at the thought of starting this business without her. The cross pendant she gave me shifted around my neck, and I had to get out of bed when the prospect of not having her in my life at all hit me with full force. *I have to do something.*

In an attempt to be as quiet as possible to keep from disturbing John, I slipped on a sweatshirt and a pair of shoes before I grabbed my keys and opened the door.

"It's about time some sense soaked into you. Go get her...." John mumbled as he turned over in his bed.

I just smiled and closed the door.

Twenty-One

HER WAY

"AVAIL, why didn't you call us?" Raine practically yelled at me after I told her and Shea about Celeste coming over here to confront me about leaving Kyle alone.

"I had no idea what Celeste would try to pull with her cousin downstairs, especially if Celeste told her to be on the lookout for the two of you. If Celeste knows where I live and how to get here, she probably also knows what you two look like. She would've remembered from seeing you at the football game last semester."

"I don't care," Shea proclaimed. If she wants to step up to me, then I'd be glad to slap the taste out of her and her cousin's mouth one good time."

Shaking my head at the thought, I told Shea, "You don't have the heart to hit a pregnant chick, and neither do I. When I opened the door and saw her standing there, I wanted to punch her, but there's something about a pregnant woman showing that reminds you that what you do to her will have an effect on the child…." I cut myself off because I didn't know if all this talk about women having babies bothered Raine being that she'd recently miscarried. I directed my attention to her and said, "Raine, does all this talk about Celeste's pregnancy bother you?"

Raine looked at me as if she had no idea what I was talking about for a split second. Recovering, she answered, "No, Avail, it doesn't. If it was meant for Reese and me to have that child, I'd still be pregnant."

Almost cautiously, Shea inquired, "How have you been dealing with the miscarriage? I mean, we still get together, hang out, go to games, and study together, but when Avail and I aren't around, are you okay?"

Raine took a deep breath before she began. "It hasn't been easy. Any unplanned pregnancy, on top of that, a pregnancy out of wedlock, isn't easy, but after the initial shock wore off, Reese and I became very comfortable with the idea of being parents while in school." She paused for a moment to gather her thoughts before continuing. "You guys know that we started making plans for what we would do. The only way I can explain it is that we know that there was a purpose in the whole thing. We miss her, but I don't think it will be the last time Reese and I experience the joys of becoming parents."

"What do you mean?" I asked immediately. "You're not actively pursuing a pregnancy now, are you?" I thought the idea sounded crazy, but since we're so cool, I felt free enough to ask.

Raine grinned before stating, "No, Avail, we're not. Actually, we're abstaining—until marriage!"

Shea's eyes shifted to Raine's ring finger on her left hand and demanded, "Are you guys engaged?"

I gasped.

"No, we're not—or, not yet, I should say—but we know we want to marry, and we have gone as far as looking at a date."

"So, when should we expect this grand event?" I inquired with a twinkle in my eye.

"We're looking at the evening of his graduation next year." We all squealed like schoolgirls before she added, "You know I'll let you know when it's official!"

We began a discussion of tentative wedding plans and commented on the fact that as bridesmaids, Shea would be coupled with Frick and I would be coupled with Grey. "Speaking of Grey," Shea interjected, "what's up with the two of you? Now that you and Kyle aren't together, the door seems to be wide open for him to slip into that vacant position as your boyfriend."

"I'm not thinking about dating anyone right now," I stated truthfully. *I'm working on getting over Kyle, and I've grown accustomed to the pain I feel anytime I think about why we broke up, but it's still too soon to consider dating anyone, including Grey.* "I'm not interested in any rebound relationships, and right now, that's what it would be. I still have too many feelings for Kyle to even give the best guy a chance with me. So, until I'm ready to be open for a lasting relationship without the drama of a crazy ex-girlfriend who happens to be the mother of the man's firstborn, then I'm not looking for a man. In fact, the Bible study I went to with Grey told us that young ladies shouldn't be doing the looking anyway!"

"You're talking about the story of Ruth and Boaz, right?" Shea asked. "I think that was the Bible study Frick and I came into late. I missed that part you're talking about."

Before I could confirm it and expand on the story, Raine interrupted, "Avail, did you say that Celeste was showing?" Her face looked puzzled as if she was trying to figure out something.

The confused look on my face joined hers as I answered, "Yeah, why?"

"How many months is she?"

"I don't know. What's your point, Raine?"

Shea's analytical mind kicked in as she asked, "Avail, when did Kyle get Celeste pregnant?"

"I don't know. I just assumed that it was sometime recently." Then the room fell quiet as we exchanged looks that spoke what we were all thinking. Even at the minimum, if Celeste was beginning her fifth month, it meant that Kyle got Celeste pregnant before coming to Whitaker…*before he met me.*

Without a word, I got up, grabbed a jacket, and left my two friends staring after me with knowing looks in their eyes.

Twenty-One

HIS WAY

It seemed my steps grew more urgent the closer I got to Avail's dorm. John had managed to convince me that I needed to talk to her before I left campus permanently. I had no idea what I would say, but something needed to be said. Leaving without attempting to explain was not an option.

I pulled out my cell phone just as I reached the back door of her dorm. I planned to call her in an attempt to convince her to come down three flights of stairs, let me in, and hear what I had to say in the middle of the night.

When I dialed her room number, an unexpected voice answered, "Hello?"

"Raine?" I asked. "I thought I called Avail's room."

"You did. She just left to see you."

This was almost a perfect setup. Avail obviously wanted to see me if she was heading over to my dorm, but I had no idea how I'd missed her since I'd taken the most direct route to her dorm. It didn't matter. I would wait for her to come back. "Raine, I'm at the back door. Can you come down and let me in?"

⁓

 A vail's door opened twenty minutes after Raine and Shea left. I swore them to secrecy about my presence in Avail's room and convinced them to find her and tell her to return to the room. As she normally did, she threw her keys on the desk and flipped on the light.

"Can we talk, Avail?"

I think I stunned her a little because she looked as if she was trying to mask her initial shock at my presence.

"Sure." She took a seat in her study chair and rolled it out to face me where I was sitting on her bed.

"Why were you heading to my dorm room this late?" I asked with a slight grin in an attempt to break the ice.

I saw a hint of a small smile before she said, "I wanted to talk to you about everything." She paused uncomfortably before she added, "I just thought about the fact that you got Celeste pregnant before you met me."

"I know; Raine and Shea told me about your conversation." I paused before I added, "I'm leaving campus tomorrow for good."

"Yes, I know. Raine and Shea told me when they found me at the locked door of your dorm. Congratulations on winning the Young Entrepreneurs Award." Her eyes reflected the confused pain she felt, as if she didn't know where to carry our conversation.

I blurted out, "Why did you think that Camden was the mother of my child?" That was one of the many things I had wondered about since out breakup scene in the Commons.

Snapping back to her usual self, she said, "I guess with all the closeness the two of you developed last semester working together added to the fact that I saw the two of you acting very close on more than one occasion this month, I felt like you were trying to play me. You knew I didn't like the way she always threw herself at you, but you kept being around her!"

Something in me snapped, and I reacted. "Well, you knew I didn't like you being around Grey, but he was always there, always around you, every time I looked up. Every time I saw you, I saw him. I asked you to do one simple thing about not being around him, and you couldn't do it—or you didn't want to do it."

"Would you have given up an opportunity to go for the award or if I had asked you to drop the class to limit your time with Camden?"

"No."

"And I didn't ask you to because it was an academic opportunity that could impact the rest of your life!" Avail screamed this last bit before pausing to breathe deeply to calm herself. "So what if my class wasn't at that level of academia! You asked me to compromise an academic pursuit because you didn't like someone in the class. You wanted me to sacrifice my intercession class, but I knew you weren't willing to do the same."

"You didn't ask me to. You could have asked me not to partner with Camden."

"Why should I have to make that request when you already know how I feel about you working with her? What would have been the point?" An uncomfortable silence answered Avail's question while I hung my head before grabbing my cross pendant and praying that this conversation would somehow take a turn for the positive. Not satisfied with my evasive answer, Avail continued, "Why did you partner with Camden anyway? You had a choice, I'm sure, and you chose to work with her. Ever since the snowball fight last semester, you knew how I felt about her interaction with you. She wants you."

"Like Grey doesn't want you—the man has told me over and over again that he'd slide right into my spot if I mishandled my relationship with you."

"Well, you have no spot now that we're not together. And we're not together because you decided to keep the pregnancy from me. Hiding such a huge secret created a separation between us that started when I left town for Christmas." She paused before she added, "Exactly when did you find out about Celeste's pregnancy?"

"The night of our Christmas date," I barely whispered.

"That explains a lot," Avail added sarcastically, but I didn't feel like challenging her. I just wanted all the outside interference and lack of communication to drift away so that we could be together again. Quietness absorbed a space of time before she continued, "Being together— that's what I wanted to talk about because somewhere in my mind, I thought it was doable. I thought that I could live with Celeste being the mother of your child and we could actually continue our relationship, but I was wrong."

The Lord did hear me! This was the turn I had prayed for! I softened my tone and said, "You're not wrong, Avail; we can do this."

I don't know how, but I know that if she wants to be with me, and I want to be with her, nothing can stop it from happening, not even Celeste.

"What about Celeste's crazy ways? What about the bond between a mother and father when their child is born? What about Camden leaving campus with you and working with you every day to establish your dream of owning a radio station? What about your subconscious feelings for Camden?"

"I don't have feelings for Camden."

Avail just shook her head as she said, "The whole point of subconscious feelings is that you have them and don't even know it." Then, she flipped the perspective: "What about you leaving me behind and wondering if Grey is making progress with me? What if I get the internship this summer in Baltimore, and you have to live with the idea that I'll spend gobs of time around Grey because my cousins hang out with him? Let's face it; long-distance relationships require a high level of trust. After what went down between Donovan and me, I don't see it happening. You and I both have trust issues when it comes to dealing with outsiders. These issues are bigger than you having a baby with Celeste."

I had to admit that everything she brought up was a valid point. Our daughter wasn't even here yet, and Celeste and I were closer now than we had ever been, sharing kisses on the cheek that crept closer and closer to our lips with each kiss. Camden would be a part of establishing the radio station simply because she was overseeing the education outreach portion of it, so yeah, she would be a part of my life for quite some time. I had to work with her.

And no, I don't trust Grey. I hate to admit it to myself, but I don't trust Avail around Grey. Even though I know she loves me, she's in denial about her feelings for Grey.

I stood up definitively and declared, "You make great points. I guess we have nothing else to talk about." I looked at my watch and said, "I have to go. I need a little rest before I drive home in a few hours." I walked toward the door.

To my back, Avail asked, "Is that it? This is how we're going to end things between us?"

I stopped in my tracks, and the cross pendant shifted under my shirt. Without turning around, I asked her, "Do you want this?"

"What do you mean?"

I turned around and pulled the pendant from under my sweatshirt. "Do you want this?"

Avail gazed at the cross that managed to catch a little light from a desk lamp she had turned on when she entered the room. "I told you that I wanted you to never take it off. So, I want you to keep it."

I planned to honor her request of wearing the cross at all times, but I felt like I had to leave one last pleasant memory with her. Stepping into her private space, I barely whispered, "But when you want this back," pausing to kiss her with all the tenderness I could gather to express my regret for us breaking up, "you know how to reach me. I love you, Avail."

Walking away from her was the hardest thing I had ever done.

Twenty-Two

HER WAY

"So Kyle has left campus, and the two of you are really over?" Grey inquired after we greeted one another after checking our mail in the student center.

It was six weeks into our spring semester, and I had barely uttered a word to anyone. Raine and Shea did their best to keep my spirits up, allowing me to confide in them, but I didn't want to bother Grey with this drama. I was glad that he understood why I decided to put some space between us while I attempted to recover from the breakup. In answer to his question, I said honestly, "Yes; he, Camden, and their partner Devin have started their project that won them the Young Entrepreneurs Award. They're in Pittsburgh and full-time online students with Whitaker now. I haven't talked to him or seen him since the end of intercession."

"Avail, I'm so sorry. With everything that has been going on with basketball, I haven't been there for you the way I'd like to be." Grey had been exceptionally busy, especially with winning the conference championship and the team going all the way to the Sweet Sixteen of the NCAA Championships. I knew that juggling schoolwork with grueling basketball practices and press interviews left him with just enough time to eat and sleep, and not much else. I wasn't trippin' about the fact that I hadn't heard from him. "Is there anything I can do?" Grey asked as he shifted through his mail.

"Not really." I looked through my pile of mail as well, noticing a thick yellow envelope from Chrys. I opened it and pulled out the copied papers that had been placed in the envelope without being folded. A hastily written note was clipped to them.

Grey noticed a package from Morgan State University. He held it out and said, "This is the announcement packet about the available internships in Baltimore that your cousins and I told you about!"

I glanced through the papers from my cousin and declared, "Apparently, Chrys received her information too and made me photocopies." Immediately, Grey and I headed for a booth in the snack area and began reading through the papers; we were anxious to find a specific internship that would give us both experience in our subject areas as well as class credit. "Look," I insisted. "On page three, there's an opportunity for me to work on drafting curriculum for specific classes in the education department."

"That sounds great," Grey affirmed, "but it sounds like a ton of research. You don't want to do something fun too? I'm looking at this internship right here that allows me to work with a basketball league while observing the psychology of the male athlete—right up my alley!"

Grey sounded so excited that I couldn't help but be happy for him. "Well, if you decide to apply for that, I hope you get it. Where will it be held?"

"It's on the campus of Morgan."

I continued to search through the paperwork Chrys had sent me, specifically looking for the opportunities that, according to her note, she thought would be perfect for me. On the last page, she circled an opportunity requesting four dance instructors. "This sounds perfect for me," I uttered under my breath.

"Which one is that?"

I pointed to the description as I said, "This one; it's a camp for inner city girls who are interested in dance. The description states that the applicant would have to use the new Common Core Standards in English Language Arts in conjunction with the skill of dance to promote reading and writing skills." I drifted off for a moment as I imagined how I would do it. Ideas flew to my mind instantly. "I could do this!" The secondary education elective I enrolled in for the spring would help me with the standards, and my dance background qualified me for the position. I shifted my attention to Grey who looked like he was a little surprised.

"Aside from dancing at parties, I didn't know you could dance—you know, formal and all."

"Yeah," I shared bashfully. "I can do just about anything but tap. I never took classes in that." We chatted excitedly as we chose our top three internships that the application required us to submit.

"Avail, if we want to be selected for our top choice, we need to apply online so that they get our applications immediately."

"Do you have your laptop with you?"

Grey grinned as he said, "I sure do. Let's apply now!"

⁓

I went to my afternoon class with a little more spark in my spirit since completing the application for the internships over the summer. Chrys sounded so excited in her note, expressing over and over again how she hoped that I would seriously consider coming back to spend a portion of the summer with her and Dill. I had to admit to myself that I loved my time with them. They were so easy to get along with, and they loved having a good time; but more than that, there was something about hanging out with Chrys that I really enjoyed. I didn't have sisters or other female family members around my age in Pittsburgh, and I supposed we had bonded for that reason. Just like with my brothers, it wasn't to say that Dill wasn't a great brother to Chrys, but there were certain things that only other young women could understand. We already had so much in common, including our two friends, Frick and Grey.

When I ran into Frick before class, he told me that he had shared the internship information with Shea and that Reese had given it to Raine as well. "Yeah, Shea and I sent in our applications during lunch," he added.

"What about Reese and Raine?" I inquired.

"When I told them that spaces fill up quickly, both of them filled out their applications on the spot. Dill, Grey, Reese, and I are talking about renting a house this summer in order to cut Grey's and my commute and to help out Reese since it'll be an extra expense for him, being that he must rent a spot since he'll come up from Atlanta. What are you planning to do for housing?"

I hadn't thought about it, but I shared, "I imagine that wherever Chrys stays, I'll stay. I'll see what Raine and Shea are thinking about doing too." Before I made too many plans in my head, I asked, "How do we know that we'll get accepted? I mean, I would think that tons of qualified students would apply for internships like these."

Frick began his sentence with a smile and said, "Those of us who have been a part of this in years past are selected first as long as we did a good job the year before. Then, if things get competitive, they ask us for recommendations of friends and family members who have applied, and who would be good for the specific programs the committee is thinking about placing them in. I think between Dill, Chrys, me, and...uh... Grey, you'll definitely be in!"

I busted out laughing before I picked at him a bit. "Why the stumbling over Grey's name?"

"Straight up?"

"Yeah, straight up," I insisted.

"Well, you know he likes you."

I played dumb on purpose and said, "Okay…and?"

He chuckled as he said, "It will be cool to see the two of you get to know each other better over the summer. During summer internships, things aren't as tense as they are around here during the school year. Everyone is much more laid back. We have time to hang, plan our futures, go to and conduct Bible studies, and travel to different cities around Baltimore. It's just a different vibe. So you'll get to meet the chilled-out Grey."

"I'd like to think that I have seen glimpses of that side of Grey already."

"And you have, but you'll see it much more."

I wasn't letting Frick off the hook so easily. "Well, what does getting to know the chilled-out Grey have to do with him liking me?"

"He'll get to meet the chilled-out, no-drama, no-boyfriend Avail." He paused before he added, "Just be aware that he's watching you, and that's a good thing." With that, Frick ran into the building because he was almost late for class, and I pondered his words.

So, Grey's watching me. Is there something in particular he's looking for in the next woman he can imagine dating? If so, do I have it? Honestly, I don't know why any guy would like me at the moment. I'm doing my best to recover from my recent breakup with Kyle, but I'm a complete mess right now. My heart is mending, but it's a painful process. My trust in guys has dropped to a newfound low, and I don't think I have the energy it takes to grow another relationship right now. Grey is wonderful, ideal even, but I've got to have my time to become whole and remember who I am, and focus on the God-given goals I want to achieve in school. I don't know for how long, but for now, I need to focus on me.

Twenty-Two

His Way

"The blueprint we will follow for the radio station will be the business plan you turned in to Dr. Delta. It was flawless, and we could not believe that two freshmen and a sophomore developed such a concept," Natalie Dunwright stated toward the end of the first meeting in our grand office space above the train station in downtown Pittsburgh. It gave us ample space for meetings and individual offices, and it even included three apartments down the hall. Devin, Camden, and I decided to take a month before we moved into the apartments, but we would work at least six days a week to begin the planning stages of our project. As she and the other members of the alumni committee stood and shook our hands, she stated, "Your first task is to decide your annual wage. This is separate from the scholarship Whitaker is giving you for winning the YEA; this money will be the salary you earn while growing your business. Salary negotiations will begin in forty-eight hours." With that, we watched them walk out the room almost military style and waited for the sound of the elevator before we expressed our elation.

"I can't believe this is happening for us!" Camden practically screamed.

Devin added, "I'm totally and completely thrilled…"

All I could do was thank God silently that they had accepted the part of the proposal where we asked for professional wages as students.

This opportunity guarantees that I'll be able to provide for my daughter without having to quit school or look for a job.

⌒

" So, how did the negotiations go? Did the three of you get what you asked for?"

With a grin, I told Celeste, "Yes, we did! I couldn't believe it. They even kicked in health and wellness benefits. It just blew me away. After we told them that we had researched the average salaries of the positions that other people in our position received, and we took into account the rent-free and utilities-free office space and apartments, they agreed that we were justified in what we asked for." I paused before adding, "Now, do you see why I had to come back to Whitaker?"

Celeste sat comfortably on one of the lounge chairs against the exposed brick wall in the waiting area of our office space with her left leg folded under her right thigh. She claimed that it was the most comfortable way for her to sit during her seventh month of pregnancy. This time in her life had served her well. The calm attitude she had chosen to adopt had given her an enhanced glow. She smiled much more and was careful about who she was around and what she said to anyone because she didn't want it to affect Kyla. *Yes, our baby daughter Kyla....* We picked out her name when Celeste insisted on naming her after me. I didn't know what the female version of Kyle would be, so I left it up to Celeste to create or find a name. When I asked about her middle name, Celeste told me that she had prayed to God so much for grace and mercy during the pregnancy that she wanted Kyla's middle name to be Grace. So our daughter's name was complete: Kyla Grace Thompson.

"I do see why you had to go back, and I'm so glad that you did. God is really blessing you, and I really don't think this would have happened if you hadn't been at Whitaker."

I had to admit to myself that over the past few months, Celeste was changing before my eyes. I always knew that God was a major factor in her life, but, for lack of a better way of acknowledging it, now she *acted* like it. On a nightly basis, she told me what she prayed over Kyla, how she repeatedly thanked God for His forgiveness, and that she asked Him for strength to make it through the remaining months of her pregnancy. Whenever I was around Celeste and we could catch a private moment, I would place my hands on her belly and we'd pray together about our little girl's future. There were several times when Kyla moved around, reacting to the prayer, and that always made my heart swell. *She is already Daddy's little girl.*

As I always did before I invaded Celeste's personal space, I asked, "May I? I have something to say to Kyla."

Celeste unfolded her leg and stood gingerly to her feet with assistance from me. I fell to my knees, positioned myself to the side of Celeste's belly, placed my hands on it and said, "Daddy did well today, Kyla, and it's all for you! God has set me up so that I can take care of you. He has provided me the overwhelming blessing of this opportunity, and I'm so grateful. Daddy's even more grateful for having you. I got to get back to work, so take a nap and stop kicking Mommy so much. I love you!"

Celeste placed her hands on her belly not too far away from mine and said, "Did you hear Daddy?" She chuckled a little before adding, "Mommy loves you too." Every word was infused with maternal kindness.

"I really do have to get back to work. Not only am I a full-time general manager of a radio station we have yet to create, but I'm a full-time student too." With all the excitement about Kyla, I tended to forget to ask Celeste how things were going with her life. "Hey, how are your classes?"

I hated the fact that Celeste insisted on going to school this semester since a majority of the semester would be during her second and third trimester. In the past, whenever she was stressed over an assignment, she complained about having stomach cramps. I made it clear to her that she would have to relax even though she was taking classes. She assured me that she would be fine because she had modified her schedule to take only electives. To appease me, she'd added a swimming class to fulfill her health and physical education core requirement, and to strengthen her body without straining it and while remaining relaxed.

"Everything's going well," she said. "I stay ahead on my assignments, and my tests haven't been giving me too many problems. The bigger I get, the better swimming is for me since it takes stress off my joints. Kyla seems to like it too. She's the most calm when we're in the water." We both grinned before she insisted, "Get to work. You have a lot to take care of." She leaned in, gave me a kiss on the cheek, and walked outside the waiting area to the elevators.

Indeed, Kyla is a lot to take care of.

Twenty-Three

HER WAY

"I got in! And I got my first choice!" Shea yelled as I opened my dorm room door an early Saturday morning, the weekend before finals for the spring semester began. The sunlight from the late April morning crept through the cracks of the blinds, forcing me to accept that I'd probably be up for the remainder of the day. The semester had been brutal due to all my professors calling for papers and projects around the same due dates. I barely had time to hang out with Raine and Shea, and I couldn't remember the last time I had joked around with Grey, Frick, and Reese. My life this past semester consisted of waking up, working out, going to class, going to the library or my work assignment to study, and coming back to my room to study a little more before passing out from everyday exhaustion. There was the occasional party, but I swapped those for rest. The only thing I didn't compromise for the sake of my studies was the Bible study I attended with Grey. The practical lessons and sharing about the topics helped me too much to let them go.

"Congratulations," I shared as Shea breezed by me to enter my room.

"Well," she inquired, "did you get in too?"

I stumbled back to bed, got under my covers, and said, "I don't know."

"Avail, check your email right now! I've gotta know if this summer has the potential of being the best summer of our lives with all of us getting to work and hang together in B'more!"

Waking up a little, I asked, "All of us? Did everyone else get in too?"

"Yep—me and Frick, Raine and Reese, and Grey. You're the last one we're waiting to hear about." She picked up my iPad and shoved it toward me, commanding, "Check your email!"

I smirked as I took the tablet and opened my mail. Part of me doubted that I had earned one of the internships. My online interview went well, but that did not mean that I'd automatically get a spot. There were always better candidates out there, and maybe I wasn't all that the program was looking for. When they asked me what literature I'd use, I automatically told them that my first choice would be the Bible. Literarily, it's the perfect blend of nonfiction via true accounts, stories through the various shared parables, and poetry from the lyrical books. Plus, the stories shared in the Bible can apply to anyone's life and connect with many of the gospel and Christian music selections that I imagined I could use in the class. Interweaving writing assignments with it would be a snap. The interviewers seemed to appreciate my answers, but I had no idea if they wanted such a strong emphasis on the Bible. Before I opened the email from Morgan State, my phone rang. I gestured for Shea to answer it.

"Avail, it's Grey. He wants to know if you opened your notification from Morgan yet." I reached my hand out for Shea to give me the phone as I clicked on the email.

"Well, did you get it? Did you get in?" Grey quizzed.

Shea looked on while I read the first few lines of the email aloud: "Miss Andrews, we are pleased to inform you that you have been granted a position in the Morgan State University Summer Enhancement Internship Program as a dance instructor in our performing arts division...."

I remembered Shea and me screaming like little girls, but I thought I caught a portion of Grey telling someone, "She got in! And she's one of the dance instructors!" I imagined that he had shared the information with Frick and Reese. "Avail, have you heard from Dill and Chrys?"

"Actually," I paused as I opened an email from Chrys, "I just did. Chrys says that both of them are in and doing elevated positions of what they did last year. We'll all be together!"

Shea added, "So I'll finally get to meet these cool cousins of yours!" I smiled at her comment as Shea got up walked to the door, "I have to run. I need to finish a final examination paper. Congratulations, Avail! This summer is going to be awesome!"

In the midst of Shea's joy, I almost forgot that Grey was still on the phone until he said, "I agree. It's going to be a great summer. I get to hang with my tightest of tight boys, m'girls, and you."

I noticed something in Grey's statement that prompted me to tease him a little. "I'm not one of your girls? And all this time, I thought we were cool."

"Avail, you know we're cool, but I look at you a little differently than I do Chrys, Shea, or Raine. You know some secrets about me they don't, so that puts you in a different category." After a small pause, he asked, "Do you see me the same way you see Frick, Reese, or even your cousin Dill?"

His question made me sit up and feel a little more alert. "No."

"So, you see what I'm saying." I nodded my head as if he could see me, but I said nothing. Without needing a reply, he said, "I'll get in touch with you before finals are over, but I gotta run now. Congrats again." I heard the smile in his good wishes.

"Okay, and thank you," was all I could say before I disconnected my end of the call.

Sliding down to the side of my bed and beginning my morning prayers, I thanked God for my family and friends, for the beautiful day He had made, and for the opportunities He'd sent my way; then I asked for strength to make it through the finals. "Lord, I'm so excited about the possibilities within the internship you just blessed me with that I don't want it to be a distraction from my studies." I paused as if God didn't already know my internal thoughts. I confessed, "And I don't want Grey or what I have with Grey to be a distraction either. Keep the two of us focused on what we need to accomplish before the end of the semester, and we'll be just fine. I need to wrap up this year on a positive note and maintain my grades, and because I know my success is only because of You, I will give You all the glory, praise, and honor for how this semester turns out. It's in Jesus's name I pray, amen."

With that, I stood to my feet and prepared myself for a day of reviewing key notes and previous readings from earlier in the semester.

Twenty-Three

HIS WAY

I nearly jumped out of my skin when Celeste's ring-tone blared in the predawn hollowness of my apartment. I'd finished moving in just a few nights ago, and I carried an exhaustion that hadn't been alleviated by the six hours of sleep I had been getting every night. After stocking the apartment with all the essentials, one of the last things I managed to set up was Kyla's crib in her small spot in my bedroom, but her presence was all over my parts of the office I shared with Devin and Camden. Kyla's playpen sat behind my desk, and her changing table found space in my private bathroom. I even carved out closet and drawer space for her since she had an entire wardrobe and toys at my place thanks to her eager grandparents.

Without realizing it, Celeste's call must have gone to voicemail, and a piece of me was thankful. I was too tired to get up and find my cell phone. I couldn't imagine what could be so important that she had to call this late. I rolled over and attempted to go back to sleep.

Then, her ringtone blared out again, and this time, the very sound seemed as if it were screaming at me, demanding me to answer the phone immediately. By this time, Camden and Devin came to my doorway to encourage me to answer the phone so they could go back to sleep just when I picked it up and said, "Celeste, what in the world are you calling so late for? What do you need?"

"It's time," she proclaimed breathlessly. "My water broke and I'm on the way to the hospital."

I jumped out of bed and nearly ran over Camden and Devin as I headed for the elevator. "What's going on?" Devin yelled at my back.

"Celeste is in labor. Kyla is on her way!"

⌒

After taking the elevator all the way down to the parking deck and realizing that I had forgotten my keys, phone, and a shirt to throw on with my pajama bottoms, Camden and Devin took the elevator down after I did, brought all the elements I was missing, including a pair of shoes, and insisted on driving me to the hospital. When we arrived, the nurses on the labor and delivery floor of Magee Women's Hospital told Devin and Camden where to take me.

A surge of emotions and feelings ran through me that I could not exactly articulate. On top of a foundation of fear, I was excited, nauseated, fearful, anxious, and thrilled. My daughter, my firstborn, was preparing to make her way into the world. Initially, I couldn't have been more disappointed with the conception of this child. I had managed to get Celeste out of my life only to keep her in it permanently by getting her pregnant months before. Then, I got involved. When I saw that first ultrasound picture, my knees buckled and Kyla became the center of my world. I worked hard to earn the Young Entrepreneurs Award because of her. I have set up a future for her. I even walked away from the love of my life for her.

Though I doubt I'll ever forget Avail, my daughter took precedence over everything in my life except God. I was getting ready to walk into the active role of being a father, and I wanted to do the best job I possibly could. I prayed constantly about the role I'd have in her life, and I read every scripture in the Bible that had anything to do with being a father. *I'm charged with the responsibility to provide for her, protect her, and raise her to be a God-fearing young lady. I need to be the example of manhood to her so that she won't fall for tricks I once pulled. I need to be the first reflection of God's love in her life, but the key thing is that I plan on being in her life, actively, every day if possible, but it will take a ton of coordination with Celeste.*

Once we reached the ward where they took Celeste, the nurses directed Camden and Devin to the waiting room, and one of them urged, "There's not much time. You've got to hurry!"

Operating room scrubs and shoe protectors seemed to instantly attach to my clothes as the nurse and I slammed into a private birthing suite where I heard the doctor say, "Okay Celeste; this next push should do it and then your baby girl will be in this world…."

Celeste's mother stepped aside and encouraged me to take Celeste's hand. With her eyes tightly shut, Celeste screamed, "Not without Kyle. Kyla is going to have to wait for him!"

I squeezed her hand with half the intensity she used on mine, bent down to her ear, and whispered, "I'm here, so push and bring Kyla into this world safely."

And she did.

Twenty-Four

HER WAY

"Avail, I apologize that I could not touch base with you before I left campus, but my parents arrived at Whitaker a little earlier than I expected," Grey began an email he sent me from Baltimore once he got home. My last final was scheduled for three hours before campus closed. While I took my final, my parents packed up my room for me. As soon as I finished, we were on our way to Pittsburgh. Only because I was so preoccupied did I not even notice the fact that I had not heard from Grey. He continued, "Frick and I are planning to look for a place to rent near Morgan for the summer. Before we know it, it'll be time to start our internships." We had only ten days between the end of our semester and the beginning of the summer program to find somewhere to stay, so timing was tight. "I'm so glad that you'll be joining us here. I can't wait to see you again."

After reading Grey's email, I slipped into a quiet, reflective mood. Since my breakup with Kyle and my pseudo-acceptance of Grey being attracted to me, I had become a little more protective of my heart. I didn't know if I could survive another breakup similar to the one I'd endured with Kyle, but I knew that if I considered dating again, I'd be vulnerable to that possibility. The only reason I thought so deeply about the idea of dating, and the possibility of dating Grey, was that the relationship itself would be a long-distance one in a year. Grey would graduate and move on to the things that were planned for his life, and I would be left behind with two more years to finish at Whitaker. Though Grey was clearly in another league compared to Donovan and Kyle, the whole concept of another long-distance relationship combined with excelling in my classes might be too much for me.

I'll have to trust that our friendship will be enough, and if we're supposed to see each other exclusively, things will work out for that to happen. For now, I'm looking forward to a fun-filled summer of doing what I love and spending time with my cousins and good friends.

$\sim$

After helping them with their bags, I immediately made introductions. "Chrys, these are my girls from Whitaker, Raine and Shea; Raine and Shea, this is my cousin, Chrys." The three of them greeted one another, and all four of us carried their bags to the room Raine and Shea would share.

We were very fortunate with the place that Uncle Bryan had found for us: a six-bedroom, six-bathroom fully furnished brownstone duplex where the women would stay on one side and Dill, Reese, Frick, and Grey would stay on the other. There were separate entrances for both sides of the duplex, but both sides shared a basement. Chyrs and I had rooms to ourselves, and Raine and Shea opted to share the last room. With four people splitting the rent and utilities for our side of the duplex, our total costs for our living space would be less than two-hundred dollars for the duration of the internship.

Another plus to finding this brownstone was its location. We were within walking distance of anything we would need. Everyone's internship was on campus, but at the last minute, my site had been moved to a local community center just a few blocks beyond Morgan. I figured that, on a daily basis, I would walk with everyone and continue my trek to my site. All the programs ended around the same time, so everyone could wait for me and we could walk home together.

"Knock, knock," I heard Dill's familiar voice as all the guys came through the front door of our side of the duplex. All of us ran downstairs and greeted them. I first ran to Dill and gave him a hug. "What's up, cuz?" he said with his usual greeting.

"Nothing much," I answered as I came out of the hug. "I'm looking forward to the summer with y'all!" I then noticed how Raine went directly to Reese and Shea glided over to Frick, and they greeted one another as if they had not seen each other in weeks.

I grinned before Dill encouraged, "Go see y' boy," referring to Grey, who finished hugging Chrys and beheld the same scene I did between the two couples.

We made eye contact, and I felt a slight blush skip across my cheeks. Instead of standing there awkwardly, I exchanged places with Chrys and stepped into a different hug from Grey. It wasn't the same brotherly hug that he normally gave me at Whitaker. I couldn't put my finger on it, but it felt a little more affectionate, a little more intimate, and much warmer than usual.

Maybe this was the difference between the on-campus Grey and the laid-back Grey that Frick said I would get to know this summer.

"Hi," I said tentatively.

"Hey," he responded, coupled with a smile. "I know you drove over to B'more with Dill and Chrys, but how was your trip to Hagerstown?"

As we slid out of the hug, Grey maintained physical contact with me by lightly lacing his fingers in mine. I bit my bottom lip as I beheld our connection, and I somehow managed to answer, "It was a smooth trip." Making eye contact with him, I confessed, "I'm glad to be here."

By 'here' I meant standing in his presence, being the object absorbing all of his attention, and apparently his affection too. His beautiful brown eyes looked relaxed, and a glow within him shone through his chocolate-hued skin. The half-smile on his face showed just enough of those bright-white teeth and demanded me to stare at those perfectly formed lips I remembered shaping with my fingers when we learned how to play the flute together. Just for a moment, I was wrapped in the enigma of friendship and attraction, wondering if this was how something between us would start and just how much interest I should show.

"It seems like it's been forever since I saw you last. I'm glad you're here too."

I didn't know if Grey was aware, but I noticed that everyone stopped what they were doing and watched us closely. It felt as if their glances were cheering us on, hoping that we'd become what they wanted us to be: a couple.

To break all the anticipation in the room, I asked, "Is anyone ready for dinner? I feel like cooking!"

With that, I unlaced my fingers from Grey's and headed to the kitchen with my cousins.

Twenty-Four

His Way

" *I*t must be nice to sleep so much every day. Enjoy it, Kyla; enjoy it, my princess."

I had just finished burping Kyla after her evening feeding before she drifted off into a nap on my shoulder. We sat in my black leather office chair, and I reclined it in such a way that the slight bouncing motion of it simulated that of a traditional rocking chair. I had a project in front of me on my desk, but my times with Kyla made everything else seem unimportant and not as pressing as when she stayed with Celeste. As I normally did with her, I hummed some of the songs that appeared on the playlist I created for the sound system near her crib, and I prayed over her, stopping to talk to her about whatever popped into my mind. When she was awake, I'd read to her, but she didn't have the privilege of hearing typical children's books. She listened to me read about business theory, how to do this or that in the radio industry, and anything I had to read for electives I chose to take. It never mattered what I read to her; the sound of my voice always caused those huge light brown eyes she got from her mother to flash with genuine interest and love.

Kyla wasn't even a month old, and she had me wrapped around all ten of her little baby fingers. I spoiled her terribly by holding her all the time. She'd fall asleep, and I knew I should put her in her crib or in her playpen, but it was hard to let her go. So, I learned how to hold her in one arm and use my other arm to complete tasks that needed my attention. On the few occasions where I had to lay her down, she would wake up fussy, as if she wondered where Daddy went. As soon as she would see me, she would calm down and wait for me to scoop her up in my arms.

I'm so in love, and though I wish the circumstances of her conception and birth were different, I can honestly say that I would not trade anything for having her in my life. She's such a blessing, and her short existence has made me strive to be a better man for her sake.

I closed my eyes for a brief moment and stroked Kyla's back while we rocked in the chair. Her breathing pattern seemed to match mine, and she slept with not a care in the world. I felt myself getting a little sleepier than normal, so in order to avoid any accidents, I walked to my apartment, placed Kyla in her crib, and grabbed the baby monitor. Before I left, I pulled out my cell phone and snapped a couple of pictures of her. It amazed me how much she had grown since her birth, and the daddy in me wanted a record of it all. I spoke a prayer of peace over her before I left the bedroom.

Once I reached the office, I looked at the pictures that I had snapped just moments before, and it occurred to me that I had yet to tell Raine and Shea about Kyla being born. I pulled up the picture I thought was the cutest of them all, attached it to an email to them, and began, "Hey, I just wanted you to know that my daughter, Kyla Grace Thompson, was born three weeks ago, and already is the center of my world! I've attached a picture of her. It's too bad that she didn't have her eyes open; they are gorgeous." I paused in my typing just to take a moment to stare at the picture of my daughter. I continued, "I hope you have a great summer, and I'll be sure to stop by and see you when I have to make stops on campus next semester. Take care."

After I finished proofreading the email, I decided to add the addresses of John, Reese, and a few of my former football teammates from Whitaker and high school. Reese and I had established a cool friendship shortly after Raine lost their baby, and before I left, he told me to keep him in the know when it came to Kyla's birth.

Before I hit Send, I contemplated the idea of sending the message to Avail. I wanted to share the news with her as well, but I thought it would be a bit cruel to send this email with the picture of Kyla attached to it.

I know she wishes me no ill will when it comes to my daughter, but if I placed myself in her shoes, and she was the one who had a baby with Donovan, I know for a fact that I wouldn't want to see pictures of the child.

Resolving not to include Avail, I sent the email.

Twenty-Five

HER WAY

"It's apparent that we're not going to go out to eat at all with all these gourmet cooks here!" Shea said after we finished our family-style meal. "Dill, that lemon herb butter salmon was unbelievable." Thankfully, Uncle Bryan had stocked the house with groceries before we arrived, so we had no reason not to cook. In addition to Dill's salmon, I sautéed a mixture of fresh zucchini and squash and placed it over a bed of rice. Raine baked a specialty of hers, mini fruit pies, and Frick contributed by making a mixture of lemonade and tropical punch Kool-Aid. Since we cooked, Chrys, Reese, Shea, and Grey agreed to clear the table and wash the dishes. In fact, we decided that we would maintain the idea that if a group cooked, the others would clean.

I had never been one to make a large mess while cooking, so as Chrys and Shea grabbed dishes off the table, I shared, "There's not too much to clean up. Most of this can go in the dishwasher, and the few pots and pans we used can be cleaned within ten minutes or so."

Grey, who had left the table moments before, came back in and announced, "I just finished the pots and pans, and Reese is in the kitchen wiping counters and sweeping the floor. After Chrys and Shea finish clearing the table, I'll wipe that down."

I took that as my cue to leave the table and relax in front of the television. I grabbed the remote and plopped down next to Dill. Before I realized, he snatched the remote out of my hand and stated, "I want to see if there are any basketball games on."

I punched him in the arm in an attempt to get the remote back, but he didn't budge. It wasn't like I didn't like basketball, but at that moment, I felt like a movie. Instead of fighting with Dill, I reached for my iPad that sat on the coffee table and decided to check my mail. "I wonder what this is," I thought aloud.

"What?" Dill asked.

"I got a list of Bible study subjects and the schedule for them from someone I don't know; they're here in Baltimore, though."

Overhearing me, Frick said, "Oh, don't trip out about that. Grey and I put you, Raine, and Shea on an email list for the Bible study we'll be attending while we're here. We figured that you would want all the study notes and other stuff that goes along with it. If you don't want to stay on the list, you can opt out of it with a link at the bottom of the email."

"I'm going to grab my tablet right now to see what subjects are on the list," Raine stated as she went up the steps.

Shea pulled out her phone and pulled up her email immediately. Let's see what we'll be studying...." Shea cut herself off and froze. Figuring that she saw something on the list that she didn't like, I leaned toward her to see what might have caused her to react the way she did. I was thankful to see topics like how to forgive people, what to do when you don't know what to do, and preparing for marriage, but I didn't see anything that would cause her to crush her own countenance.

When Raine returned downstairs, she sat next to me on the couch and remarked, "Let's see this list." She was silent and moment, and then she proclaimed, "Hey, I got an email from Kyle."

"I did too," Reese stated as he took his rest in an oversized recliner. After punching buttons on his phone, he added, "There's some type of attachment."

I turned my attention toward my inbox and immediately noticed that Kyle hadn't sent me the email that he'd sent Raine and Reese. Most likely, Shea had it as well, and I wondered if that had made her freeze.

Out of sheer curiosity, and in an attempt to make it seem like I could handle hearing Kyle's name, I asked, "What's going on with him?"

No one responded. Rained had a pained expression on her face, while Reese feverishly replied to Kyle, looking as if he'd heard great news from him. Shea gave me a poignant look and said, "You don't want to know."

"Why wouldn't I want to?" Then I actually saw why Shea said what she did. I could see on Raine's tablet a photo of one of the most beautiful baby girls I had ever seen. I had to assume that the child in the picture was Kyle's daughter. She lay sleeping peacefully in a crib decorated with pink and turquoise bed linens, her little body snug and warm in footed white pajamas. Her full head of hair displayed ebony ringlets that framed her peaceful café-au-lait face. Her whole body was relaxed, and it almost looked as if she was smiling in her sleep. She had a right to sleep with such happiness, because I knew that Kyle was doing a bang-up job as a father.

Then it hit me—the finality of our relationship had culminated in the birth of his daughter and the deceit he dwelled in when he found out about her. I felt my eyes water right before my body went numb. Dill shifted his attention toward me and asked, "What's wrong, cuz?"

I couldn't even turn my head to meet his gaze. "I'm just a little tired. I'm going to bed now." I stood to go up the stairs but told Shea, "Tell him I said congratulations," as I disappeared to my room.

Before I left earshot of the conversation, I heard Grey ask, "What's wrong with Avail?" when he came into the living room.

"This is," Shea shared, showing Grey the picture of Kyle's daughter, I imagined.

*W*hat will it take for Avail to finally get over her relationship with Kyle? Will Grey be able to control his growing anger toward Kyle while attempting to show Avail the love God has designed for her? Has the birth of Kyla really changed Celeste, or is that a front to get Kyle back? Will Kyle and Celeste unite, forsaking all others, to raise Kyla together? How will the lessons from Bible study manage to uncover secrets and principles that no one wants to face? These and many other questions will be answered in the third installment of The K(no)w Series, *A Wonderful Change.*

So, what did you think? Care to share your thoughts about this or any book by E. Marie Sanders? You can by doing any of the following:

1. Write a review on the book at www.amazon. com. Many self-published authors like E. Marie depend on the reviews from readers like you. Potential readers want to know what you really thought about this read!

2. Post your comments in the guestbook on E. Marie's web site, www.emariesanders.com. Visitors to the web site sometimes look through the comments left there by other visitors and decide to buy and read the books based on your feedback. Don't forget to sign up for her mailing list in order to stay in the know with all things E. Marie.

3. Email E. Marie! She loves to hear from her readers and will reply to as many as she can. She can be reached at author@emariesanders. com.

Are you into social media? So is E. Marie. Connect with her here:

Facebook

E. Marie Sanders (regular and fan page)

Twitter

EMarieWrites

Pintrest

E Marie

E. Marie Sanders is available for speaking engagements, book talks, panel discussions, and literary workshops. Email her at author@emariesanders.com to inquire about these services and more.

Made in the USA
Columbia, SC
11 March 2024